SEARCH FOR EURYDICE:

SCREENPLAY & GRAPHIC NOVEL

By Karl Smith

...oh x

orphic house
* UNITED KINGDOM *

SEARCH FOR EURYDICE:

SCREENPLAY & GRAPHIC NOVEL

First published in Great Britain by
Orphic House
95 Longhirst, Middlesbrough TS80TD

Creative Director: Karl Peter Smith

© 2010 Karl Peter Smith
First Edition

Previous title *OF MEN AND MYTH*:

Writers Guild of America, west, Inc.
OF MEN AND MYTH
By KARL PETER SMITH – writer
Registration #: 1160182
Effective Date: 10/11/06

Library of Congress
United States Copyright Office
101 Independence Avenue SE
Washington, DC 20559-6000
Registration Number: PA 1-607-940
Effective date of registration: August 28, 2008
Performing Arts title: OF MEN AND MYTH

The British Library
Legal Deposit Office
Boston Spa, Wetherby
West Yorkshire
LS23 7BY

Orphic House

        British Library Cataloguing in Publication Data

Smith, Karl Peter.
  Search for Eurydice : screenplay & graphic novel.
  1. Orpheus (Greek mythology)--Comic books, strips, etc.--
  Fiction. 2. Eurydice (Greek mythology)--Comic books,
  strips, etc.--Fiction. 3. Orpheus (Greek mythology)--
  Drama. 4. Eurydice (Greek mythology)--Drama. 5. Graphic
  novels.
  I. Title
  741.5-dc22

ISBN-13: 978-0-9566156-0-2

Also available in HARDBACK
ISBN-13: 978-0-9566156-6-4

DOWNLOAD
www.lulu.com

'Encourage the turning of a page.'
- Orphic House

SPECIAL ACKNOWLEDGEMENTS

Special thanks to
Juliana Seminova
Moscow, Russia

"Eurydice"
(Uri-dee-chee)

Brief script reading refresher...

Location line:
- o **INT.** (interior) or **EXT.** (exterior)
- o Locations are always listed from **LARGER** to **SMALLER**.
- o **DAY** or **NIGHT** (other times like **DAWN** are unnecessary).
- o **DAYDREAM** or **ANCIENT TIMES** can help a reader visualise.

Description:
- o **Describe the environment in the present tense.**
- o **Movement** and **actions** of actors.
- o Possibly a point-of-view **POV** specific to one character.
- o An actor's first appearance is **CAPITALIZED** with a **(micro description)**.

Character name:
- o Always CAPITALIZED when followed by dialogue.
- o Multiple names appearing on the same line means **actors talk together.**

Dialogue:
- o **(parenthicals)** guidelines for the unobvious delivery of dialogue.
- o **(…)** three dots **(ellipsis)** OR **(beat)** a **pause** the length of a drum beat.

Pronunciation guide...

Eurydice   (uri-dee-chee)
Persephone   (pur-sef-uh-nee)

Useful information:

Orpheus: Minstrel, and famous Argonaut.
Search for Eurydice: Underworld journey in order to rescue his wife, Eurydice.
Agonautica Orphica: The 'Argonautica' poem as told from Orpheus's perspective.

" Whilst visiting my local library I asked a lovely old lady what attracts her to a novel; she said she always likes to read something about the author and as an attractive young man I should use my picture on the cover. Continuing our conversation she revealed that she did not have her glasses but could still read. Flattered, yet on a serious note; I soon realised I had forgotten to tell one thing... *my true story.* "

"I didn't think it <u>the time</u> or <u>the place</u> to mention my sister's death...
...or my screaming which was drowned out by the music of the pool hall.
My mouth frozen open, screaming...
...yet all the gods could hear is the most sorrowful song."

Karl Smith, *Author.*   *"One man had been here before me: Orpheus."*

CONTENTS

Search for Eurydice

Graphic Novel

Screenplay

Search for Eurydice

METROPOLITAN MUSEUM

ARGONAUTICA ORPHICA
(Ορφεως Αργοναυτικα)

An 'Argonautica Orphica' banner spans the grand entrance.
STUDENTS (Teens) disembark the SCHOOL BUS. A smart TEACHER
with event program in hand leads them up the museum steps.

Everyone here? Listen up people.

Ok then, today's exhibits will aid the more kinesthetic of you to literally grasp the heroes by the Greeks.

To expand on the teachings of Aristotle you will be able to touch and feel the very tools of the Greek heroes, some of you will even be able to kiss the very lips of the gorgeous heroes some of us have come across in the classroom.

MURMURING CROWD

YOUNG ORPHEUS carries a GUITAR.

YOUNG EURYDICE sports a port wine birthmark.

That's what I call first-hand evidence.

I said touch not touch-up. Your father waxing lyrical at every governors meeting does not mean that you can do the same over my narration, that understood ?

Yes sir.

Now where are we? Ah-yes front entrance is where we are at. And gallery three is where we are to be. Follow me.

FADE IN:

EXT. METROPOLITAN MUSEUM   SCHOOL BUS   DAY

An 'Argonautica Orphica' banner spans the grand entrance. STUDENTS (Teens) disembark the SCHOOL BUS. A smart TEACHER with event program in hand leads them up the museum steps.

YOUNG ORPHEUS carries a GUITAR.

YOUNG EURYDICE sports a port wine birthmark.

> TEACHER
> Everyone here? Listen up people.
> (beat)
> Ok then, today's exhibits will aid the more kinesthetic of you to literally grasp the heroes by the Greeks.
> (beat)
> To expand on the teachings of Aristotle you will be able to touch and feel the very tools of the Greek heroes, some of you will even be able to kiss the very lips of the gorgeous heroes some of us have come across in the classroom.

> YOUNG ORPHEUS
> That's what I call first-hand evidence.

> TEACHER
> I said touch not touch-up. Your father waxing lyrical at every governors meeting does not mean that you can do the same over my narration, understood?

> YOUNG ORPHEUS
> Yes sir.

> TEACHER
> Now where are we? Ah yes front entrance is where we are at. And gallery three is where we are to be. Follow me.

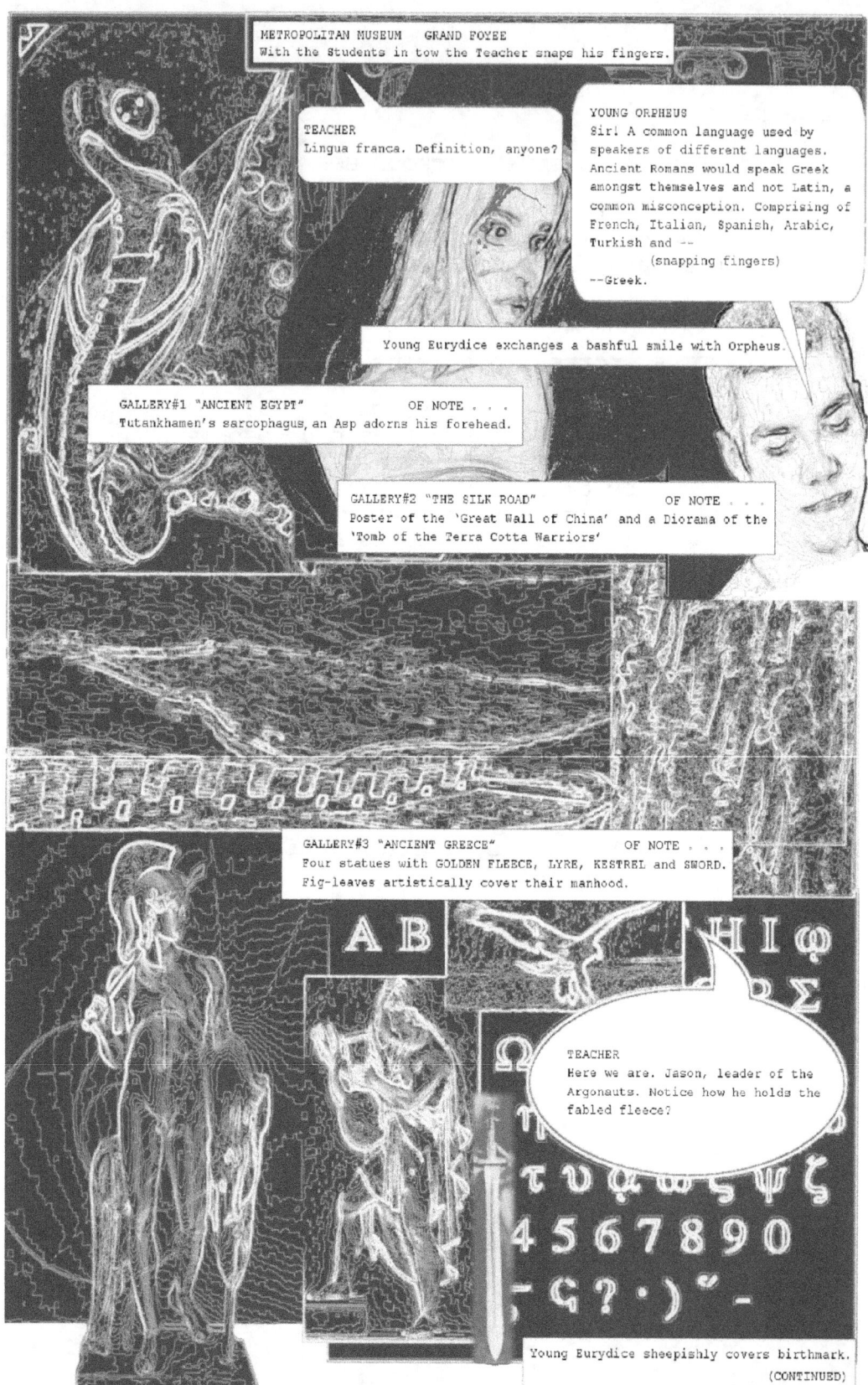

INT. METROPOLITAN MUSEUM   GRAND FOYEE   DAY

With the Students in tow the Teacher snaps his fingers.

                    TEACHER
          Lingua franca. Definition, anyone?

                    YOUNG ORPHEUS
          Sir! A common language used by
          speakers of different languages.
          Ancient Romans would speak Greek
          amongst themselves and not Latin, a
          common misconception. Comprising of
          French, Italian, Spanish, Arabic,
          Turkish and --
                    (snapping fingers)
          --Greek.

Young Eurydice exchanges a bashful smile with Orpheus.

INT. GALLERY#1 "ANCIENT EGYPT"   DAY

Tutankhamen's sarcophagus, an Asp adorns his forehead.

INT. GALLERY#2 "THE SILK ROAD"   DAY

Poster of the 'Great Wall of China' and a Diorama of the
'Tomb of the Terra Cotta Warriors'

INT. GALLERY#3 "ANCIENT GREECE"   DAY

Four statues with GOLDEN FLEECE, LYRE, KESTREL and SWORD.
Fig-leaves artistically cover their manhood.

                    TEACHER
          Here we are. Jason, leader of the
          Argonauts. Notice how he holds the
          fabled fleece?

Young Eurydice sheepishly covers birthmark.

                                        (CONTINUED)

CONTINUED:

> YOUNG EURYDICE
> Sir, they have no clothes on.

> YOUNG ORPHEUS
> Are-go-<u>nuts</u>.

Students laugh.

> TEACHER
> Simmer down, let's be mature. The correct pronunciation is Ar-go-nawts, after the ship's designer 'Argus'. A fine architect of his day. Crotch pouches were the day's designer garments.

Young Eurydice elbows Young Orpheus.

> TEACHER
> There were fifty Argonauts sailing with Jason, searching for the Golden Fleece, the fleece of an actual magical lamb.

> YOUNG ORPHEUS
> A sheep. Ba-a-a-h!

> TEACHER
> This <u>is</u> on everyone's history paper. And individuals wishing to not partake in my elite history group better listen up or escape my wrath.
> (note in hand)
> Isn't there a scheduled music festival you must attend Orpheus?

> YOUNG ORPHEUS
> Yes sir. Music to my ears. Adios.

Young Orpheus blows Young Eurydice a kiss.

> YOUNG EURYDICE
> A lame excuse to bunk.
> (to Teacher)
> Sir, why did Jason wish to find the fleece?

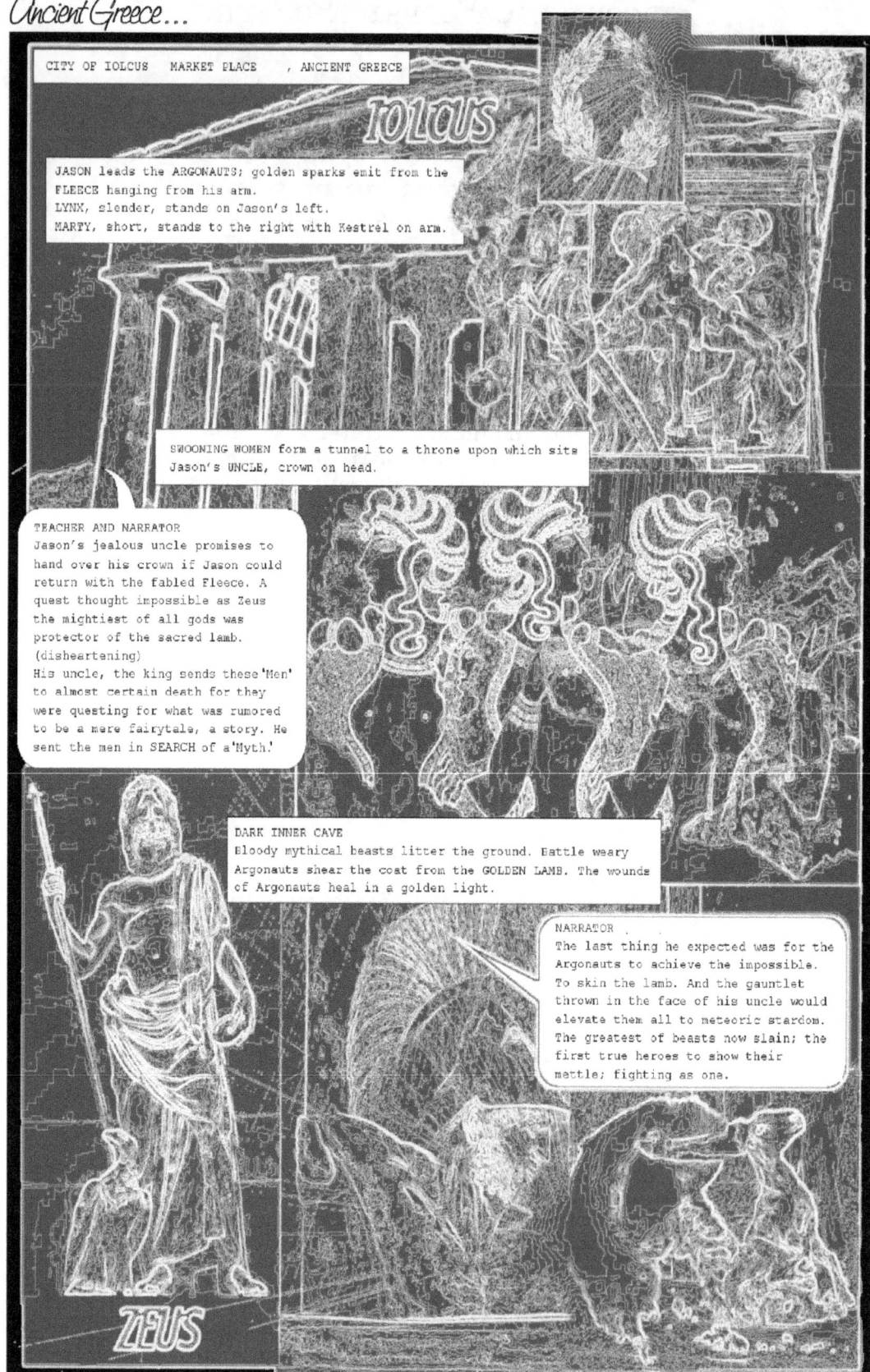

CITY OF IOLCUS   MARKET PLACE   , ANCIENT GREECE

IOLCUS

JASON leads the ARGONAUTS; golden sparks emit from the
FLEECE hanging from his arm.
LYNX, slender, stands on Jason's left.
MARTY, short, stands to the right with Kestrel on arm.

SWOONING WOMEN form a tunnel to a throne upon which sits
Jason's UNCLE, crown on head.

TEACHER AND NARRATOR
Jason's jealous uncle promises to
hand over his crown if Jason could
return with the fabled Fleece. A
quest thought impossible as Zeus
the mightiest of all gods was
protector of the sacred lamb.
(disheartening)
His uncle, the king sends these 'Men'
to almost certain death for they
were questing for what was rumored
to be a mere fairytale, a story. He
sent the men in SEARCH of a 'Myth.'

DARK INNER CAVE
Bloody mythical beasts litter the ground. Battle weary
Argonauts shear the coat from the GOLDEN LAMB. The wounds
of Argonauts heal in a golden light.

NARRATOR .
The last thing he expected was for the
Argonauts to achieve the impossible.
To skin the lamb. And the gauntlet
thrown in the face of his uncle would
elevate them all to meteoric stardom.
The greatest of beasts now slain; the
first true heroes to show their
mettle; fighting as one.

ZEUS

EXT. CITY OF IOLCUS   MARKET PLACE   DAY, ANCIENT GREECE

JASON leads the ARGONAUTS; golden sparks emit from the
FLEECE hanging from his arm.

LYNX, slender, stands on Jason's left.

MARTY, short, stands to the right with Kestrel on arm.

SWOONING WOMEN form a tunnel to a throne upon which sits
Jason's UNCLE, crown on head.

>   TEACHER AND NARRATOR
> Jason's jealous uncle promises to
> hand over his crown if Jason could
> return with the fabled Fleece. A
> quest thought impossible as Zeus
> the mightiest of all gods was
> protector of the sacred lamb.
>   (disheartening)
> His uncle, the king sends these'Men'
> to almost certain death for they
> were questing for what was rumored
> to be a mere fairytale, a story. He
> sent the men in SEARCH of a 'Myth'.

INT. DARK INNER CAVE   NIGHT

Bloody mythical beasts litter the ground. Battle weary
Argonauts shear the coat from the GOLDEN LAMB.   The wounds
of Argonauts heal in a golden light.

>   NARRATOR (V.O.)
> The last thing he expected was for the
> Argonauts to achieve the impossible.
> To skin the lamb. And the gauntlet
> thrown in the face of his uncle would
> elevate them all to meteoric stardom.
> The greatest of beasts now slain; the
> first true heroes to show their
> mettle; fighting as one.

ORPHEUS AND EURYDICE

IOLCUS   GRASSY HILLSIDE MEADOW
BIRDS fill the air with courting songs.

NARRATOR
For a time, they had conquered the beast.

ORPHEUS a handsome athlete sits playing a Lyre; grasses sway to the sweet vibrations.

EURYDICE with pre-Raphaelite beauty seductively twiddles a buttercup in her fingertips.

EURYDICE
I love you. You fill that space god can't fill.

ORPHEUS
Show me.

Drawing his lips to hers she straddles him. A CADUCEUS CHARM hangs from her neck.

A note twangs off-key making the grasses rise to create a shelter.
Giggles emanate from the grassy cocoon.

Caduceus Charm
(SNAKES INTERTWINED)

NARRATOR
When two of the greatest armies to ever amass were to fight at the city of Troy; two Gods could not resist on a wager.

INT. IOLCUS   GRASSY HILLSIDE MEADOW   DAY

BIRDS fill the air with courting songs.

> NARRATOR (V.O.)
> For a time, they had conquered the
> beast.

ORPHEUS a handsome athlete sits playing a Lyre; grasses sway
to the sweet vibrations.

EURYDICE with pre-Raphaelite beauty seductively twiddles a
buttercup in her fingertips. She kneels.

> EURYDICE
> I love you. You fill that space god
> can't fill.

> ORPHEUS
> Show me.

Drawing his lips to hers she straddles him. A CADUCEUS CHARM
hangs from her neck.

A note twangs off-key making the grasses rise to create a shelter.

Giggles emanate from the grassy cocoon.

> NARRATOR (V.O.)
> When two of the greatest armies to
> ever amass were to fight at the
> city of Troy; two Gods could not
> resist on a wager.

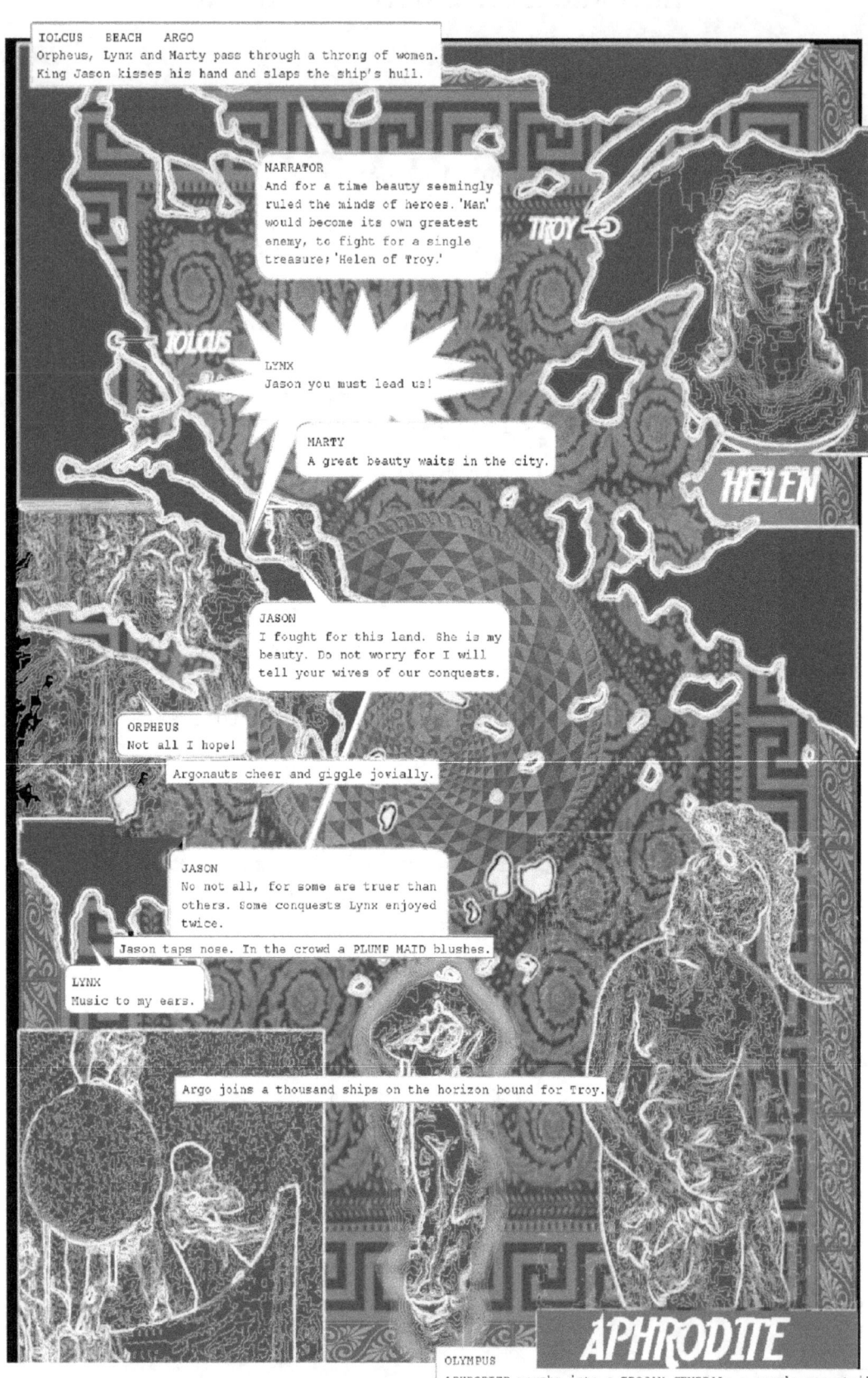

IOLCUS   BEACH   ARGO
Orpheus, Lynx and Marty pass through a throng of women.
King Jason kisses his hand and slaps the ship's hull.

NARRATOR
And for a time beauty seemingly
ruled the minds of heroes. 'Man'
would become its own greatest
enemy, to fight for a single
treasure; 'Helen of Troy.'

TROY

IOLCUS

HELEN

LYNX
Jason you must lead us!

MARTY
A great beauty waits in the city.

JASON
I fought for this land. She is my
beauty. Do not worry for I will
tell your wives of our conquests.

ORPHEUS
Not all I hope!

Argonauts cheer and giggle jovially.

JASON
No not all, for some are truer than
others. Some conquests Lynx enjoyed
twice.

Jason taps nose. In the crowd a PLUMP MAID blushes.

LYNX
Music to my ears.

Argo joins a thousand ships on the horizon bound for Troy.

APHRODITE

OLYMPUS
APHRODITE morphs into a TROJAN GENERAL; a purple pony-tail
adorns her open-faced helmet.

INT. IOLCUS   BEACH   ARGO   DAY

Orpheus, Lynx and Marty pass through a throng of women.

King Jason kisses his hand and slaps the ship's hull.

> NARRATOR (V.O.)
> And for a time beauty seemingly
> ruled the minds of heroes. Man
> would become its own greatest
> enemy, to fight for a single
> treasure; Helen of Troy.

> LYNX
> Jason you must lead us!

> MARTY
> A great beauty waits in the city.

> JASON
> I fought for this land. She is my
> beauty. Do not worry for I will
> tell your wives of our conquests.

> ORPHEUS
> Not all I hope!

Argonauts cheer and giggle jovially.

> JASON
> No not all, for some are truer than
> others. Some conquests Lynx enjoyed
> twice.

Jason taps nose. In the crowd a PLUMP MAID blushes.

> LYNX
> Music to my ears.

Argo joins a thousand ships on the horizon bound for Troy.

EXT. OLYMPUS   DAY

APHRODITE morphs into a TROJAN GENERAL; a purple pony-tail
adorns her open-faced helmet.

EXT: TROY   PALACE   BALCONY   DAY

HELEN OF TROY in sheer gown looks out across the great city
to the empty ocean once occupied by a thousand ships.

INT. TROY   INSIDE TROJAN HORSE   DAY

Orpheus, Lynx, and Marty rock side to side. Huge wooden
wheels grind.

                    LYNX
          Tell me again why we cut the ships
          up to make a wooden pony?

                    MARTY
          Who's breathing in my face? This is
          so gay.

A hefty jerk causes the men to tumble. Sound of ropes.

                    LYNX
          Uh, get off me!

                    MARTY
          I hope this new closeness doesn't
          affect our professional soldiering?

                    ORPHEUS
          Shhh, they've snared us.

                    LYNX
          I told you this wouldn't work.

EXT. TROY   GATEHOUSE   DAY

Aphrodite commands SOLDIERS that pull in a gargantuan Horse.

                    APHRODITE
          A fine piñata. A lovely creation.
                    (with venom)
          I will give it a loving crush.

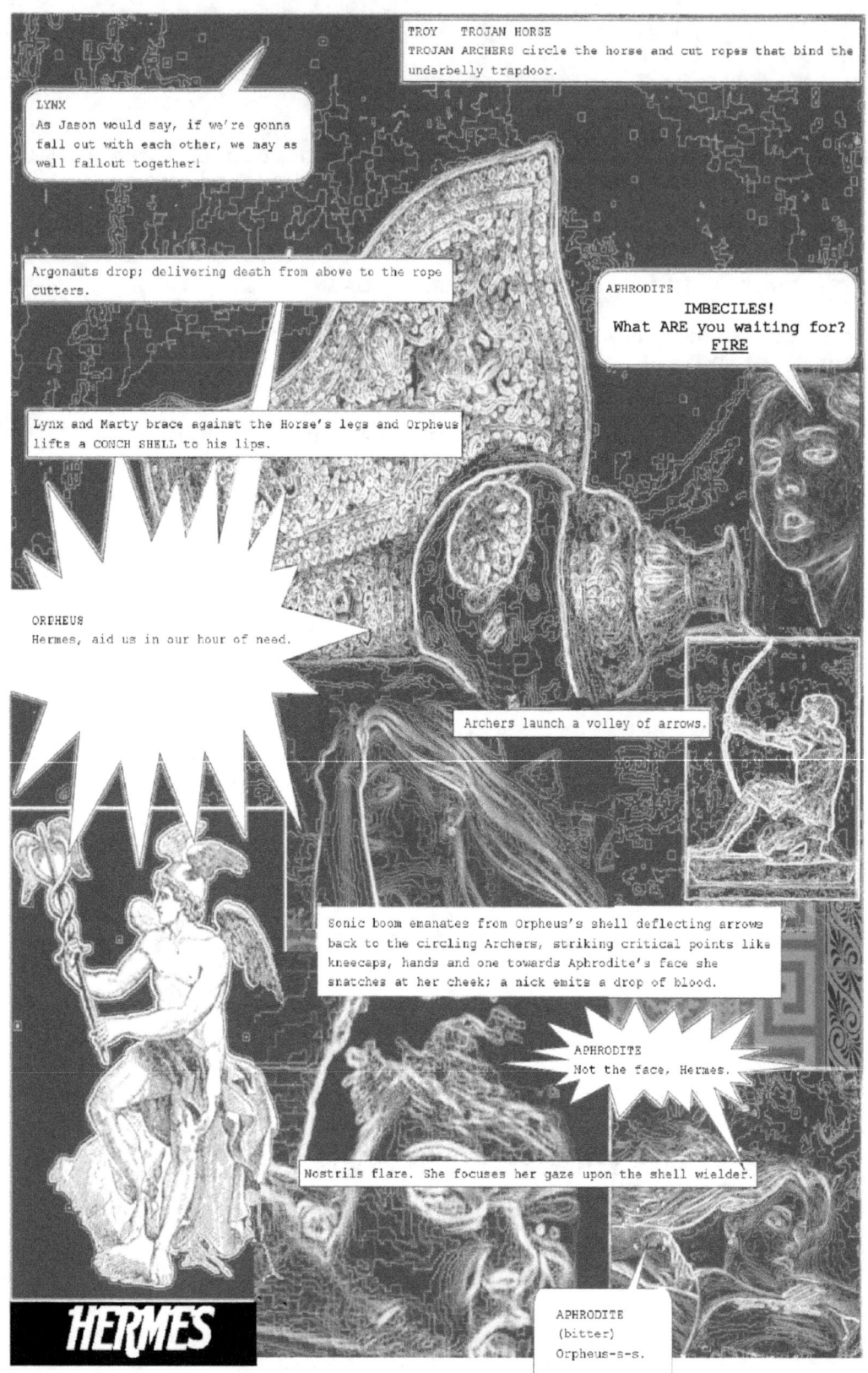

TROY   TROJAN HORSE
TROJAN ARCHERS circle the horse and cut ropes that bind the
underbelly trapdoor.

LYNX
As Jason would say, if we're gonna
fall out with each other, we may as
well fallout together!

Argonauts drop; delivering death from above to the rope
cutters.

APHRODITE
        IMBECILES!
What ARE you waiting for?
        FIRE

Lynx and Marty brace against the Horse's legs and Orpheus
lifts a CONCH SHELL to his lips.

ORPHEUS
Hermes, aid us in our hour of need.

Archers launch a volley of arrows.

Sonic boom emanates from Orpheus's shell deflecting arrows
back to the circling Archers, striking critical points like
kneecaps, hands and one towards Aphrodite's face she
snatches at her cheek; a nick emits a drop of blood.

APHRODITE
Not the face, Hermes.

Nostrils flare. She focuses her gaze upon the shell wielder.

HERMES

APHRODITE
(bitter)
Orpheus-s-s.

EXT. TROY   TROJAN HORSE   NIGHT

TROJAN ARCHERS circle the horse and cut ropes that bind the underbelly trapdoor.

                         LYNX (O.S.)
               As Jason would say, if we're gonna
               fall out with each other, we may as
               well fallout together!

Argonauts drop; delivering death from above to the rope cutters.

                         APHRODITE
               Imbeciles! What ARE you waiting for?
                         (beat)
               Fire!

Lynx and Marty brace against the Horse's legs and Orpheus lifts a CONCH SHELL to his lips.

                         ORPHEUS
               Hermes, aid us in our hour of need.

Archers launch a volley of arrows.

Sonic boom emanates from Orpheus's shell deflecting arrows back to the circling Archers, striking critical points like kneecaps, hands and one towards Aphrodite's face she snatches at her cheek; a nick emits a drop of blood.

                         APHRODITE
               Not the face, Hermes.

Nostrils flare. She focuses her gaze upon the shell wielder.

                         APHRODITE
                         (bitter)
               Orpheus-s-s.

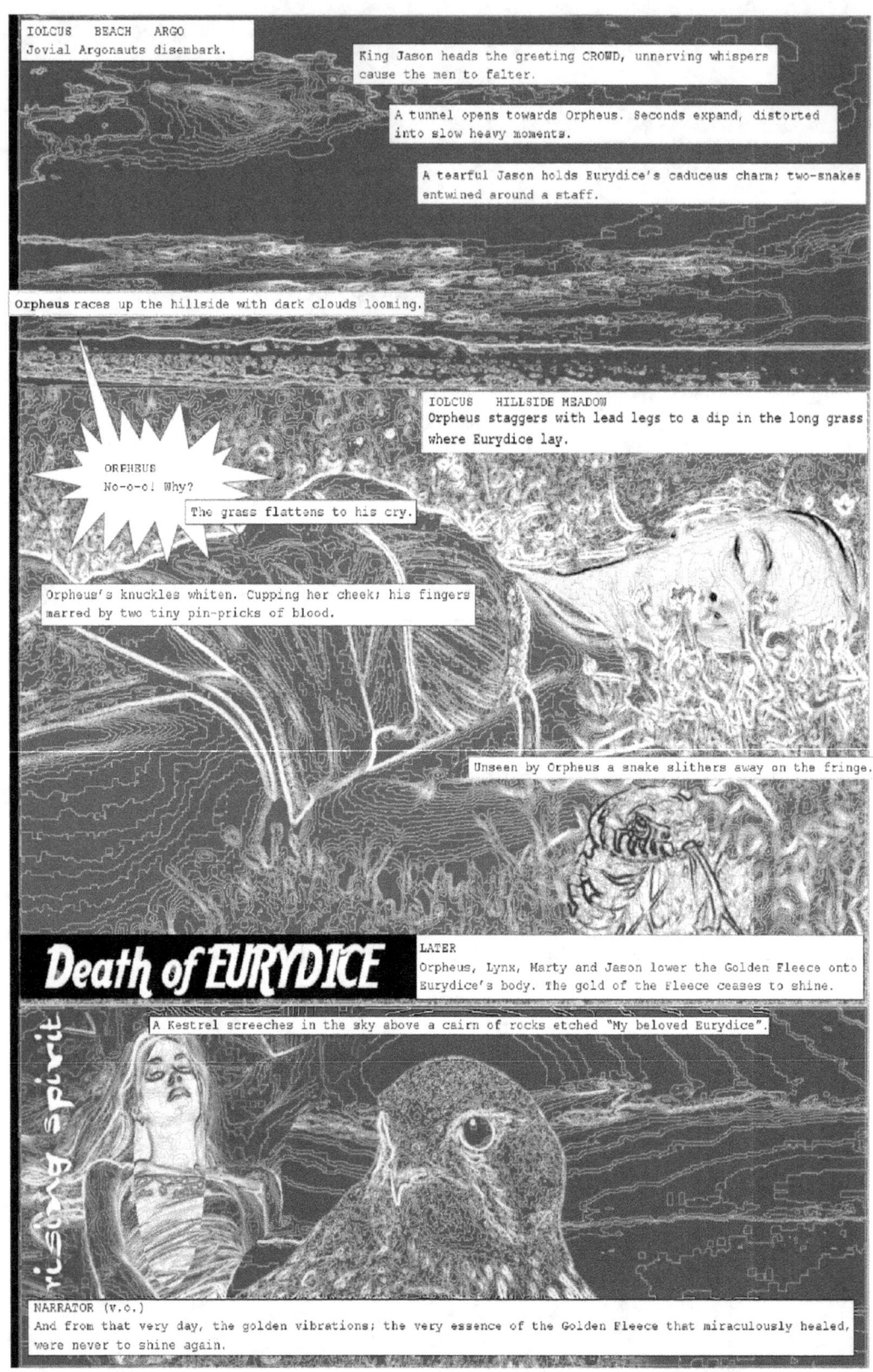

EXT. IOLCUS   BEACH   ARGO   DAY

Jovial Argonauts disembark.

King Jason heads the greeting CROWD, unnerving whispers
cause the men to falter.

A tunnel opens towards Orpheus. Seconds expand, distorted
into slow heavy moments.

A tearful Jason holds Eurydice's caduceus charm; two-snakes
entwined around a staff.

Orpheus races up the hillside with dark clouds looming.

EXT. IOLCUS   HILLSIDE MEADOW   DAY

Orpheus staggers with lead legs to a dip in the long grass
where Eurydice lay.

                    ORPHEUS
          NO-O-O!

The grass flattens to his cry.

Orpheus's knuckles whiten. Cupping her cheek; his fingers
marred by two tiny pin-pricks of blood.

Unseen by Orpheus a snake slithers away on the fringe.

LATER

Orpheus, Lynx, Marty and Jason lower the Golden Fleece onto
Eurydice's body. The gold of the Fleece ceases to shine.

A Kestrel screeches in the sky above a cairn of rocks etched
"My beloved Eurydice".

                    NARRATOR (V.O.)
          And from that very day, the golden
          vibrations; the very essence of the
          Golden Fleece that miraculously
          healed, were never to shine again.

HIS SORROW...

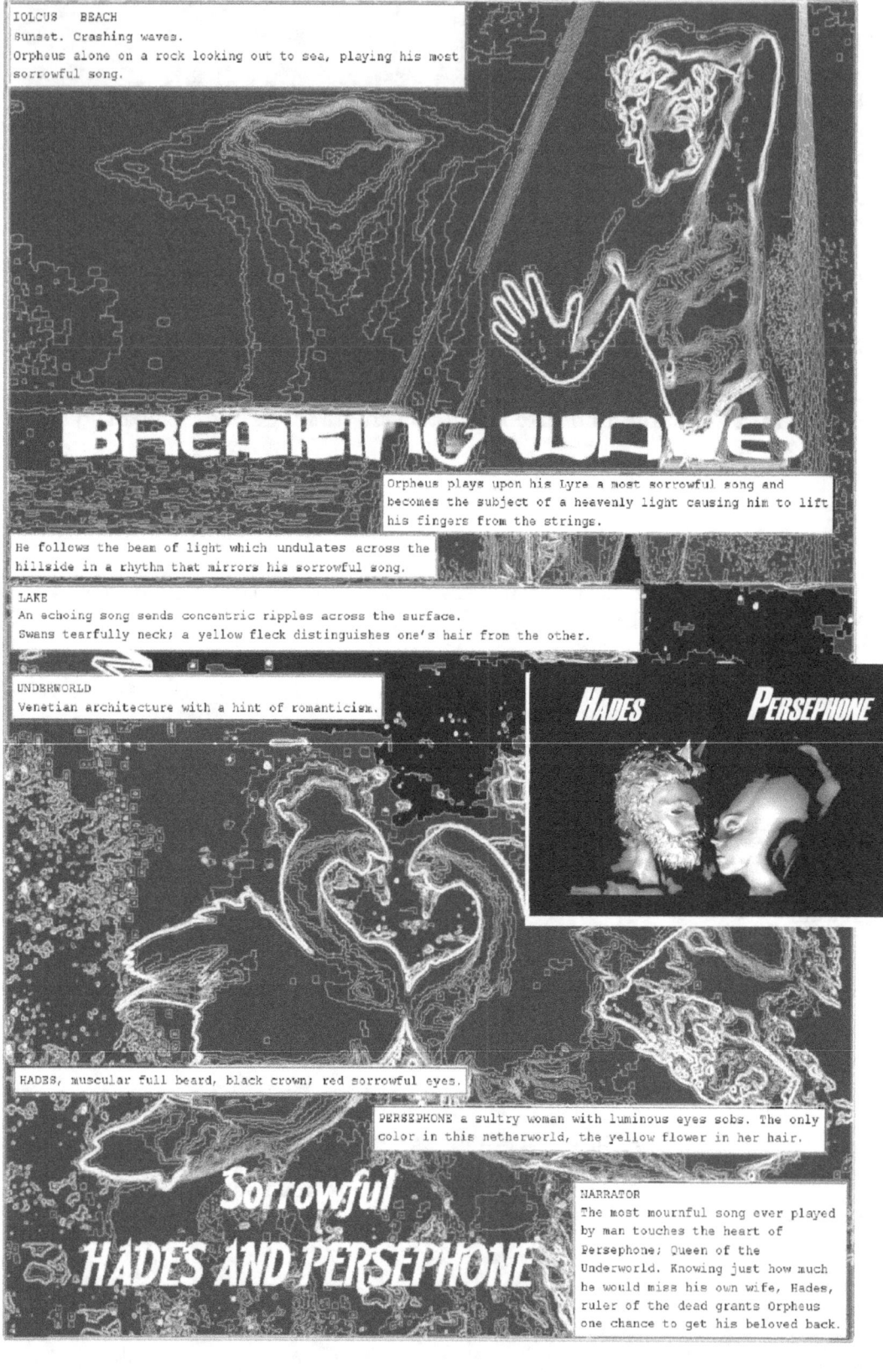

IOLCUS   BEACH
Sunset. Crashing waves.
Orpheus alone on a rock looking out to sea, playing his most
sorrowful song.

BREAKING WAVES

Orpheus plays upon his Lyre a most sorrowful song and
becomes the subject of a heavenly light causing him to lift
his fingers from the strings.

He follows the beam of light which undulates across the
hillside in a rhythm that mirrors his sorrowful song.

LAKE
An echoing song sends concentric ripples across the surface.
Swans tearfully neck; a yellow fleck distinguishes one's hair from the other.

UNDERWORLD
Venetian architecture with a hint of romanticism.

HADES   PERSEPHONE

HADES, muscular full beard, black crown; red sorrowful eyes.

PERSEPHONE a sultry woman with luminous eyes sobs. The only
color in this netherworld, the yellow flower in her hair.

Sorrowful
HADES AND PERSEPHONE

NARRATOR
The most mournful song ever played
by man touches the heart of
Persephone; Queen of the
Underworld. Knowing just how much
he would miss his own wife, Hades,
ruler of the dead grants Orpheus
one chance to get his beloved back.

HIS SORROW . . .   20.

EXT. IOLCUS   BEACH   DAY

Sunset. Crashing waves.

Orpheus alone on a rock looking out to sea, playing his most
sorrowful song.

Orpheus plays upon his Lyre a most sorrowful song and
becomes the subject of a heavenly light causing him to lift
his fingers from the strings.

He follows the beam of light which undulates across the
hillside in a rhythm that mirrors his sorrowful song.

EXT. LAKE   DAY

An echoing song sends concentric ripples across the surface.

Swans tearfully neck; a yellow fleck distinguishes
one's hair from the other.

INT. UNDERWORLD   NIGHT

Venetian architecture with a hint of romanticism.

HADES, muscular full beard, black crown; red sorrowful eyes.

PERSEPHONE a sultry woman with luminous eyes sobs. The only
color in this netherworld, the yellow flower in her hair.

                    NARRATOR (V.O.)
          The most mournful song ever played
          by man touches the heart of
          Persephone; Queen of the
          Underworld. Knowing just how much
          he would miss his own wife, Hades,
          ruler of the dead grants Orpheus
          one chance to get his beloved back.

Valley of the Dead...

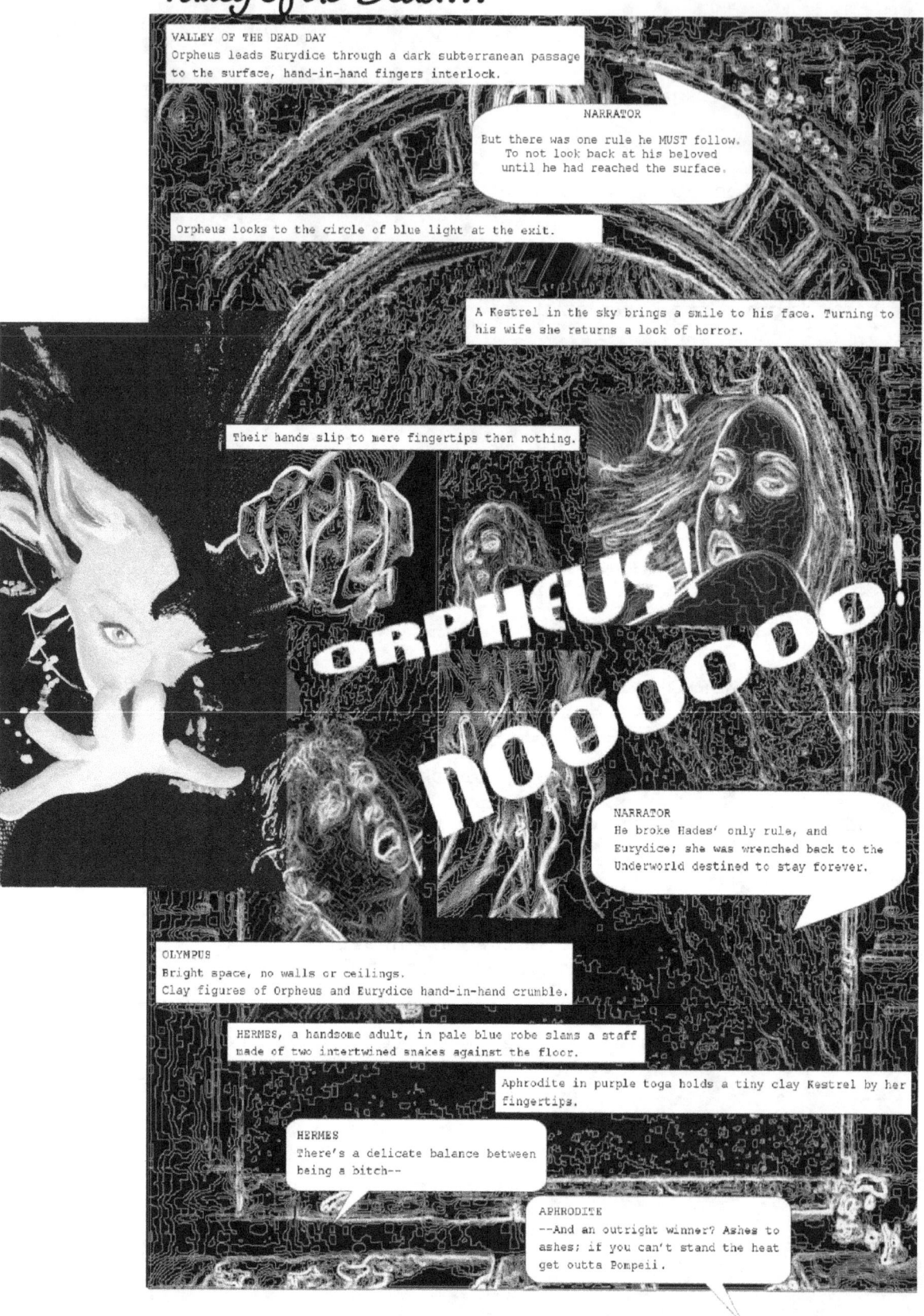

VALLEY OF THE DEAD DAY
Orpheus leads Eurydice through a dark subterranean passage
to the surface, hand-in-hand fingers interlock.

NARRATOR
But there was one rule he MUST follow.
To not look back at his beloved
until he had reached the surface.

Orpheus looks to the circle of blue light at the exit.

A Kestrel in the sky brings a smile to his face. Turning to
his wife she returns a look of horror.

Their hands slip to mere fingertips then nothing.

ORPHEUS!
NOOOOOO!

NARRATOR
He broke Hades' only rule, and
Eurydice; she was wrenched back to the
Underworld destined to stay forever.

OLYMPUS
Bright space, no walls or ceilings.
Clay figures of Orpheus and Eurydice hand-in-hand crumble.

HERMES, a handsome adult, in pale blue robe slams a staff
made of two intertwined snakes against the floor.

Aphrodite in purple toga holds a tiny clay Kestrel by her
fingertips.

HERMES
There's a delicate balance between
being a bitch--

APHRODITE
--And an outright winner? Ashes to
ashes; if you can't stand the heat
get outta Pompeii.

EXT. VALLEY OF THE DEAD   DAY

Orpheus leads Eurydice through a dark subterranean passage
to the surface, hand-in-hand fingers interlock.

                    NARRATOR (V.O.)
          But there was one rule. To not look
          back at his beloved until he had
          reached the surface.

Orpheus looks to the circle of blue light at the exit.

A Kestrel in the sky brings a smile to his face. Turning to
his wife she returns a look of horror.

Their hands slip to mere fingertips then nothing.

          EURYDICE   ORPHEUS
       Orpheus-s-s!   No-o-o!

                    NARRATOR (V.O.)
          He broke Hades' only rule, and
          Eurydice; she was wrenched back to the
          Underworld destined to stay forever.

INT. OLYMPUS   DAY

Bright space, no walls or ceilings.

Clay figures of Orpheus and Eurydice hand-in-hand crumble.

HERMES, a handsome adult, in pale blue robe slams a staff
made of two intertwined snakes against the floor.

Aphrodite in purple toga holds a tiny clay Kestrel by her
fingertips.

                    HERMES
          There's a delicate balance between
          being a bitch--

                    APHRODITE
          --And an outright winner? If you
          can't stand the heat get outta
          Pompeii, now that's one hole I'll
          be plugging up. Ashes to ashes as
          they say.

1930's...

POMPEII   ARCHAEOLOGICAL DIG   CAVE
At the entrance in a circle of light stands JASON leaning
upon a shovel and peering down into the darkness.

Behind Jason, in the air flies a Kestrel.

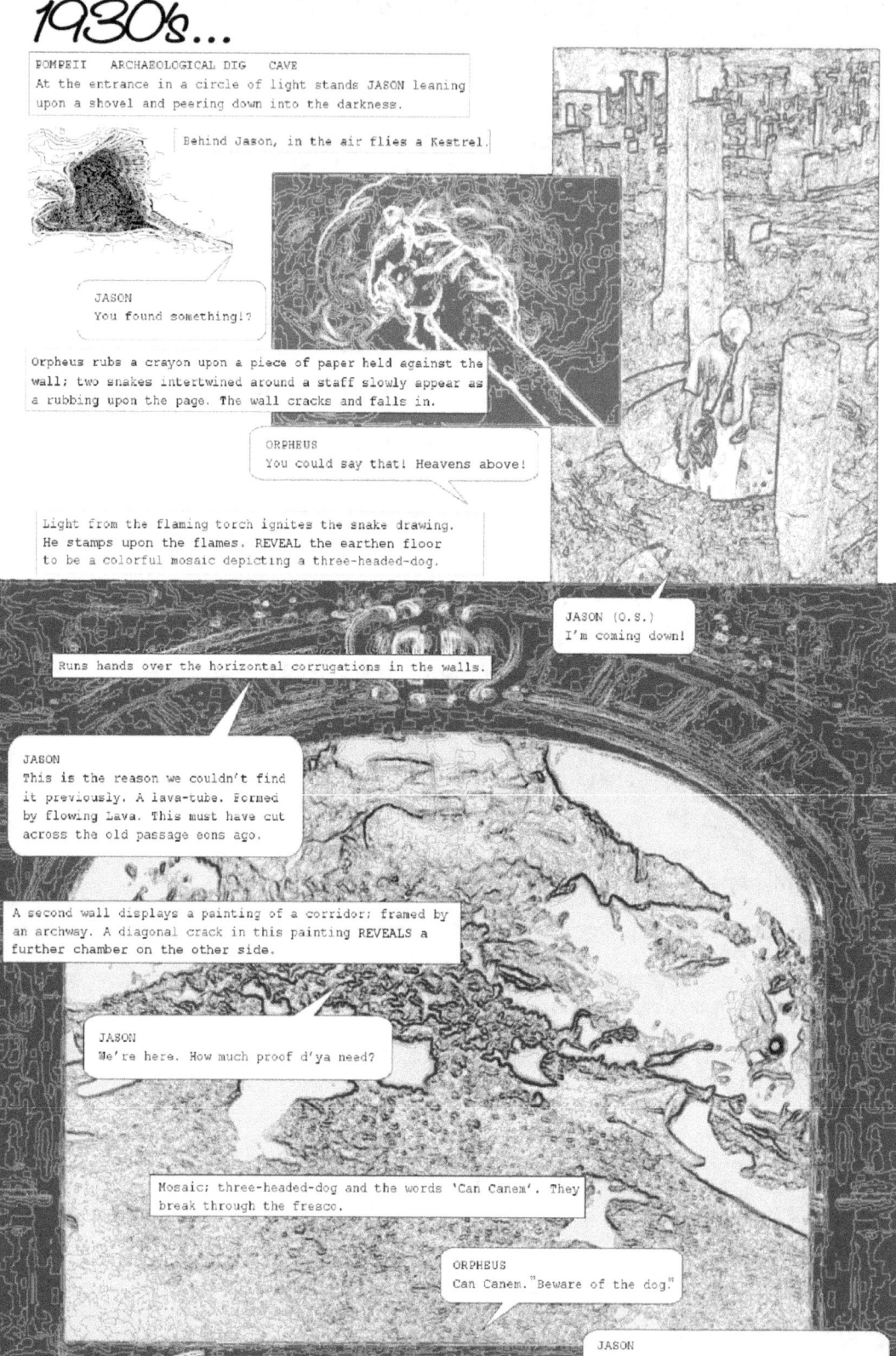

JASON
You found something!?

Orpheus rubs a crayon upon a piece of paper held against the
wall; two snakes intertwined around a staff slowly appear as
a rubbing upon the page. The wall cracks and falls in.

ORPHEUS
You could say that! Heavens above!

Light from the flaming torch ignites the snake drawing.
He stamps upon the flames. REVEAL the earthen floor
to be a colorful mosaic depicting a three-headed-dog.

JASON (O.S.)
I'm coming down!

Runs hands over the horizontal corrugations in the walls.

JASON
This is the reason we couldn't find
it previously. A lava-tube. Formed
by flowing lava. This must have cut
across the old passage eons ago.

A second wall displays a painting of a corridor; framed by
an archway. A diagonal crack in this painting REVEALS a
further chamber on the other side.

JASON
We're here. How much proof d'ya need?

Mosaic; three-headed-dog and the words 'Can Canem'. They
break through the fresco.

ORPHEUS
Can Canem. "Beware of the dog."

JASON
Acherusia right? The only way for a
living being to reach the Underworld.

INT. POMPEII   ARCHAEOLOGICAL DIG   CAVE   DAY, 1930'S

At the entrance in a circle of light stands JASON leaning
upon a shovel and peering down into the darkness.

Behind Jason, in the air flies a Kestrel.

> JASON
> You found something!?

Orpheus rubs a crayon upon a piece of paper held against the
wall; two snakes intertwined around a staff slowly appear as
a rubbing upon the page. The wall cracks and falls in.

> ORPHEUS
> You could say that! Heavens above!

Light from the flaming torch ignites the snake drawing.
He stamps upon the flames. REVEAL the earthen floor to be a
colorful mosaic depicting a threeheaded dog.

> JASON (O.S.)
> I'm coming down!

Runs hands over the horizontal corrugations in the walls.

> JASON
> This is the reason we couldn't find
> it previously. A lava-tube. Formed
> by flowing Lava. This must have cut
> across the old passage eons ago.

A second wall displays a painting of a corridor; framed by
an archway. A diagonal crack in this painting REVEALS a
further chamber on the other side.

> JASON
> We're here. How much proof d'ya need?

Mosaic; three-headed-dog and the words 'Can Canem'. They
break through the fresco.

> ORPHEUS
> Can Canem. "Beware of the dog."

> JASON
> Acherusia right. The only way for a
> living being to reach the Underworld.

LAIR OF MEDUSA 1930'S
Tall supporting pillars. A skylight drops light onto a stone
font. Unusual animal statues; mountain goat, sheep and bear.

MEDUSA (O.S.)
H-s-s-s.

HAIRS RISE on the arms of both Jason and Orpheus.

JASON
Who turned the heating off?

(eyes fearfully wide)
YEEARGH!

Solidification sound. Orpheus faces a stone statue of Jason
wearing an expression of terror. A blow to the side of his
head forces him to the floor and he momentarily sees the
slender legs of MEDUSA in bronze studded cat suit.

Light dances up a super-ancient dagger held to his throat.

MEDUSA
I too wield a gift from the gods.
Except unlike you Orpheus this one
is all singing and dancing.

Blue sparks emit from the charm.

ORPHEUS
Urgah-h-h.

The bloodied charm lands broken on the ground.

OLYMPUS
Hades appears in a black mist and removes the clay
simulacrum of Orpheus from the table. Aphrodite and Hermes
look on.

HADES
I rule over the dead. He is in my
domain now. Game over.

INT. LAIR OF MEDUSA   DAY, 1930'S

Tall supporting pillars. A skylight drops light onto a stone font. Unusual animal statues; mountain goat, sheep and bear.

                        MEDUSA (O.S.)
          H-s-s-s.

HAIRS RISE on the arms of both Jason and Orpheus.

                        JASON
               Who turned the heating off?
                    (eyes fearfully wide)
               YEEARGH!

Solidification sound. Orpheus faces a stone statue of Jason wearing an expression of terror. A blow to the side of his head forces him to the floor and he momentarily sees the slender legs of MEDUSA in bronze studded cat suit.

Light dances up a super-ancient dagger held to his throat.

                        MEDUSA
               I too wield a gift from the gods.
               Except unlike you Orpheus this one
               is all singing and dancing.

Blue sparks emit from the charm.

                        ORPHEUS
               Urgah-h-h.

The bloodied charm lands broken on the ground.

INT. OLYMPUS   DAY

Hades appears in a black mist and removes the clay simulacrum of Orpheus from the table. Aphrodite and Hermes look on.

                        HADES
               I rule over the dead. He is in my
               domain now. Game over.

                                        (CONTINUED)

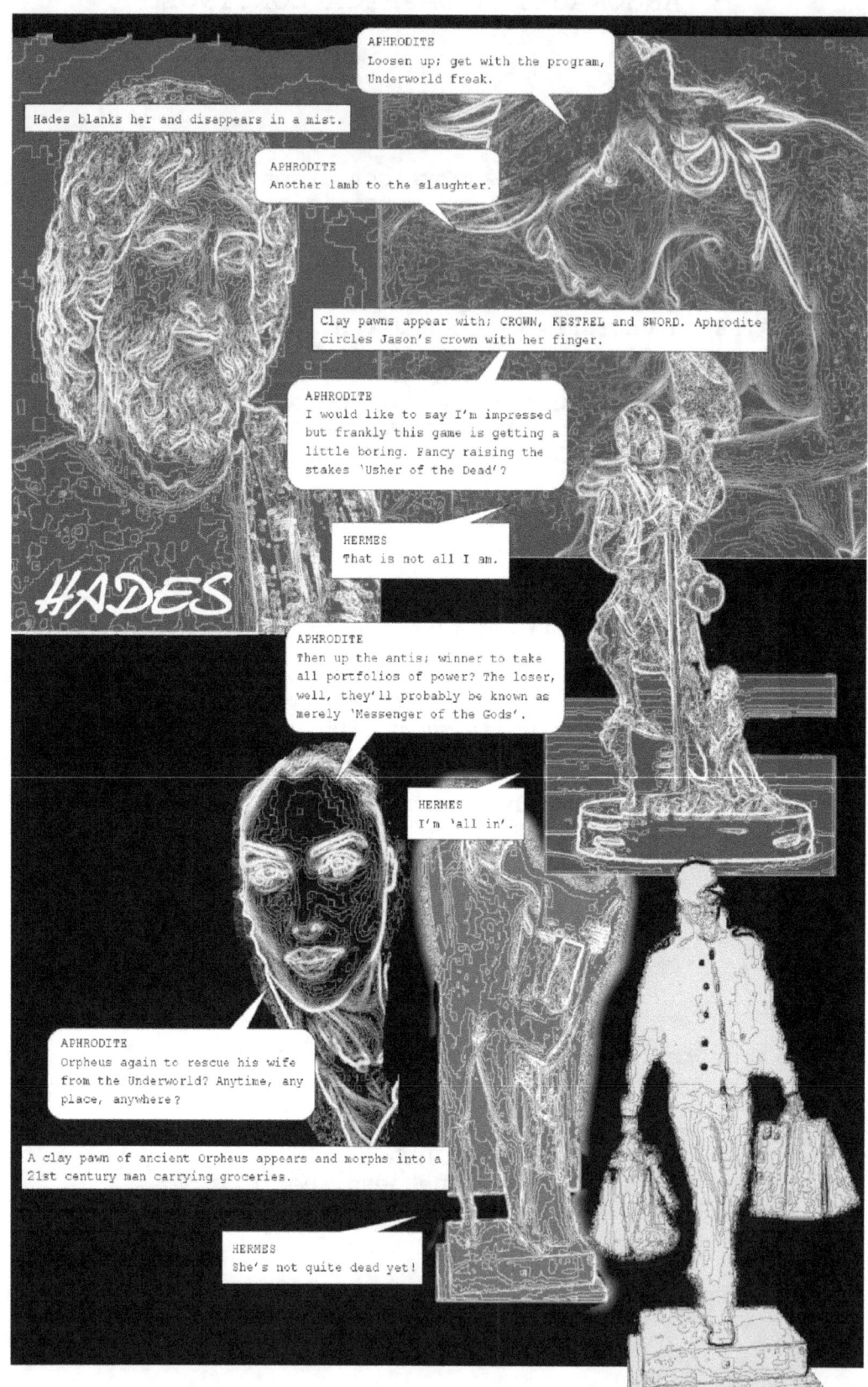

CONTINUED:

> APHRODITE
> Loosen up; get with the program,
> Underworld freak.

Hades blanks her and disappears in a mist.

> APHRODITE
> Another lamb to the slaughter.

Clay pawns appear with; CROWN, KESTREL and SWORD. Aphrodite
circles Jason's crown with her finger.

> APHRODITE
> I would like to say I'm impressed
> but frankly this game is getting a
> little boring. Fancy raising the
> stakes 'Usher of the Dead'?

> HERMES
> That is not all I am.

> APHRODITE
> Then up the antis; winner to take
> all portfolios of power? The loser,
> well, they'll probably be known as
> merely 'Messenger of the Gods'.

> HERMES
> I'm 'all in'.

> APHRODITE
> Orpheus again to rescue his wife
> from the Underworld? Anytime, any
> place, anywhere?

A clay pawn of ancient Orpheus appears and morphs into a
21st century man carrying groceries.

> HERMES
> She's not quite dead yet!

Present day...

ORPHEUS'S HOUSE   DRIVEWAY
Orpheus unloads a car; groceries in hand.

A rumble of thunder makes BIRDS take flight. Hermes's face
dissolves amongst the clouds.

INDOORS, a ringing telephone.

EURYDICE (O.S.)
Orpheus, Jason on the line!

ORPHEUS'S HOUSE   LIVING ROOM
Eurydice, head towel and bathroom gown, cotton wool between
her toes; juggling nail varnish and phone in one hand.

EURYDICE
And a happy birthday to you. (beat)
Oh, me, you know, I'm sat here all
done up like a Christmas tree. If
your wife could pop round and pin my
new dress back from the dry cleaners
I would much appreciate it.

Enter Orpheus groceries in hand, dress in the other.

ORPHEUS
And I got some seeds for that weedy lawn.

She kisses him.

Orpheus takes the phone.

JASON ON THE TELEPHONE
The hunting trip we've always been
planning since we were kids. See
those clear skies. Must be my
birthday or something.

EXT. ORPHEUS'S HOUSE   DRIVEWAY   PRESENT DAY

Orpheus unloads a car; groceries in hand.

A rumble of thunder makes BIRDS take flight. Hermes's face dissolves amongst the clouds.

INDOORS, a ringing telephone.

> EURYDICE (O.S.)
> Orpheus! Jason on the line.

INT. ORPHEUS'S HOUSE   LIVING ROOM   DAY

Eurydice, head towel and bathroom gown, cotton wool between her toes; juggling nail varnish and phone in one hand.

> EURYDICE
> And a happy birthday to you. (beat)
> Oh, me, you know, I'm sat here all
> done up like a Christmas tree. If
> your wife could pop round and pin my
> new dress back from the dry cleaners
> I would much appreciate it.

Enter Orpheus groceries in hand, dress in the other.

> ORPHEUS
> And I got some seeds for that weedy
> lawn.

She kisses him.

Orpheus takes the phone.

> JASON (O.S.)
> (filtered)
> The hunting trip we've always been
> planning since we were kids. See
> those clear skies. Must be my
> birthday or something.

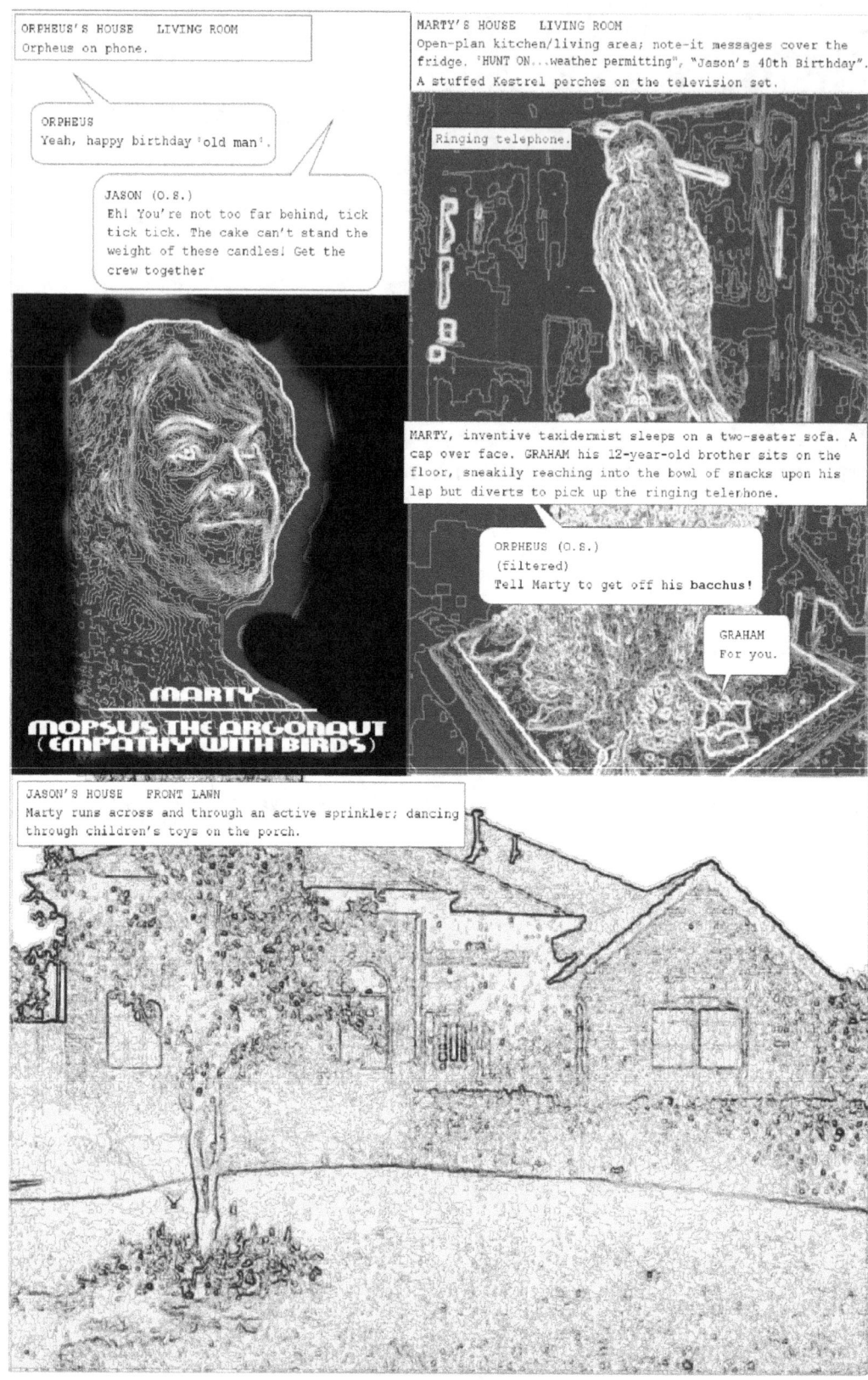

ORPHEUS'S HOUSE   LIVING ROOM
Orpheus on phone.

ORPHEUS
Yeah, happy birthday 'old man'.

JASON (O.S.)
Eh! You're not too far behind, tick tick tick. The cake can't stand the weight of these candles! Get the crew together

MARTY

MOPSUS THE ARGONAUT
(EMPATHY WITH BIRDS)

MARTY'S HOUSE   LIVING ROOM
Open-plan kitchen/living area; note-it messages cover the fridge. 'HUNT ON...weather permitting", "Jason's 40th Birthday". A stuffed Kestrel perches on the television set.

Ringing telephone.

MARTY, inventive taxidermist sleeps on a two-seater sofa. A cap over face. GRAHAM his 12-year-old brother sits on the floor, sneakily reaching into the bowl of snacks upon his lap but diverts to pick up the ringing telephone.

ORPHEUS (O.S.)
(filtered)
Tell Marty to get off his bacchus!

GRAHAM
For you.

JASON'S HOUSE   FRONT LAWN
Marty runs across and through an active sprinkler; dancing through children's toys on the porch.

INT. ORPHEUS'S HOUSE · LIVING ROOM   DAY

Orpheus on phone.

                    ORPHEUS
          Yeah, happy birthday 'old man'.

                    JASON (O.S.)
                (filtered)
          Eh! You're not too far behind, tick
          tick tick. The cake can't stand the
          weight of these candles! Get the
          crew together.

INT. MARTY'S HOUSE   LIVING ROOM   DAY

Open-plan kitchen/living area; note-it messages cover the
fridge. "HUNT ON...weather permitting", "Jason's 40th Birthday".
A stuffed Kestrel perches on the television set.

Ringing telephone.

MARTY, inventive taxidermist sleeps on a two-seater sofa. A
cap over face. GRAHAM his 12-year-old brother sits on the
floor, sneakily reaching into the bowl of snacks upon his
lap but diverts to pick up the ringing telephone.

                    ORPHEUS (O.S.)
                (filtered)
          Tell Marty to get off his bacchus!

                    GRAHAM
          For you.

EXT. JASON'S HOUSE   FRONT LAWN   DAY

Marty runs across and through an active sprinkler; dancing
through children's toys on the porch.

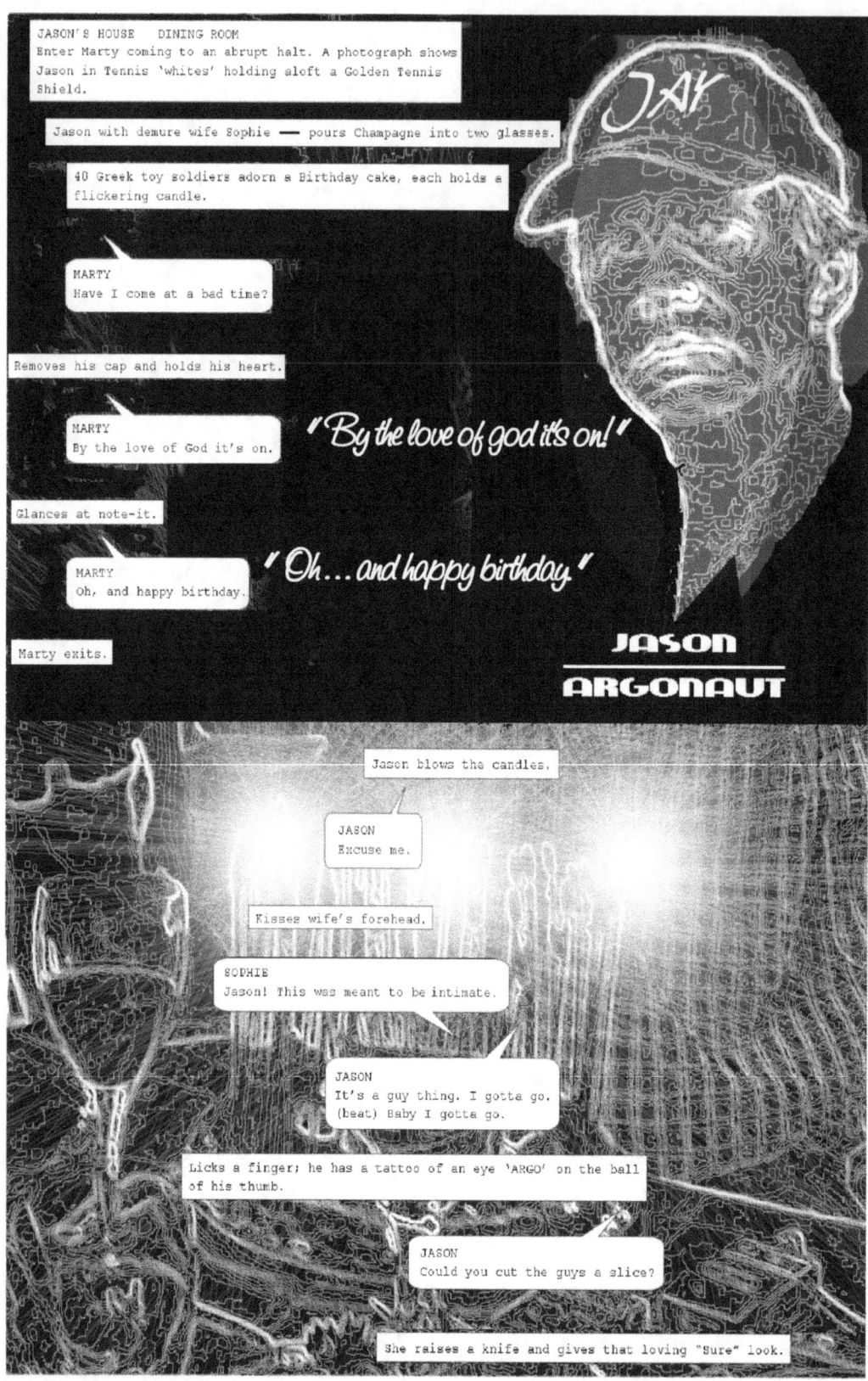

INT. JASON'S HOUSE   DINING ROOM   DAY

Enter Marty coming to an abrupt halt. A photograph shows
Jason in Tennis 'whites' holding aloft a Golden Tennis
Shield.

Jason with demure wife Sophie — pours Champagne into two
glasses.

40 Greek toy soldiers adorn a Birthday cake, each holds a
flickering candle.

> MARTY
> Have I come at a bad time?

Removes his cap and holds his heart.

> MARTY
> By the love of God it's on.

Glances at note-it.

> MARTY
> Oh, and happy birthday.

Marty exits.

Jason blows the candles.

> JASON
> Excuse me.

Kisses wife's forehead.

> SOPHIE
> Jason! This was meant to be
> intimate.

> JASON
> It's a guy thing. I gotta go.
> (beat) Baby I gotta go.

Licks a finger; he has a tattoo of an eye 'ARGO' on the ball
of his thumb.

> JASON
> Could you cut the guys a slice?

She raises a knife and gives that loving "Sure" look.

DRIVEWAY/LYNX'S HOUSE
Marty emerges, hotly pursued by LYNX; various patches
decorate his leather jacket. He bites at the straps on his
boxing gloves and pats his pockets.

LYNX
Keys, money. Rock 'n' Roll!

LYNX'S HOUSE   DRIVEWAY
Marty vaults into the rear of a PICK-UP.
Lynx shadow boxes into the wing-mirror then jumps up-front.
Engine revs and they reverse across the street.

JASON'S HOUSE   FRONT LAWN DAY
Jason adjusts a sprinkler. Holds cake in one hand.

Lynx and Marty reverse over the edge of his lawn.
Child's toy squeaks underneath the rear wheel.

JASON
Damn it guys! Watch the lawn.

LYNX
It's dead weight Marty here riding
shotgun.

JASON
I'll give you a bleedin' shotgun.

Under the rear wheel, the whine from a toy snake expanding
back into shape.

LYNX
ARGONAUT

EXT./INT. DRIVEWAY/LYNX'S HOUSE   DAY

Marty emerges, hotly pursued by LYNX; various patches
decorate his leather jacket. He bites at the straps on his
boxing gloves and pats his pockets.

> LYNX
> Keys, money. Rock 'n' Roll!

EXT. LYNX'S HOUSE   DRIVEWAY   DAY

Marty vaults into the rear of a PICK-UP.

Lynx shadow boxes into the wing-mirror then jumps up-front.

Engine revs and they reverse across the street.

EXT. JASON'S HOUSE   FRONT LAWN   DAY

Jason adjusts a sprinkler. Holds cake in one hand.

Lynx and Marty reverse over the edge of his lawn.

Child's toy squeaks underneath the rear wheel.

> JASON
> Damn it guys! Watch the lawn.

> LYNX
> It's dead weight Marty here riding
> shotgun.

> JASON
> I'll give you a bleedin' shotgun.

Under the rear wheel, the whine from a toy snake expanding
back into shape.

DINER DAY
Uncomfortable tables.

Jason deals four beer coasters, one to Marty, one to Lynx,
himself and an empty chair.

Marty and Lynx look at each other, then to Jason.

JASON
Orpheus.

LYNX
Orpheus.

MARTY
Orpheus.

JASON
Give him a call Marty!

MARTY
Why's it always me?

MOMENTS LATER
On his cell phone.

MARTY
Hi, it's (beat) yeah it's me, his
best friend, Marty.

Mouths "it's Eurydice" to Lynx and Jason who wince.

MARTY
Yeah, is he home?

Just myself, Lynx and Jason.

No women, just hunting. It's a guy
thing, let him out; it'll give you
more time to underpin that wedding
dress.

Yes, sorry, he did mention it.

INT. DINER   DAY

Uncomfortable tables.

Jason deals four beer coasters, one to Marty, one to Lynx,
himself and an empty chair.

Marty and Lynx look at each other, then to Jason.

              JASON   LYNX   MARTY
         Orpheus.   Orpheus.   Orpheus.

                        JASON
              Give him a call Marty!

                        MARTY
              Why's it always me?

MOMENTS LATER

On his cell phone.

                        MARTY
              Hi, it's (beat) yeah it's me, his
              best friend, Marty.

Mouths "it's Eurydice" to Lynx and Jason who wince.

                        MARTY
              Yeah, is he home?
                   (beat)
              Just myself, Lynx and Jason.
                   (beat)
              No women, just hunting. It's a guy
              thing, let him out; it'll give you
              more time to underpin that wedding
              dress.
                   (beat)
              Yes, sorry, he did mention it.

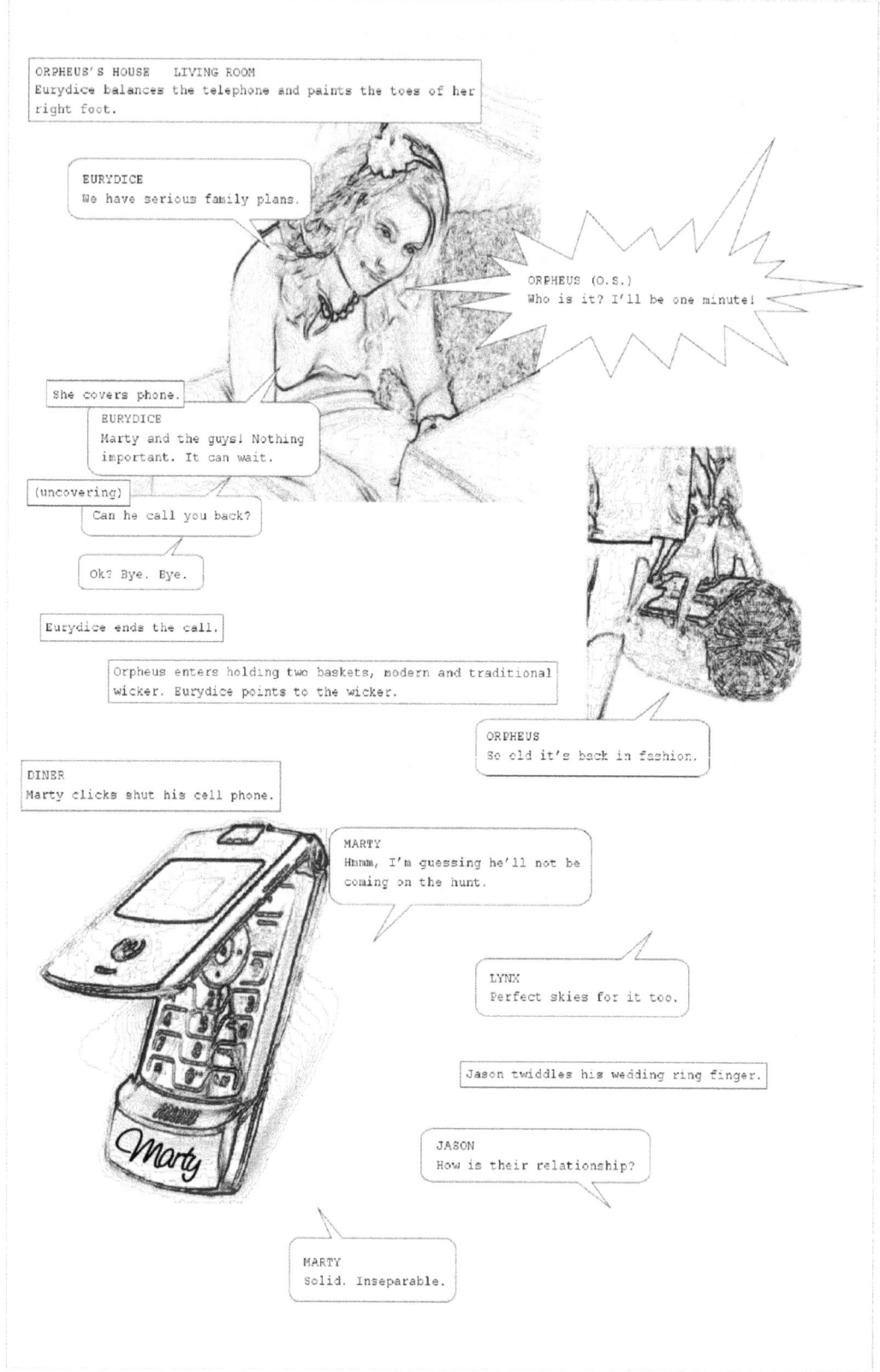

ORPHEUS'S HOUSE   LIVING ROOM
Eurydice balances the telephone and paints the toes of her
right foot.

EURYDICE
We have serious family plans.

ORPHEUS (O.S.)
Who is it? I'll be one minute!

She covers phone.

EURYDICE
Marty and the guys! Nothing
important. It can wait.

(uncovering)
Can he call you back?

Ok? Bye. Bye.

Eurydice ends the call.

Orpheus enters holding two baskets, modern and traditional
wicker. Eurydice points to the wicker.

ORPHEUS
So old it's back in fashion.

DINER
Marty clicks shut his cell phone.

MARTY
Hmmm, I'm guessing he'll not be
coming on the hunt.

LYNX
Perfect skies for it too.

Jason twiddles his wedding ring finger.

JASON
How is their relationship?

MARTY
Solid. Inseparable.

INT. ORPHEUS'S HOUSE   LIVING ROOM   DAY

Eurydice balances the telephone and paints the toes of her
right foot.

                    EURYDICE
          We have serious family plans.

                    ORPHEUS (O.S.)
          Who is it? I'll be one minute!

She covers phone.

                    EURYDICE
          Marty and the guys! Nothing
          important. It can wait.
                    (uncovering)
          Can he call you back?
                    (beat)
          Ok? Bye. Bye.

Eurydice ends the call.

Orpheus enters holding two baskets, modern and traditional
wicker. Eurydice points to the wicker.

                    ORPHEUS
          So old it's back in fashion.

INT. DINER   DAY

Marty clicks shut his cell phone.

                    MARTY
          Hmmm, I'm guessing he'll not be
          coming on the hunt.

                    LYNX
          Perfect skies for it too.

Jason twiddles his wedding ring finger.

                    JASON
          How is their relationship?

                    MARTY
          Solid. Inseparable.

ORPHEUS'S HOUSE   LIVING ROOM
Orpheus hums a tune, takes a sepia lake photograph of a
woman sat in a boat from a dusty box.

Eurydice face reflects in the picture.

He places a caduceus CHARM in her palm.

EURYDICE
I think your grandfather would have
wanted you to keep it.

ORPHEUS
Yeah, it always reminded him of
GRAN; as did this picture. Is a
shame to keep this all boxed up.

Swaps the picture with one above the fireplace.

EURYDICE
Can you remember anything?

ORPHEUS
I must have been really young that
day she drowned, or maybe I just
dreamt the whole thing.

In the box, a CONCH SHELL in newspaper obscures a JOURNAL
whose cover depicts a two-legged snake.

EURYDICE
Keep-sakes?

ORPHEUS
The love of his life. Just couldn't
let her go.

I want you to have it. It meant so
much to him. You are the love of my
life too.

Conch Shell...

Taking the charm... squeezing it with white
knuckles. She nuzzles into him, holding him tight

EURYDICE
God you make me feel so special.

INT. ORPHEUS'S HOUSE   LIVING ROOM   DAY

Orpheus hums a tune, takes a sepia lake photograph of a
woman sat in a boat from a dusty box.

Eurydice face reflects in the picture.

He places a caduceus CHARM in her palm.

> EURYDICE
> I think your grandfather would have
> wanted you to keep it.

> ORPHEUS
> Yeah, it always reminded him of
> GRAN; as did this picture. Is a
> shame to keep this all boxed up.

Swaps the picture with one above the fireplace.

> EURYDICE
> Can you remember anything?

> ORPHEUS
> I must have been really young that
> day she drowned, or maybe I just
> dreamt the whole thing.

In the box, a CONCH SHELL in newspaper obscures a JOURNAL
whose cover depicts a two-legged snake.

> EURYDICE
> Keep-sakes?

> ORPHEUS
> The love of his life. Just couldn't
> let her go.
>   (beat)
> I want you to have it. It meant so
> much to him. You are the love of my
> life too.

Taking the charm... squeezing it with white
knuckles. She nuzzles into him, holding him tight

> EURYDICE
> God you make me feel so special.

DINER DAY
Lynx splits open a large bag of monkey-nuts.

Jason deals out four beer coasters depicting a crossbow,
dart, rifle and dagger.

Marty's cellular phone hums. He flips it open. A Kestrel
emblem adorns the cover.

With a mouthful of nuts.

MARTY
Yup?

ORPHEUS (O.S.)
(filtered)
Jason?

MARTY
No, it's Marty.

ORPHEUS (O.S.)
(filtered)
I'll catch all you guys up later.
I'm torn. She's got her heart set
on the lakes, it's our anniversary
and I don't wanna let her down.

MARTY
No problem. Take care of number one.

ORPHEUS
In a week, weather permitting - I'm
'good to go'. You guys will still
be there right?

MARTY
Does a bear drop a Titan in
the woods? . . . Stay true.

Closes phone.

MARTY
Sounds like he's taking his beloved
to Cozy-Cabins. He's torn. What can
the man do, he loves her to bits.

INT. DINER   DAY

Lynx splits open a large bag of monkey-nuts.

Jason deals out four beer coasters depicting a crossbow, dart, rifle and dagger.

Marty's cellular phone hums. He flips it open. A Kestrel emblem adorns the cover.

With a mouthful of nuts.

                    MARTY
          Yup?

                    ORPHEUS (O.S.)
                  (filtered)
          Jason?

                    MARTY
          No, it's Marty.

                    ORPHEUS (O.S.)
                  (filtered)
          I'll catch all you guys up later.
          I'm torn. She's got her heart set
          on the lakes, it's our anniversary
          and I don't wanna let her down.

                    MARTY
          No problem. Take care of number
          one.

                    ORPHEUS

          In a week, weather permitting - I'm
          'good to go'. You guys will still
          be there right?

                    MARTY

          **Does a bear drop a Titan in
          the woods? (beat) Stay true.**

Closes phone.

                    MARTY
          Sounds like he's taking his beloved
          to Cozy-Cabins. He's torn. What can
          the man do, he loves her to bits.

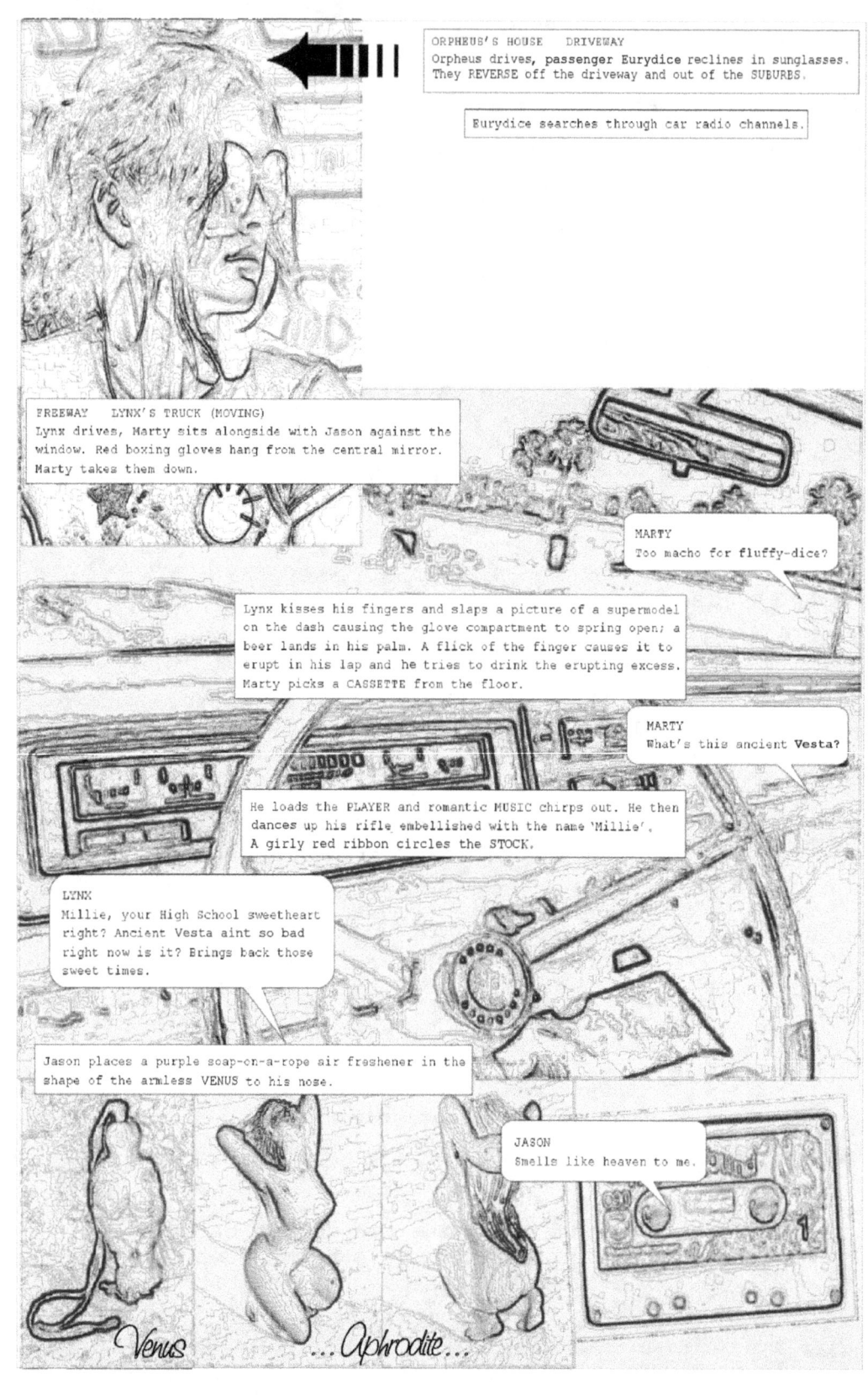

ORPHEUS'S HOUSE   DRIVEWAY
Orpheus drives, passenger Eurydice reclines in sunglasses.
They REVERSE off the driveway and out of the SUBURBS.

Eurydice searches through car radio channels.

FREEWAY   LYNX'S TRUCK (MOVING)
Lynx drives, Marty sits alongside with Jason against the
window. Red boxing gloves hang from the central mirror.
Marty takes them down.

MARTY
Too macho for fluffy-dice?

Lynx kisses his fingers and slaps a picture of a supermodel
on the dash causing the glove compartment to spring open; a
beer lands in his palm. A flick of the finger causes it to
erupt in his lap and he tries to drink the erupting excess.
Marty picks a CASSETTE from the floor.

MARTY
What's this ancient Vesta?

He loads the PLAYER and romantic MUSIC chirps out. He then
dances up his rifle embellished with the name 'Millie'.
A girly red ribbon circles the STOCK.

LYNX
Millie, your High School sweetheart
right? Ancient Vesta aint so bad
right now is it? Brings back those
sweet times.

Jason places a purple soap-on-a-rope air freshener in the
shape of the armless VENUS to his nose.

JASON
Smells like heaven to me.

Venus   ...Aphrodite...

EXT. ORPHEUS'S HOUSE   DRIVEWAY   DAY

Orpheus drives, passenger Eurydice reclines in sunglasses.
They REVERSE off the driveway and out of the SUBURBS.

Eurydice searches through car radio channels.

INT. FREEWAY   LYNX'S TRUCK (MOVING)   DAY

Lynx drives, Marty sits alongside with Jason against the
window. Red boxing gloves hang from the central mirror.
Marty takes them down.

                    MARTY
          Too macho for fluffy-dice?

Lynx kisses his fingers and slaps a picture of a supermodel
on the dash causing the glove compartment to spring open; a
beer lands in his palm. A flick of the finger causes it to
erupt and he tries to drink the excess.

Marty picks up a CASSETTE from the floor.

                    MARTY
          What's this ancient Vesta?

He loads the PLAYER and romantic MUSIC chirps out. He then
dances up his rifle embellished with the name 'Millie'.
A girly red ribbon circles the STOCK.

                    LYNX
          Millie, your High School sweetheart
          right? Ancient **Vesta aint so bad**
          right now is it? Brings back those
          sweet times.

Jason places a purple soap-on-a-rope air freshener in the
shape of the armless VENUS to his nose.

                    JASON
          Smells like heaven to me.

Lynx slaps the dashboard supermodel.

                                        (CONTINUED)

LYNX
Now hasn't she the beauty of
Aphrodite?

Lynx's face distorts. Reaching inside the glove compartment.

LYNX
Forget fresh-air.
How about beers?!

FREEWAY - ORPHEUS'S CAR (MOVING)
Eurydice raises sunscreen, her nostrils flare; looks to
Orpheus who closes the window exhaling in short breaths.

ORPHEUS
You really think that was me?
Something just hit one gargantuan
fan. Mine smell of roses.

In a nearby field, a spreader flips out manure.

FREEWAY - LYNX'S TRUCK (MOVING)
Jason shakes his head at Marty. Lynx drives.

JASON
Caliber is a substitute for sexual
inadequacy.

Marty puts his hands down his pants and pulls out a long fat
rifle-silencer.

MARTY
No one will hear this thing coming.

LYNX
Sorry to change the tune a little.
Jay, how is it your wife lets you
come on these outings?
(CONTINUED)

CONTINUED:

> LYNX
> Now hasn't she the beauty of
> Aphrodite?

Lynx's face distorts. Reaching inside the glove compartment.

> LYNX
> Forget fresh air. How about beers?!

EXT. FREEWAY   ORPHEUS'S CAR (MOVING)   DAY

Eurydice raises sunscreen, her nostrils flare; looks to
Orpheus who closes the window exhaling in short breaths.

> ORPHEUS
> You really think that was me?
> Something just hit one gargantuan
> fan. Mine smell of roses.

In a nearby field, a spreader flips out manure.

EXT. FREEWAY   LYNX'S TRUCK (MOVING)   DAY

Jason shakes his head at Marty. Lynx drives.

> JASON
> Caliber is a substitute for sexual
> inadequacy.

Marty puts his hands down his pants and pulls out a long fat
rifle-silencer.

> MARTY
> No one will hear this thing coming.

> LYNX
> Sorry to change the tune a little.
> Jay, how is it your wife lets you
> come on these outings?

(CONTINUED)

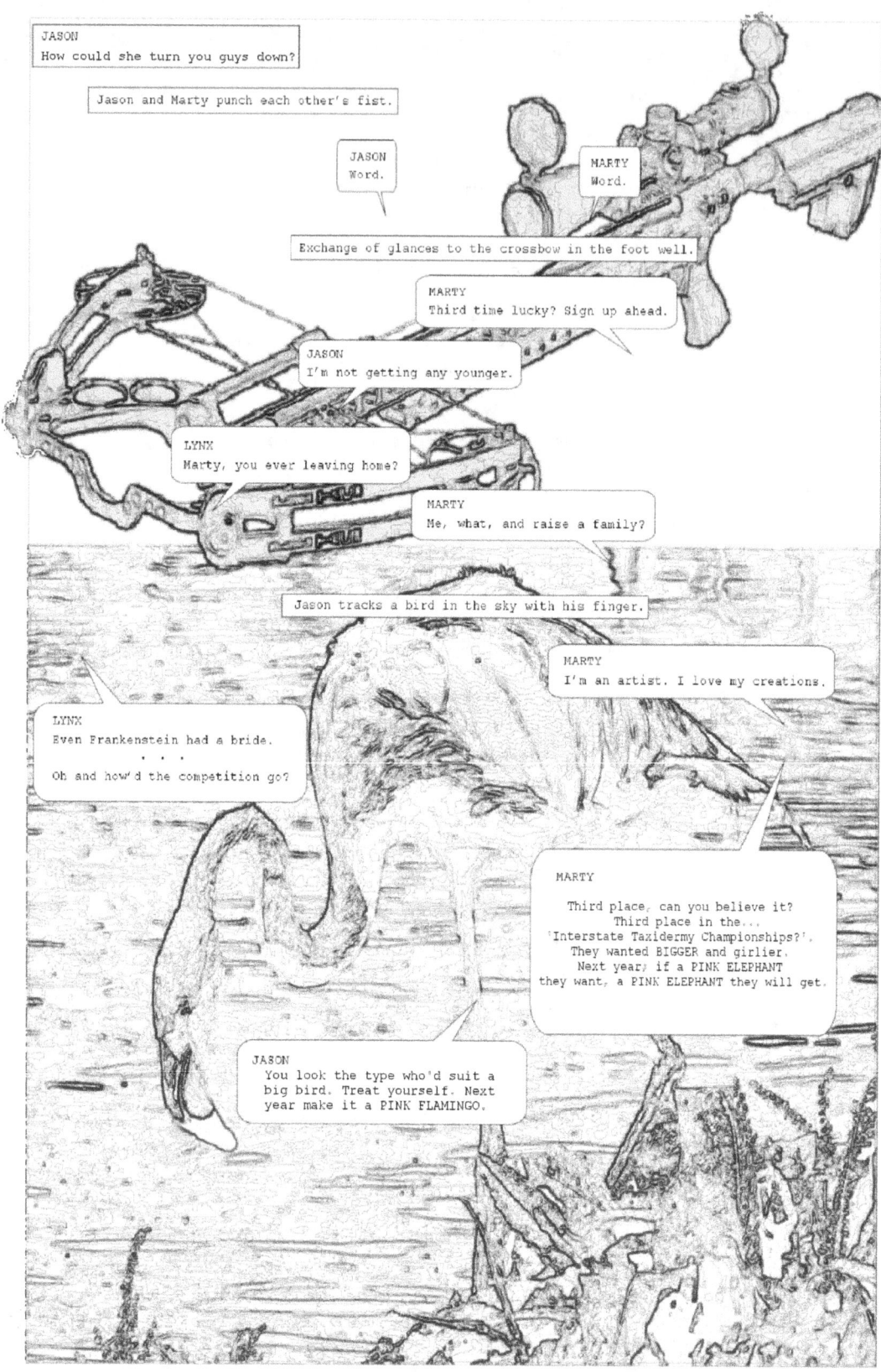

JASON
How could she turn you guys down?

Jason and Marty punch each other's fist.

JASON
Word.

MARTY
Word.

Exchange of glances to the crossbow in the foot well.

MARTY
Third time lucky? Sign up ahead.

JASON
I'm not getting any younger.

LYNX
Marty, you ever leaving home?

MARTY
Me, what, and raise a family?

Jason tracks a bird in the sky with his finger.

MARTY
I'm an artist. I love my creations.

LYNX
Even Frankenstein had a bride.
. . .
Oh and how'd the competition go?

MARTY
Third place, can you believe it?
Third place in the...
`Interstate Taxidermy Championships?'.
They wanted BIGGER and girlier.
Next year, if a PINK ELEPHANT
they want, a PINK ELEPHANT they will get.

JASON
You look the type who'd suit a
big bird. Treat yourself. Next
year make it a PINK FLAMINGO.

CONTINUED:

>   JASON
>   How could she turn you guys down?

Jason and Marty punch each other's fist.

>   JASON   MARTY
>   Word.   Word.

Exchange of glances to the crossbow in the foot well.

>   MARTY
>   Third time lucky? Sign up ahead.

>   JASON
>   I'm not getting any younger.

>   LYNX
>   Marty, you ever leaving home?

>   MARTY
>   Me, what, and raise a family?

Jason tracks a bird in the sky with his finger.

>   MARTY
>   I'm an artist. I love my creations,

>   LYNX
>   Even Frankenstein had a bride.
>   (beat)
>   Oh and how'd the competition go?

>   MARTY
>   Third place, can you believe it?
>   Third place in the...
>   'Interstate Taxidermy Championships?'.
>   They wanted BIGGER and girlier.
>   Next year; if a PINK ELEPHANT they want,
>   a PINK ELEPHANT they will get.

>   JASON
>   You look the type who'd suit a
>   big bird. Treat yourself. Next
>   year make it a PINK FLAMINGO.

(CONTINUED)

CONTINUED:
Jason smiles behind Marty.

MARTY
You think?

JASON
How about one in flight; may not
impress the judges but would
impress the hell outta me.

Sign reads "Hunting cabin - we'll do anything for a BUCK",
with a picture of a male deer.

Jason fires, his bolt strikes the BUCK in the forehead.

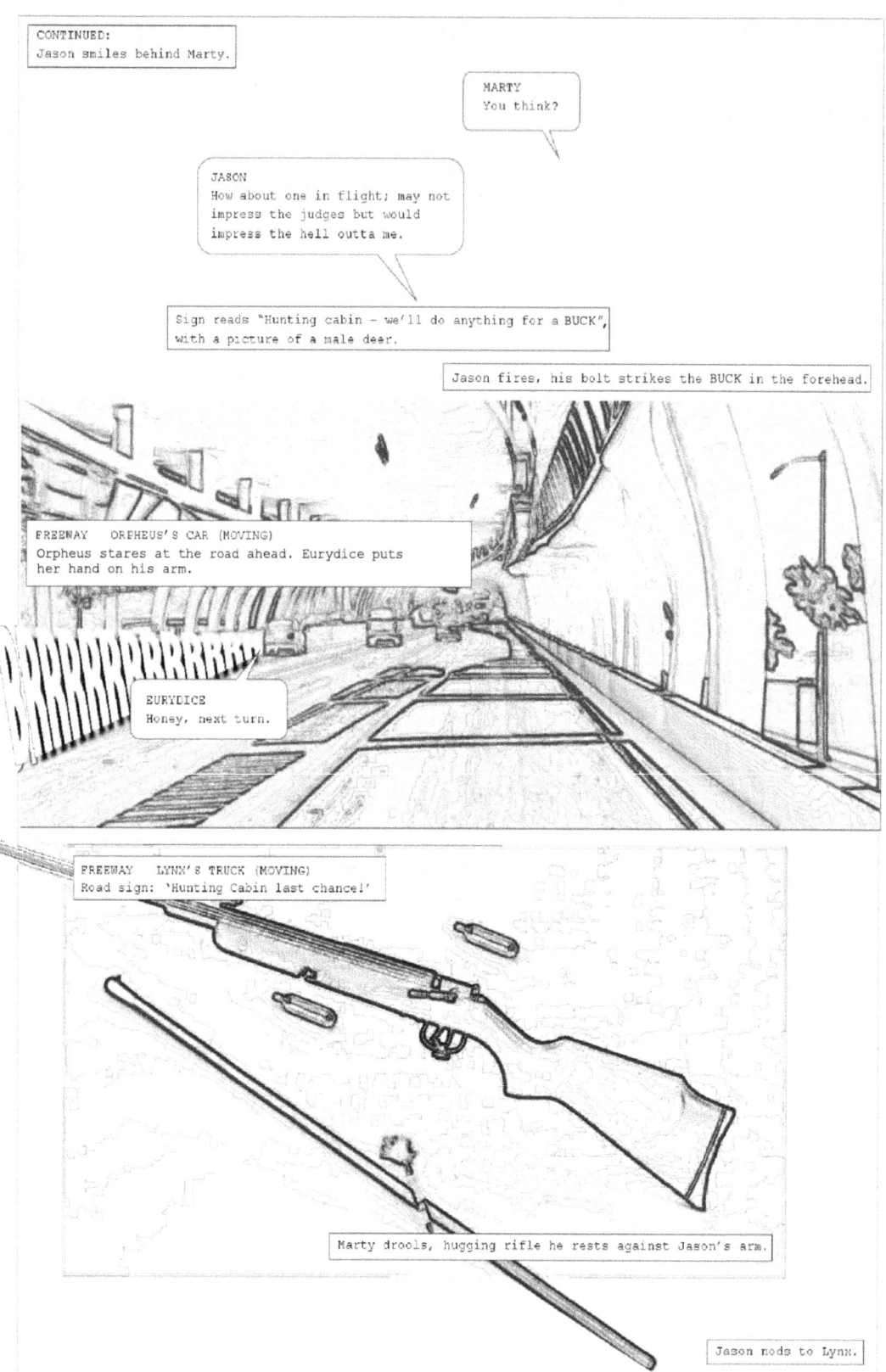

FREEWAY   ORPHEUS'S CAR (MOVING)
Orpheus stares at the road ahead. Eurydice puts
her hand on his arm.

EURYDICE
Honey, next turn.

FREEWAY   LYNX'S TRUCK (MOVING)
Road sign: 'Hunting Cabin last chance!'

Marty drools, hugging rifle he rests against Jason's arm.

Jason nods to Lynx.

CONTINUED:

Jason smiles behind Marty.

>   MARTY
>   You think?

>   JASON
>   How about one in flight; may not
>   impress the judges but would
>   impress the hell outta me.

Sign reads "Hunting cabin - we'll do anything for a BUCK"
with a picture of a male deer.

Jason fires, his bolt strikes the BUCK in the forehead.

EXT. FREEWAY   ORPHEUS'S CAR (MOVING)   DAY
Orpheus stares at the road ahead. Eurydice puts her hand
on his arm.

>   EURYDICE
>   Honey, next turn.

EXT. FREEWAY   LYNX'S TRUCK (MOVING)   DAY

Road sign: 'Hunting Cabin last chance!'

Marty drools, hugging rifle he rests against Jason's arm.

Jason nods to Lynx.

Swerving onto the verge Marty jerks hysterically awake.

They hit the dirt road, foliage brushing the side of the
vehicle to the sound of cranked up MUSIC.

Ancien times...

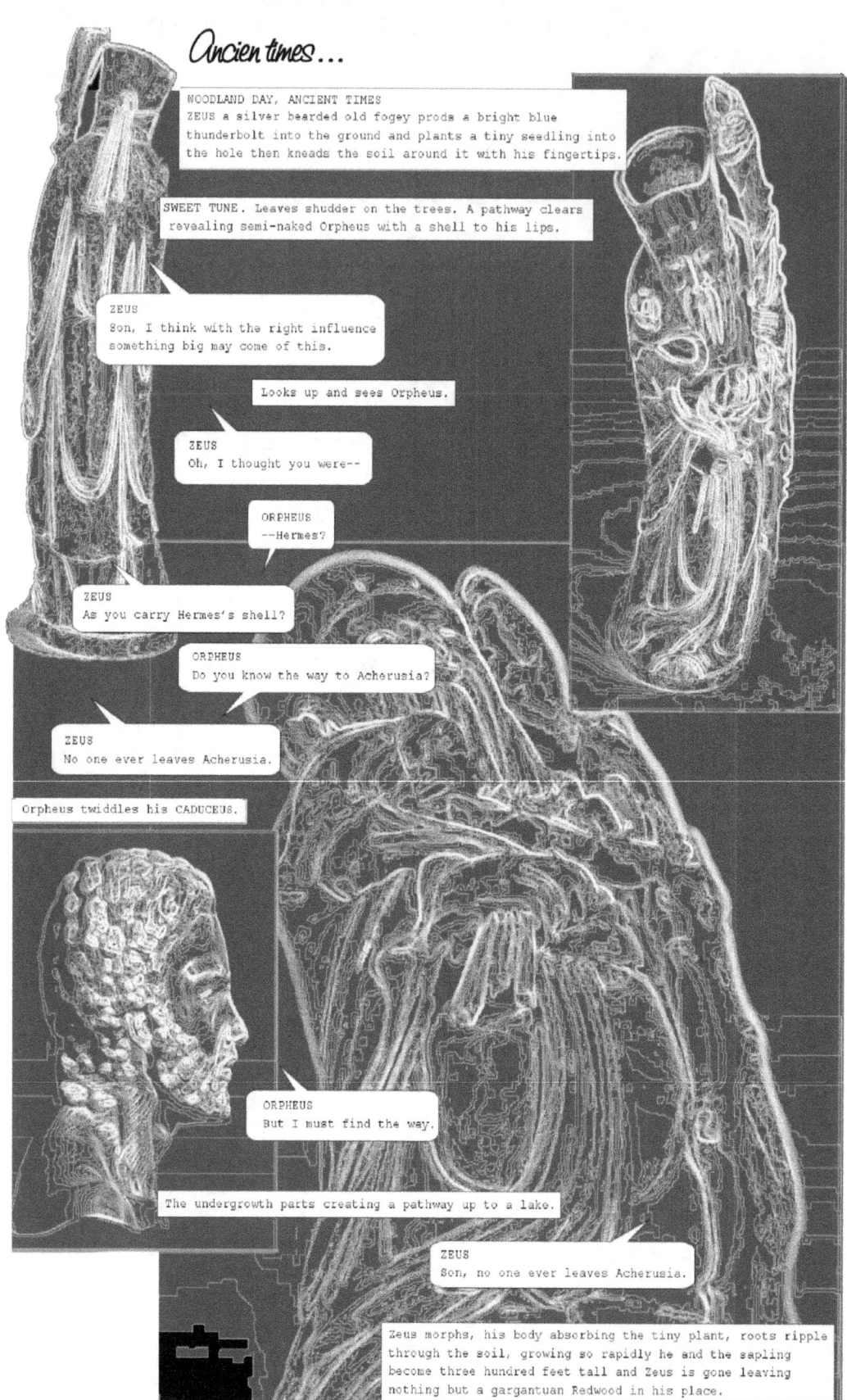

WOODLAND DAY, ANCIENT TIMES
ZEUS a silver bearded old fogey prods a bright blue
thunderbolt into the ground and plants a tiny seedling into
the hole then kneads the soil around it with his fingertips.

SWEET TUNE. Leaves shudder on the trees. A pathway clears
revealing semi-naked Orpheus with a shell to his lips.

ZEUS
Son, I think with the right influence
something big may come of this.

Looks up and sees Orpheus.

ZEUS
Oh, I thought you were--

ORPHEUS
--Hermes?

ZEUS
As you carry Hermes's shell?

ORPHEUS
Do you know the way to Acherusia?

ZEUS
No one ever leaves Acherusia.

Orpheus twiddles his CADUCEUS.

ORPHEUS
But I must find the way.

The undergrowth parts creating a pathway up to a lake.

ZEUS
Son, no one ever leaves Acherusia.

Zeus morphs, his body absorbing the tiny plant, roots ripple
through the soil, growing so rapidly he and the sapling
become three hundred feet tall and Zeus is gone leaving
nothing but a gargantuan Redwood in his place.

. . . A CRACK OF LIGHTNING STRIKES THE TREE.

EXT. WOODLAND   DAY, ANCIENT TIMES

ZEUS a silver bearded old fogey prods a bright blue
thunderbolt into the ground and plants a tiny seedling into
the hole then kneads the soil around it with his fingertips.

SWEET TUNE. Leaves shudder on the trees. A pathway clears
revealing semi-naked Orpheus with a shell to his lips.

                    ZEUS
          Son, I think with the right influence
          something big may come of this.

Looks up and sees Orpheus.

                    ZEUS
          Oh, I thought you were--

                    ORPHEUS
          --Hermes?

                    ZEUS
          As you carry Hermes's shell?

                    ORPHEUS
          Do you know the way to Acherusia?

                    ZEUS
          No one ever leaves Acherusia.

Orpheus twiddles his CADUCEUS.

                    ORPHEUS
          But I must find the way.

The undergrowth parts creating a pathway up to a lake.

                    ZEUS
          Son, no one ever leaves Acherusia.

Zeus morphs, his body absorbing the tiny plant, roots ripple
through the soil, growing so rapidly he and the sapling
become three hundred feet tall and Zeus is gone leaving
nothing but a gargantuan Redwood in his place.

A CRACK OF LIGHTNING STRIKES THE TREE.

EXT. GREAT REDWOOD TREE   ORPHEUS'S CAR (MOVING)   DAY

Sign reads 'One thousand year-old great redwood'. Orpheus
and Eurydice pass through a tunnel in the tree and up to a
lake visible in the distance.

                    EURYDICE
          Hurry honey we'll miss the ferry.

EXT. LAKE SHOP   ORPHEUS'S CAR   DAY

Signs "Hourly crossing" and "Do not feed animals".

Orpheus carries basket to Eurydice who lays out a tablecloth
on one of the surrounding picnic tables.

Enter Zeus rattling a bunch of keys on the veranda.

                    ZEUS
          Staying long?

                    ORPHEUS
          Maybe a week.

                    EURYDICE
          Are there really Grizzlies?

Zeus hands over a number thirteen cabin-key.

                    ZEUS
          Grizzlies no? But wait till you see
          the size of them spiders. Chalets
          across the lake. Enjoy your stay.

LATER

Orpheus at one of the picnic tables studies the floaters in
his eyes with a far away expression.

                    ORPHEUS
          Cabin thirteen, nothing to hunt;
          enjoy your stay. What a jinx.

HUNTING CABIN
A teasingly delicious aroma wafts from a barbecue. Jason complete with 'white mushroom hat' plays Chef. He scorches a finger on a burger that hisses back.

Lynx and Marty laugh and swap pictures of their last stag hunting week.

Beers in hand, smacking lips.

JASON
Round one!

Lynx licks the excess from his burger in a bun.

LYNX
Palatable but is there anything adventurous to spice this up?

Lynx pops the lid off a jar and spoons on relish.

LAKE SHOP   PICNIC AREA
Orpheus reads a Toppling Springs 'Wildlife' brochure.
FRONT COVER 'The Hunt is on! Deer Season!'

LAKE SHOP   WINDOW
Miscellaneous bric-a-brac, seasonal shop flotsam; fishing rods, reels and various bate hooks.

"Palatable but is there anything adventurous to spice this up?"

EURYDICE
Orpheus?

"Orrpheus?"

Weird animal head trophies hang behind the counter.

EXT. HUNTING CABIN   DAY

A teasingly delicious aroma wafts from a barbecue. Jason
complete with 'white mushroom hat' plays Chef. He scorches a
finger on a burger that hisses back.

Lynx and Marty laugh and swap pictures of their last stag
hunting week.

Beers in hand, smacking lips.

                    JASON
          Round one!

Lynx licks the excess from his burger in a bun.

                    LYNX
          Palatable but is there Anything
          adventurous to spice this up?

Lynx pops the lid off a jar and spoons on relish.

EXT. LAKE SHOP   PICNIC AREA   DAY

Orpheus reads a *Toppling Springs* 'Wildlife' brochure.
FRONT COVER 'The Hunt is on! Deer Season!'

EXT. LAKE SHOP   WINDOW   DAY

Miscellaneous bric-a-brac, seasonal shop flotsam; fishing
rods, reels and various bate hooks.

                    EURYDICE
          Orpheus?

Weird animal head trophies hang behind the counter.

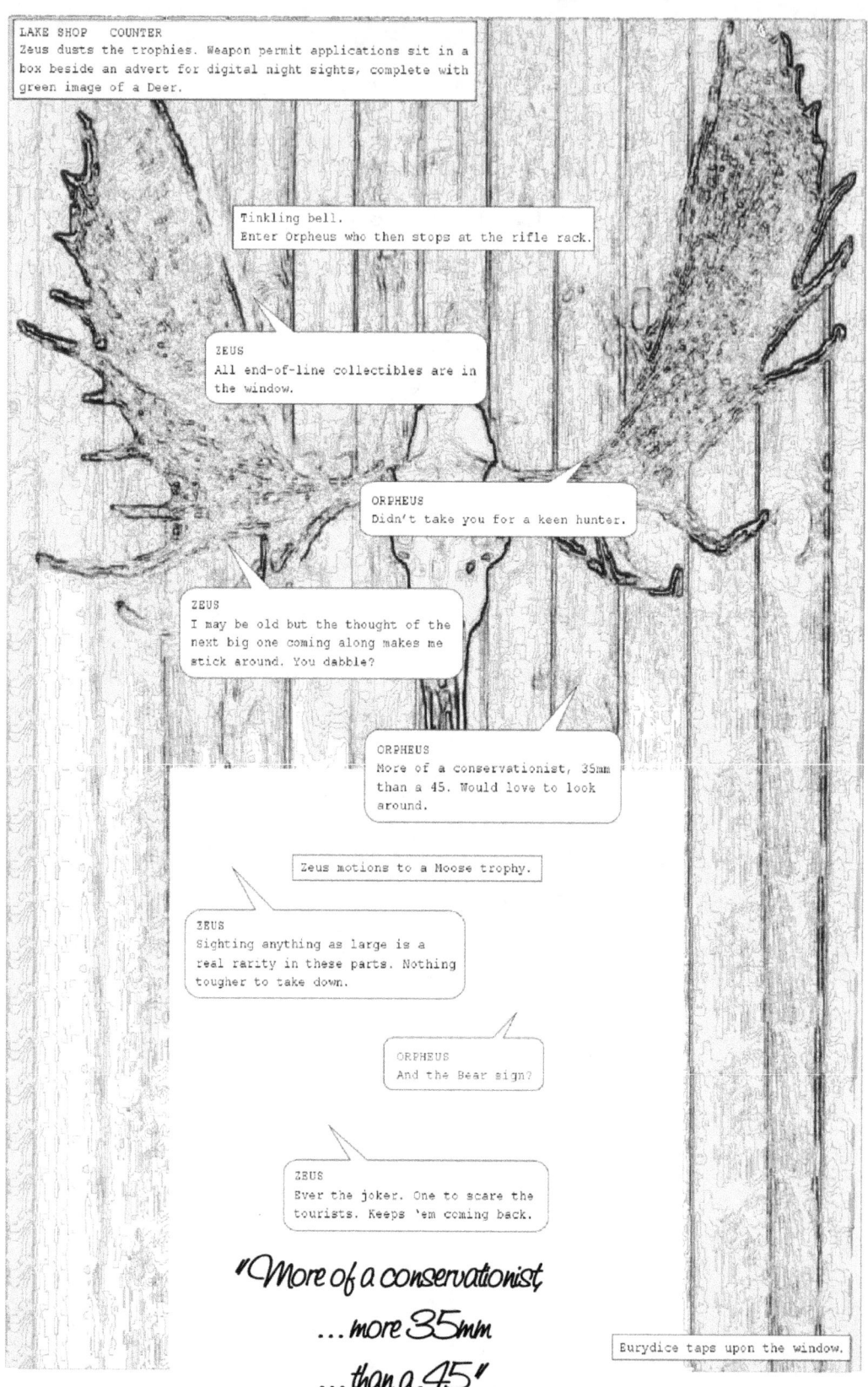

LAKE SHOP   COUNTER
Zeus dusts the trophies. Weapon permit applications sit in a box beside an advert for digital night sights, complete with green image of a Deer.

Tinkling bell.
Enter Orpheus who then stops at the rifle rack.

ZEUS
All end-of-line collectibles are in the window.

ORPHEUS
Didn't take you for a keen hunter.

ZEUS
I may be old but the thought of the next big one coming along makes me stick around. You dabble?

ORPHEUS
More of a conservationist, 35mm than a 45. Would love to look around.

Zeus motions to a Moose trophy.

ZEUS
Sighting anything as large is a real rarity in these parts. Nothing tougher to take down.

ORPHEUS
And the Bear sign?

ZEUS
Ever the joker. One to scare the tourists. Keeps 'em coming back.

"More of a conservationist,
... more 35mm
... than a .45"

Eurydice taps upon the window.

INT. LAKE SHOP   COUNTER   DAY

Zeus dusts the trophies. Weapon permit applications sit in a box beside an advert for digital night sights, complete with green image of a Deer.

Tinkling bell.

Enter Orpheus who then stops at the rifle rack.

> ZEUS
> All end-of-line collectibles are in
> the window.

> ORPHEUS
> Didn't take you for a keen hunter.

> ZEUS
> I may be old but the thought of the
> next big one coming along makes me
> stick around. You dabble?

> ORPHEUS
> More of a conservationist, 35mm
> than a 45. Would love to look
> around.

Zeus motions to a Moose trophy.

> ZEUS
> Sighting anything as large is a
> real rarity in these parts. Nothing
> tougher to take down.

> ORPHEUS
> And the Bear sign?

> ZEUS
> Ever the joker. One to scare the
> tourists. Keeps 'em coming back.

Eurydice taps upon the window.

The Rematch...

LAKE SHOP - PICNIC AREA
Orpheus exits the shop empty-handed. Eurydice stands beside
a 'To let' sign for an old lake boathouse.

Ferry horn.

EURYDICE
Honey the Ferry.

LAKE - FERRY
Orpheus and Eurydice board with other TOURISTS, of note is
Hermes in fishing garb, REEL in hand, SICKLE in the other.

EURYDICE
Orpheus, Honey?

She holds two sticks, wiggling one over the water's edge.

EURYDICE
Loser pays for dinner.

Orpheus takes one.

EURYDICE
One, two--

Her stick falls prematurely.

ORPHEUS
--What the! You cheat.

She chuckles.

EURYDICE
Ok. Rematch, start again.

Eurydice rushes from one side of the Ferry to the other.

Crouching; leg lowering, the water bubbles.

PLOP
PLOP
PLOP

The stick emerges an inch from her wriggling toes.
(CONTINUED)

" Ok Rematch start again"

The Rematch . . .   62.

EXT. LAKE SHOP   PICNIC AREA   DAY

Orpheus exits the shop empty-handed. Eurydice stands beside
a 'To let' sign for an old lake boathouse.

Ferry horn.

                         EURYDICE
                  Honey the Ferry.

EXT. LAKE   FERRY   DAY

Orpheus and Eurydice board with other TOURISTS, of note is
Hermes in fishing garb, REEL in hand, SICKLE in the other.

                         EURYDICE
                  Orpheus, Honey?

She holds two sticks, wiggling one over the water's edge.

                         EURYDICE
                  Loser pays for dinner.

Orpheus takes one.

                         EURYDICE
                  One, two--

Her stick falls prematurely.

                         ORPHEUS
                  --What the! You cheat.

She chuckles.

                         EURYDICE
                  Ok. Rematch, start again.

Eurydice rushes from one side of the Ferry to the other.

Crouching; leg lowering, the water bubbles.

The stick emerges an inch from her wriggling toes.

                                          (CONTINUED)

WHOOSH!

CONTINUED:
A toothy HYDRA erupts with a WHOOSH; chisel-like teeth seize
her by the ankle.

Orpheus looks to a space where his wife once stood.

Eurydice gasps air at the water's surface. She reaches for
the deck, nails splintering.

Orpheus pushes through the crowd; seconds expand.

Eurydice thrashes in the water.

EURYDICE
Argh-h-h!

Snake-like undulations move around her, the water darkening.
She reaches out and he grabs her wrist.

His grip slips from wrist to fingertips.

His other hand gains a grip of the safety rail but the deck
splinters where it meets the rotten deck. Both he and the
rail join Eurydice in the water.

LAKE   FERRY
Passengers scream.

PLOP
PLOP
PLOP

Orpheus gulps down water.

ORPHEUS
God save us!

ARGHH!!
AAAHHHH!

A strong hand from Hermes drags him aboard.

Behind, surfacing in a whirlpool of blood, thrown back and
forth like a rag-doll; she reaches out to him.

EURYDICE
Orpheus-s-s!
(CONTINUED)

CONTINUED:

A toothy HYDRA erupts with a WHOOSH; chisel-like teeth seize
her by the ankle.

Orpheus looks to a space where his wife once stood.

Eurydice gasps air at the water's surface. She reaches for
the deck, nails splintering.

Orpheus pushes through the crowd; seconds expand.

Eurydice thrashes in the water.

                    EURYDICE
          Argh-h-h!

Snake-like undulations move around her, the water darkening.

She reaches out and he grabs her wrist.

His grip slips from wrist to fingertips.

His other hand gains a grip of the safety rail but the deck
splinters where it meets the rotten deck. Both he and the
rail join Eurydice in the water.

EXT. LAKE   FERRY   DAY

Passengers scream.

Orpheus gulps down water.

                    ORPHEUS
          God save us!

A strong hand from Hermes drags him aboard.

Behind, surfacing in a whirlpool of blood, thrown back and
forth like a rag-doll; she reaches out to him.

                    EURYDICE
          Orpheus-s-s!

                                        (CONTINUED)

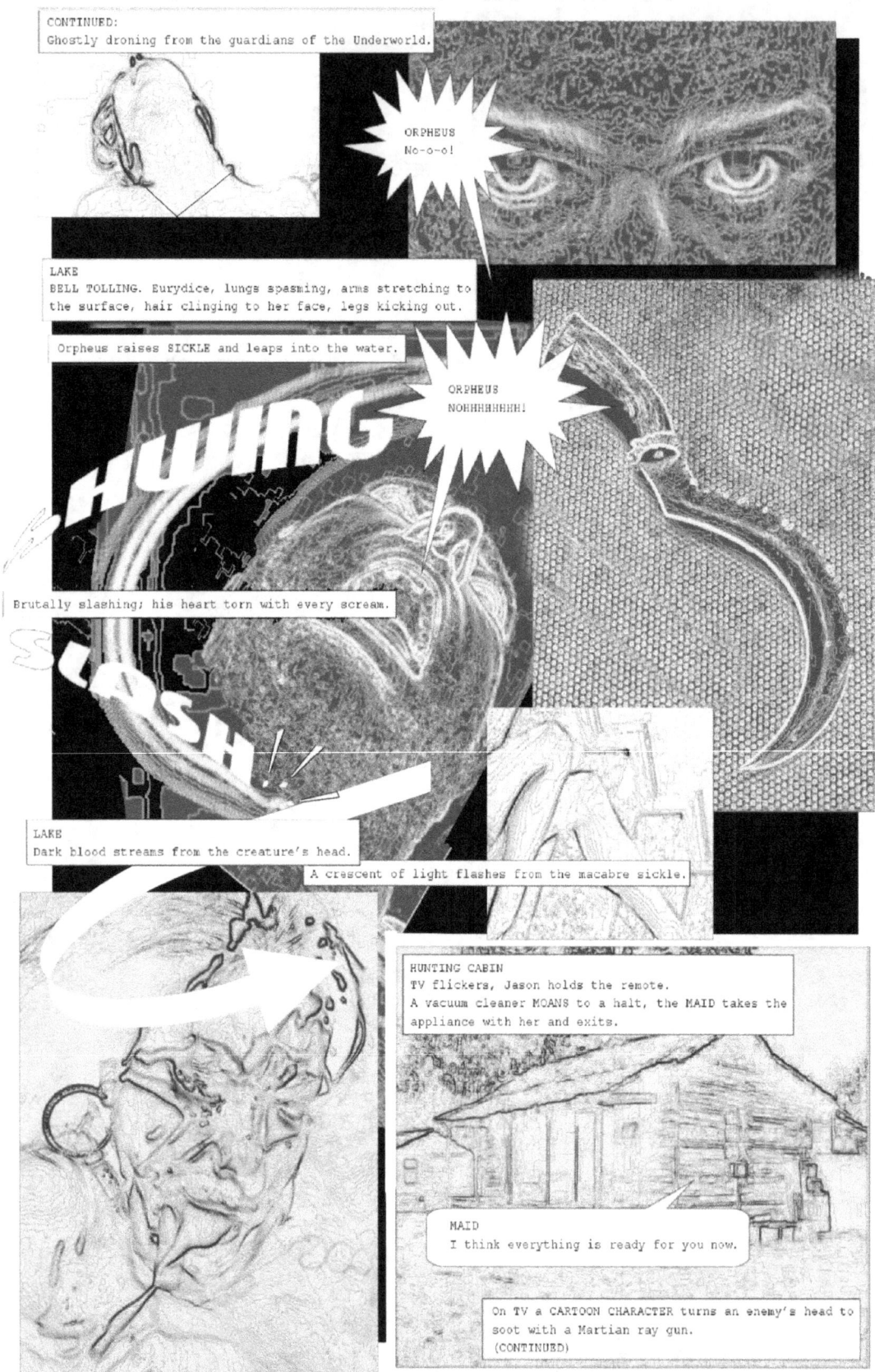

CONTINUED:

Ghostly droning from the guardians of the Underworld.

                    ORPHEUS
          No-o-o!

EXT. LAKE   DAY

BELL TOLLING. Eurydice, lungs spasming, arms stretching to
the surface, hair clinging to her face, legs kicking out.

Orpheus raises SICKLE and leaps into the water.

                    ORPHEUS
          NOHHHHHHHH!

Brutally slashing; his heart torn with every scream.

INT. LAKE   DAY

Dark blood streams from the creature's head.

A crescent of light flashes from the macabre sickle.

INT. HUNTING CABIN   DAY

TV flickers, Jason holds the remote.

A vacuum cleaner MOANS to a halt, the MAID takes the
appliance with her and exits.

                    MAID
          I think everything is ready for you
          now.

On TV a CARTOON CHARACTER turns an enemy's head to
soot with a Martian ray gun.

                              (CONTINUED)

Onscreen caption 'Breaking news'.

NEWS BROADCASTER
Toppling Springs Wildlife Foundation
responded to reports of not only a
sighting but an attack from a lake
serpent upon a lady known to us only
as Eurydice. Rangers attending the
scene can not dismiss a connection
with a similar attack in the same
place, to a lady of the same name way
back in the '30's. A compelling story
of mythic proportions; brought to you
by Ron Garland reporting for
'Toppling Springs' broadcasting.

Jason's mouth hovers inches above his burger.

" Eurydice?"

LAKE   SECLUDED SHORELINE
Orpheus sits in a few inches of bloody water. Incoming waves
from a search boat shunt ripples up his body. Tongue gagging
at the roof of his mouth. With the limp head of Eurydice
resting on his shoulder he tentatively grooms her hair.

ORPHEUS
Why take her from me! If there is a
God in this world he will bring her
back to me.

White knuckles snap the caduceus from around her neck
and he throws it far into the lake.

SKY   SECLUDED SHORELINE
POV from EURYDICE'S SOUL rising. Orpheus's whimpers become
less audible. The blue-green colors of the lake blur with
the deeper greens of surrounding trees.

Looking back through the clouds the Earth resembles an onyx green
rock floating in a vast open space.

CONTINUED:

Onscreen caption 'Breaking news'.

                    NEWS BROADCASTER
          Toppling Springs Wildlife Foundation
          responded to reports of not only a
          sighting but an attack from a lake
          serpent upon a lady known to us only
          as Eurydice. Rangers attending the
          scene can not dismiss a connection
          with a similar attack in the same
          place, to a lady of the same name way
          back in the '30's. A compelling story
          of mythic proportions; brought to you
          by Ron Garland reporting for
          'Toppling Springs' broadcasting.

Jason's mouth hovers inches above his burger.

EXT. LAKE   SECLUDED SHORELINE   DAY

Orpheus sits in a few inches of bloody water. Incoming waves
from a search boat shunt ripples up his body. Tongue gagging
at the roof of his mouth. With the limp head of Eurydice
resting on his shoulder he tentatively grooms her hair.

                    ORPHEUS
          Why take her from me! If there is a
          God in this world he will bring her
          back to me.

White knuckles snap the caduceus from around her neck and
he throws it far into the lake.

EXT. SKY   SECLUDED SHORELINE   DAY

POV from EURYDICE'S SOUL rising. Orpheus's whimpers become
less audible. The blue-green colors of the lake blur with
the deeper greens of surrounding trees.

Looking back through the clouds the Earth resembles an onyx-
green rock floating in a vast open space.

On the back of a celestial turtle...

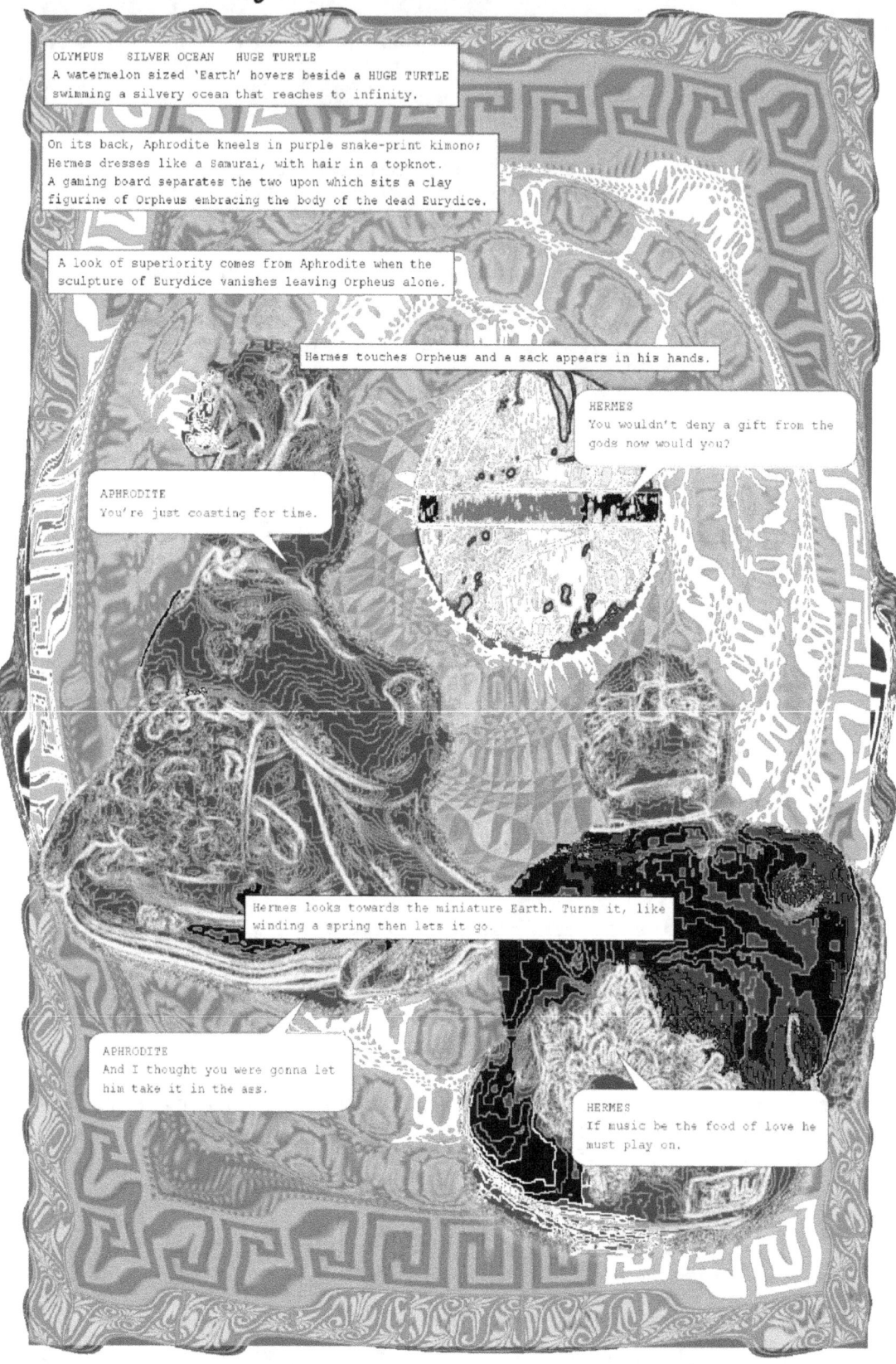

OLYMPUS   SILVER OCEAN   HUGE TURTLE
A watermelon sized 'Earth' hovers beside a HUGE TURTLE
swimming a silvery ocean that reaches to infinity.

On its back, Aphrodite kneels in purple snake-print kimono;
Hermes dresses like a Samurai, with hair in a topknot.
A gaming board separates the two upon which sits a clay
figurine of Orpheus embracing the body of the dead Eurydice.

A look of superiority comes from Aphrodite when the
sculpture of Eurydice vanishes leaving Orpheus alone.

Hermes touches Orpheus and a sack appears in his hands.

HERMES
You wouldn't deny a gift from the
gods now would you?

APHRODITE
You're just coasting for time.

Hermes looks towards the miniature Earth. Turns it, like
winding a spring then lets it go.

APHRODITE
And I thought you were gonna let
him take it in the ass.

HERMES
If music be the food of love he
must play on.

INT. OLYMPUS   SILVER OCEAN   HUGE TURTLE   DAY

A watermelon sized 'Earth' hovers beside a HUGE TURTLE
swimming a silvery ocean that reaches to infinity.

On its back, Aphrodite kneels in purple snake-print kimono;
Hermes dresses like a Samurai, with hair in a topknot.

A gaming board separates the two upon which sits a clay
figurine of Orpheus embracing the body of the dead Eurydice.

A look of superiority comes from Aphrodite when the
sculpture of Eurydice vanishes leaving Orpheus alone.

Hermes touches Orpheus and a sack appears in his hands.

                    HERMES
          You wouldn't deny a gift from the
          gods now would you?

                    APHRODITE
          You're just coasting for time.

Hermes looks towards the miniature Earth. Turns it, like
winding a spring then lets it go.

                    HERMES
          If music be the food of love he
          must play on.

                    APHRODITE
          And I thought you were gonna let
          him take it in the ass.

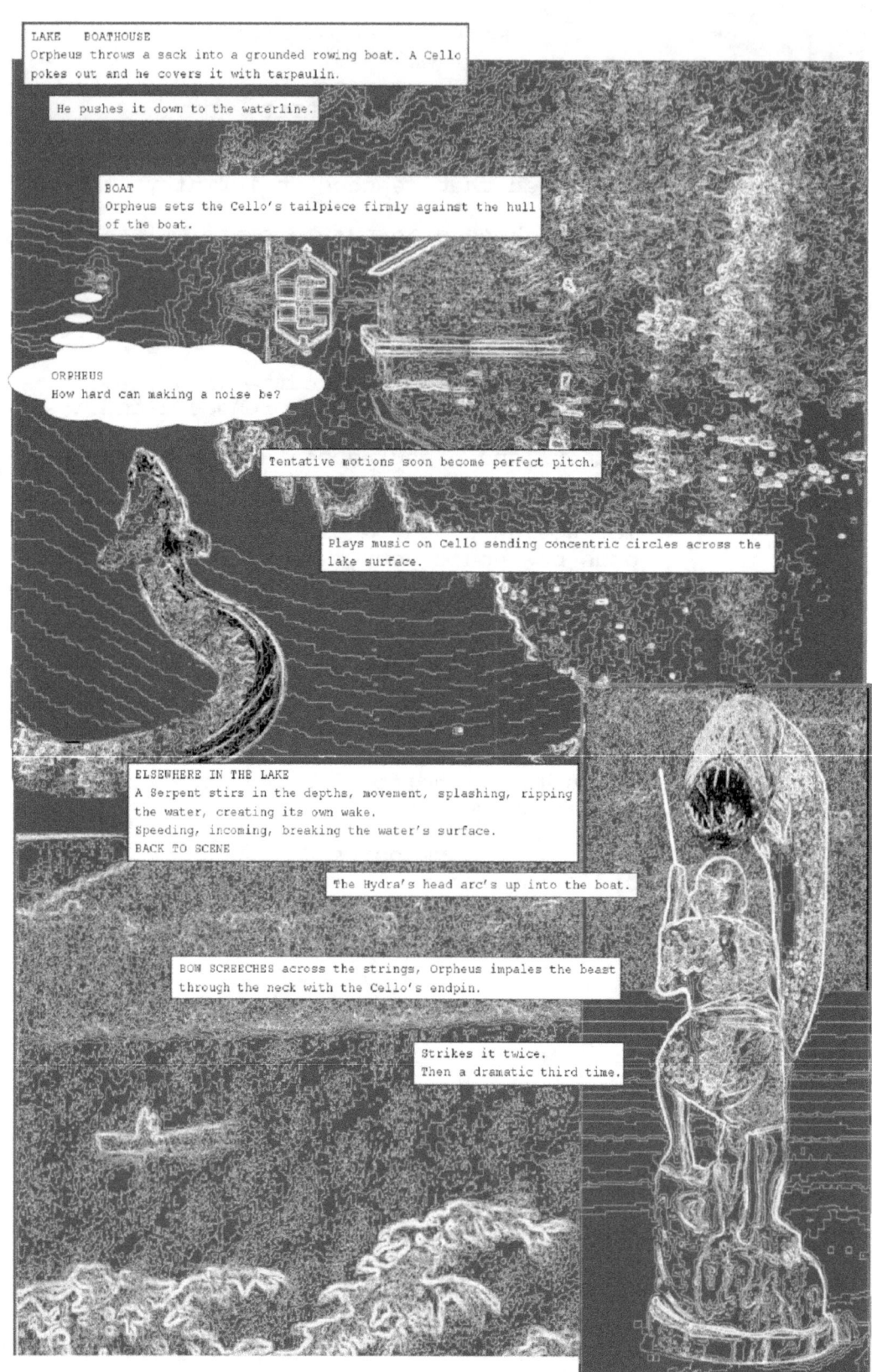

LAKE   BOATHOUSE
Orpheus throws a sack into a grounded rowing boat. A Cello
pokes out and he covers it with tarpaulin.

He pushes it down to the waterline.

BOAT
Orpheus sets the Cello's tailpiece firmly against the hull
of the boat.

ORPHEUS
How hard can making a noise be?

Tentative motions soon become perfect pitch.

Plays music on Cello sending concentric circles across the
lake surface.

ELSEWHERE IN THE LAKE
A Serpent stirs in the depths, movement, splashing, ripping
the water, creating its own wake.
Speeding, incoming, breaking the water's surface.
BACK TO SCENE

The Hydra's head arc's up into the boat.

BOW SCREECHES across the strings, Orpheus impales the beast
through the neck with the Cello's endpin.

Strikes it twice.
Then a dramatic third time.

. . . SILENCE

EXT. LAKE   BOATHOUSE   NIGHT

Orpheus throws a sack into a grounded rowing boat. A Cello
pokes out and he covers it with tarpaulin.

He pushes it down to the waterline.

EXT. LAKE   BOAT   NIGHT

Orpheus sets the Cello's tailpiece firmly against the hull
of the boat.

                    ORPHEUS
          How hard can making a noise be?

Tentative motions soon become perfect pitch.

Plays music on Cello sending concentric circles across the
lake surface.

ELSEWHERE IN THE LAKE

A Serpent stirs in the depths, movement, splashing, ripping
the water, creating its own wake.

Speeding, incoming, breaking the water's surface.

BACK TO SCENE

The Hydra's head arc's up into the boat.

BOW SCREECHES across the strings, Orpheus impales the beast
through the neck with the Cello's endpin.

Strikes it twice.

Then a dramatic third time.

SILENCE

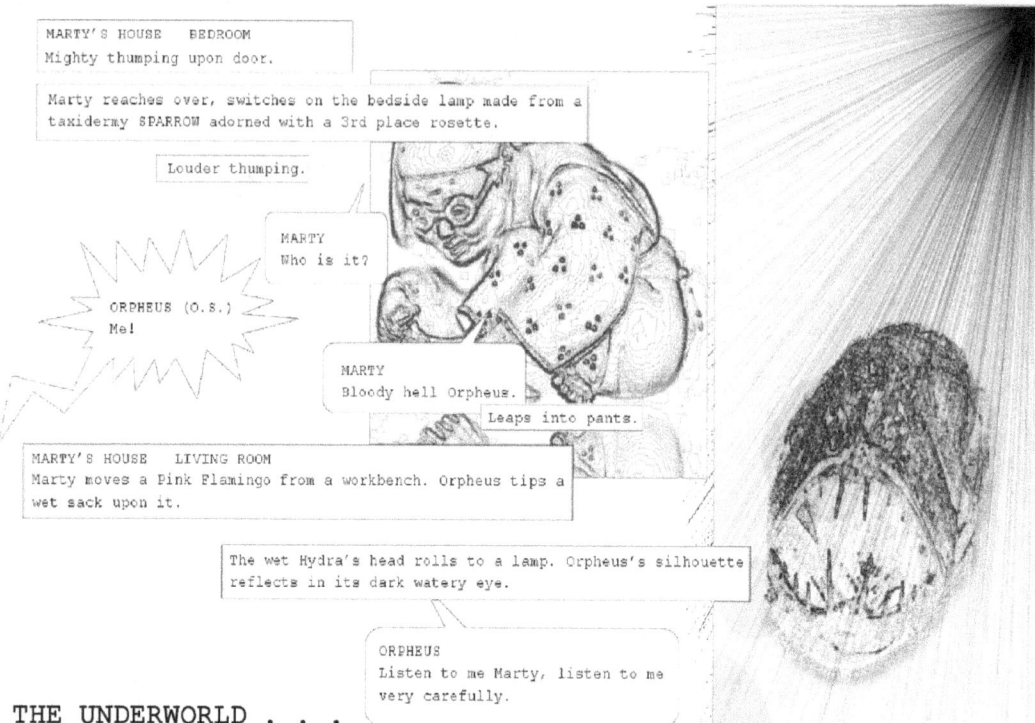

MARTY'S HOUSE BEDROOM
Mighty thumping upon door.

Marty reaches over, switches on the bedside lamp made from a
taxidermy SPARROW adorned with a 3rd place rosette.

Louder thumping.

MARTY
Who is it?

ORPHEUS (O.S.)
Me!

MARTY
Bloody hell Orpheus.

Leaps into pants.

MARTY'S HOUSE LIVING ROOM
Marty moves a Pink Flamingo from a workbench. Orpheus tips a
wet sack upon it.

The wet Hydra's head rolls to a lamp. Orpheus's silhouette
reflects in its dark watery eye.

ORPHEUS
Listen to me Marty, listen to me
very carefully.

IN THE UNDERWORLD . . .

UNDERWORLD BOARDROOM
Subtle red up-lighters illuminate the area.

Enter Persephone, rolling her eyes at the statue in the
foyee; of Hades abducting her from the surface world.
Peering through dark eye shadow; her jaw-line beauty spot
finishes off her femme fatale image. She carries a pumpkinsized
parcel wrapped in newspaper and hums Orpheus's music.

(CONTINUED)

Hades abducting Persephone from the upper world...

INT. MARTY'S HOUSE   BEDROOM   NIGHT

Mighty thumping upon door.

Marty reaches over, switches on the bedside lamp made from a taxidermy SPARROW adorned with a 3rd place rosette.

Louder thumping.

>   MARTY
>   Who is it?

>   ORPHEUS (O.S.)
>   Me!

>   MARTY
>   Bloody hell Orpheus.

Leaps into pants.

INT. MARTY'S HOUSE   LIVING ROOM   NIGHT

Marty moves a Pink Flamingo from a workbench. Orpheus tips a wet sack upon it.

The wet Hydra's head rolls to a lamp. Orpheus's silhouette reflects in its dark watery eye.

>   ORPHEUS
>   Listen to me Marty, listen to me
>   very carefully.

INT. UNDERWORLD   BOARDROOM   DAY

Subtle red up-lighters illuminate the area.

Enter Persephone, rolling her eyes at the statue in the foyee; of Hades abducting her from the surface world. Peering through dark eye shadow; her jaw-line beauty spot finishes off her femme fatale image. She carries a pumpkin-sized parcel wrapped in newspaper and hums Orpheus's music.

                                   (CONTINUED)

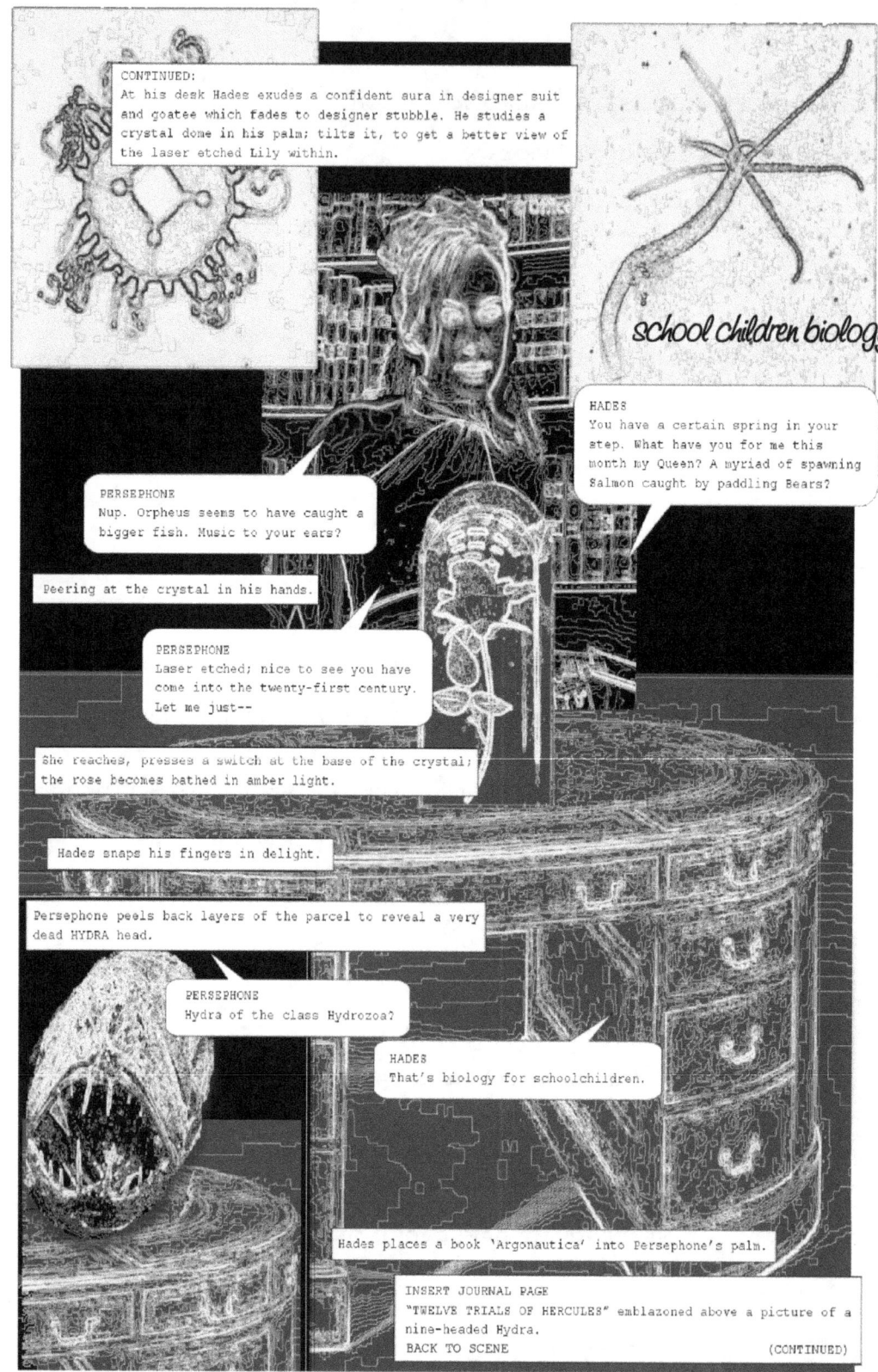

CONTINUED:
At his desk Hades exudes a confident aura in designer suit
and goatee which fades to designer stubble. He studies a
crystal dome in his palm; tilts it, to get a better view of
the laser etched Lily within.

school children biology

HADES
You have a certain spring in your
step. What have you for me this
month my Queen? A myriad of spawning
Salmon caught by paddling Bears?

PERSEPHONE
Nup. Orpheus seems to have caught a
bigger fish. Music to your ears?

Peering at the crystal in his hands.

PERSEPHONE
Laser etched; nice to see you have
come into the twenty-first century.
Let me just--

She reaches, presses a switch at the base of the crystal;
the rose becomes bathed in amber light.

Hades snaps his fingers in delight.

Persephone peels back layers of the parcel to reveal a very
dead HYDRA head.

PERSEPHONE
Hydra of the class Hydrozoa?

HADES
That's biology for schoolchildren.

Hades places a book 'Argonautica' into Persephone's palm.

INSERT JOURNAL PAGE
"TWELVE TRIALS OF HERCULES" emblazoned above a picture of a
nine-headed Hydra.
BACK TO SCENE   (CONTINUED)

CONTINUED:

At his desk Hades exudes a confident aura in designer suit
and goatee which fades to designer stubble. He studies a
crystal dome in his palm; tilts it, to get a better view of
the laser etched Lily within.

>   HADES
>   You have a certain <u>spring</u> in your
>   step. What have you for me this
>   month my Queen? A myriad of spawning
>   Salmon caught by paddling Bears?

>   PERSEPHONE
>   Nup. Orpheus seems to have caught a
>   bigger fish. Music to your ears?

Peering at the crystal in his hands.

>   PERSEPHONE
>   Laser etched; nice to see you have
>   come into the twenty-first century.
>   Let me just--

She reaches, presses a switch at the base of the crystal;
the rose becomes bathed in amber light.

Hades snaps his fingers in delight.

Persephone peels back layers of the parcel to reveal a very
dead HYDRA head.

>   PERSEPHONE
>   Hydra of the class Hydrozoa?

>   HADES
>   That's biology for schoolchildren.

Hades places a book 'Argonautica' into Persephone's palm.

INSERT JOURNAL PAGE

"TWELVE TRIALS OF HERCULES" emblazoned above a picture of a
nine-headed Hydra.

BACK TO SCENE

                                        (CONTINUED)

. . . TAPS FINGERNAILS ON HIS DESK

CONTINUED 2:

>   HADES
>   Killed in a time when heroes were
>   half-man half-god.

>   PERSEPHONE
>   Demi-gods?

Hades points implying, "You got it!"

>   PERSEPHONE
>   Does this still exist?

>   HADES
>   A real bad mother, but Zeus let her
>   live; left to challenge all the
>   wannabie heroes. I get a feeling
>   someone is stepping on my toes!

>   PERSEPHONE
>   Our toes, baby. Lucky this Orpheus
>   sent it back before all hell broke
>   loose.

>   HADES
>   This Hydra is only one of the
>   children of Echidna, the mother of
>   all beasts. A beast of beasts.

>   PERSEPHONE
>   Major she-bitch.

>   HADES
>   In every sense.
>   (beat)
>   Someone upstairs's messing with me.

>   PERSEPHONE
>   Messing with us.

TAPS FINGERNAILS ON HIS DESK.

MEANWHILE . . .

ORPHEUS'S HOUSE　STUDY
Orpheus pins the poster of the Nine-headed Hydra over
pictures of other monsters. The Nemean Lion, Cerberus,
Ladon, hundred headed dragon, Chimera, and the Sphinx.
Corkboard map of the world; Orpheus adds a pin to Toppling
Springs.

ORPHEUS'S HOUSE　ATTIC
Light pours down through cobwebs.

Orpheus pulls an oar off a dusty traveller's chest.
Delicately removes a fist-sized conch shell in newspaper
from a bound journal with a two-legged snake on the cover.

OPENS JOURNAL
B&W photograph of his grandmother in a boat 1930, hinged
over an ancient pencil drawing of Eurydice. He lifts the
photo, and then lays it flat. Repeating it twice.

Turns to next page.
Illustration of Eurydice and Orpheus fleeing from the
Underworld. Title on page "Valley of Acherusia".

ORPHEUS
The only way for a living being to
reach the Underworld.

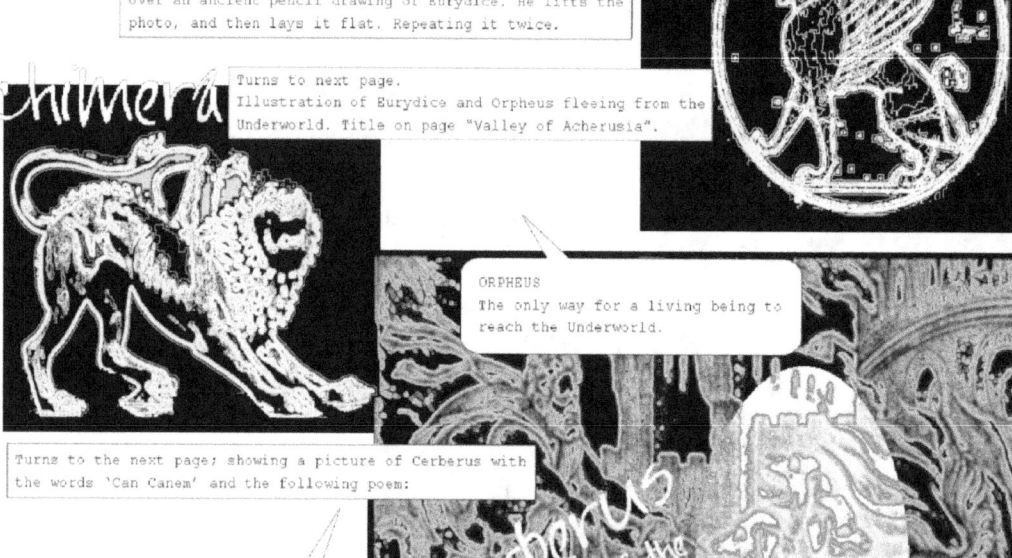

Turns to the next page; showing a picture of Cerberus with
the words 'Can Canem' and the following poem:

ORPHEUS
The dog which still is hovering
nigh, repeating the same timid cry.
This dog, in three directions face.
A dweller in this savage place.
Cerberus guardian of the Underworld.

MEANWHILE . . .

INT. ORPHEUS'S HOUSE   STUDY   DAY

Orpheus pins the poster of the Nine-headed Hydra over
pictures of other monsters. The Nemean Lion, Cerberus,
Ladon, hundred headed dragon, Chimera, and the Sphinx.

Corkboard map of the world; Orpheus adds a pin to Toppling
Springs.

INT. ORPHEUS'S HOUSE   ATTIC   DAY

Light pours down through cobwebs.

Orpheus pulls an oar off a dusty traveller's chest.

Delicately removes a fist-sized conch shell in newspaper
from a bound journal with a two-legged snake on the cover.

OPENS JOURNAL

B&W photograph of his grandmother in a boat 1930, hinged
over an ancient pencil drawing of Eurydice. He lifts the
photo, and then lays it flat. Repeating it twice.

Turns to next page.

Illustration of Eurydice and Orpheus fleeing from the
Underworld. Title on page "Valley of Acherusia".

                    ORPHEUS
          The only way for a living being to
          reach the Underworld.

Turns to the next page; showing a picture of Cerberus with
the words 'Can Canem' and the following poem:

                    ORPHEUS
          The dog which still is hovering
          nigh, repeating the same timid cry.
          This dog, in three directions face.
          A dweller in this savage place.
          Cerberus guardian of the Underworld.

Footnote:
Musical inspiration for journal scene . . . Ave Maria, Cuccini/Mercurio, Andrea Bocelli.

Persephone influences Orpheus with a dream sequence . . .

HILL OVERLOOKING ORPHEUS'S HOUSE DAY, ORPHEUS'S DREAM
Orpheus and Eurydice weave up a path to the summit.

Eurydice's golden curls bounce down around her smile. She
giggles at a yellow flower that springs from underfoot.

EURYDICE
Quite bouncy for something that has
taken a trampling.

Kneeling, peering at the flower.

Plucks it.

In her hand she smells its perfume. The flower's vibrant
yellow color reflects in her flawless skin.

Foot flexing on the grass.

EURYDICE
May be better to repair the lawns
with the seeds from this more
robust grass?

Flexing his foot on the grass.

ORPHEUS
Sure bounces back.

ORPHEUS'S HOUSE   LAWN, DREAM CONTINUED
Orpheus pants hard, unable to hold back his tears. His hand
grasps down upon a dark patch of resilient hill-grass.

Enter Persephone, her long black hair morphs into Eurydice's
golden curls.

She crouches, touching his hand.

PERSEPHONE AS EURYDICE
(whispers)
You must find me Orpheus.
(CONTINUED)

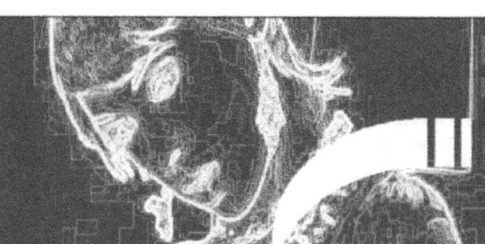
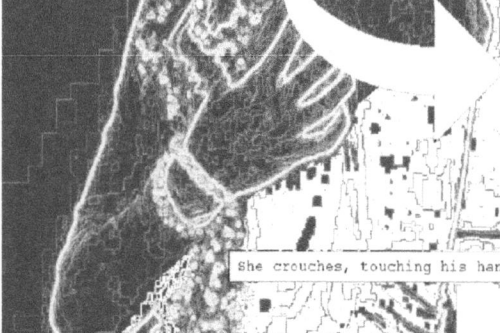

MONTAGE DREAM SEQUENCE

EXT. HILL OVERLOOKING ORPHEUS'S HOUSE   DAY, ORPHEUS'S DREAM

Orpheus and Eurydice weave up a path to the summit.

Eurydice's golden curls bounce down around her smile. She
giggles at a yellow flower that springs from underfoot.

> EURYDICE
> Quite bouncy for something that has
> taken a trampling.

Kneeling, peering at the flower.

Plucks it.

In her hand she smells its perfume. The flower's vibrant
yellow color reflects in her flawless skin.

Foot flexing on the grass.

> EURYDICE
> May be better to repair the lawns
> with the seeds from this more
> robust grass?

Flexing his foot on the grass.

> ORPHEUS
> Sure bounces back.

EXT. ORPHEUS'S HOUSE   LAWN   DAY, DREAM CONTINUED

Orpheus pants hard, unable to hold back his tears. His hand
grasps down hard upon a dark patch of resilient hill-grass.

Enter Persephone, her long black hair morphs into Eurydice's
golden curls.

She crouches, touching his hand.

> PERSEPHONE AS EURYDICE
> (whispers)
> You must find me Orpheus.

(CONTINUED)

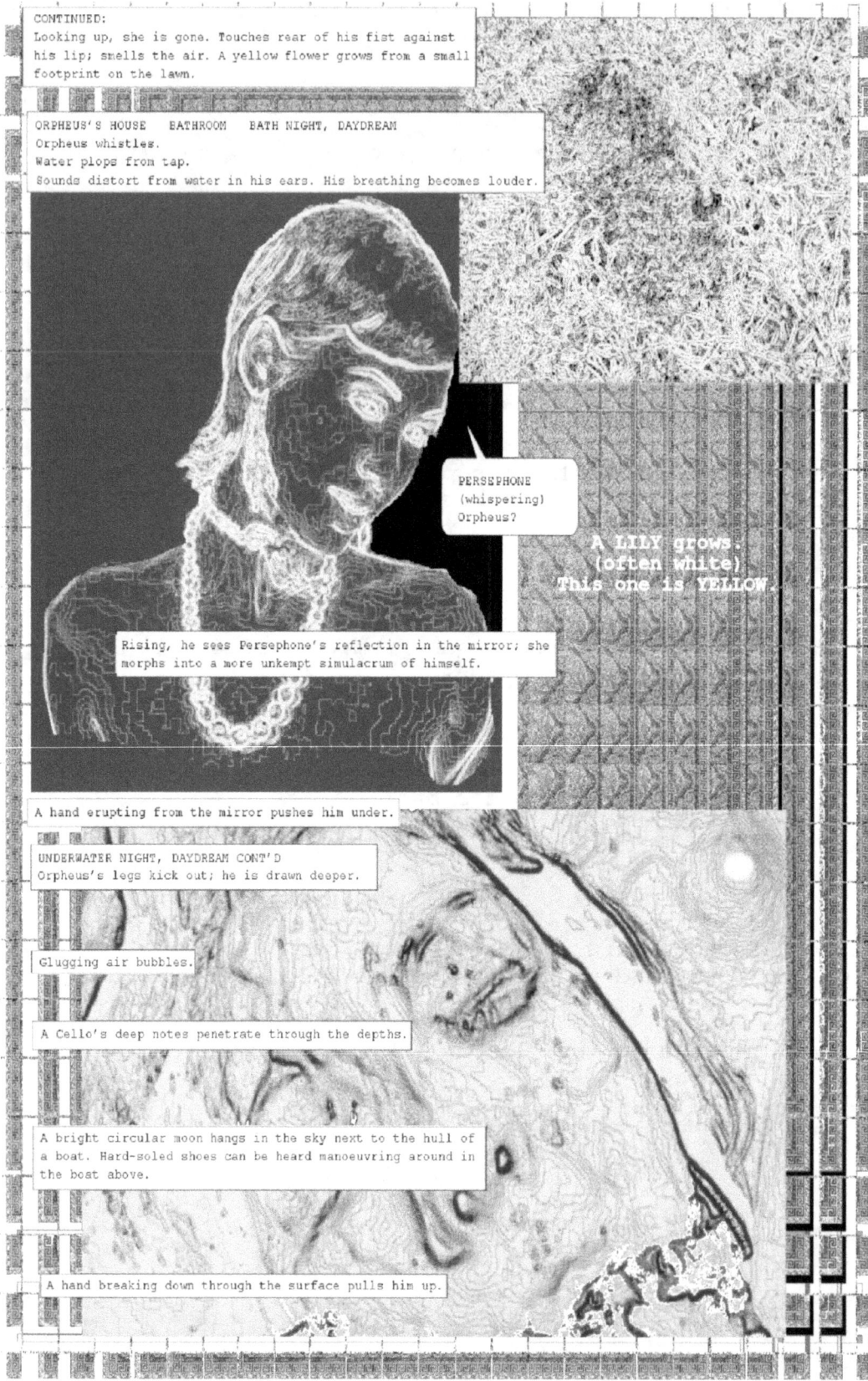

CONTINUED:
Looking up, she is gone. Touches rear of his fist against
his lip; smells the air. A yellow flower grows from a small
footprint on the lawn.

ORPHEUS'S HOUSE   BATHROOM   BATH NIGHT, DAYDREAM
Orpheus whistles.
Water plops from tap.
Sounds distort from water in his ears. His breathing becomes louder.

PERSEPHONE
(whispering)
Orpheus?

A LILY grows.
(often white)
This one is YELLOW.

Rising, he sees Persephone's reflection in the mirror; she
morphs into a more unkempt simulacrum of himself.

A hand erupting from the mirror pushes him under.

UNDERWATER NIGHT, DAYDREAM CONT'D
Orpheus's legs kick out; he is drawn deeper.

Glugging air bubbles.

A Cello's deep notes penetrate through the depths.

A bright circular moon hangs in the sky next to the hull of
a boat. Hard-soled shoes can be heard manoeuvring around in
the boat above.

A hand breaking down through the surface pulls him up.

CONTINUED:

Looking up, she is gone. Touches rear of his fist against
his lip; smells the air. A yellow flower grows from a small
footprint on the lawn.

INT. ORPHEUS'S HOUSE   BATHROOM   BATH   NIGHT, DAYDREAM

Orpheus whistles.

Water plops from tap.

Sounds distort from water in his ears. His breathing becomes
louder.

                    PERSEPHONE O.S.
                   (whispering)
          Orpheus?

Rising, he sees Persephone's reflection in the mirror; she
morphs into a more unkempt simulacrum of himself.

A hand erupting from the mirror pushes him under.

EXT. LAKE   UNDERWATER NIGHT, DAYDREAM CONT'D

Orpheus's legs kick out; he is drawn deeper.

Glugging air bubbles.

A Cello's deep notes penetrate through the depths.

A bright circular moon hangs in the sky next to the hull of
a boat. Hard-soled shoes can be heard manoeuvring around in
the boat above.

A hand breaking down through the surface pulls him up.

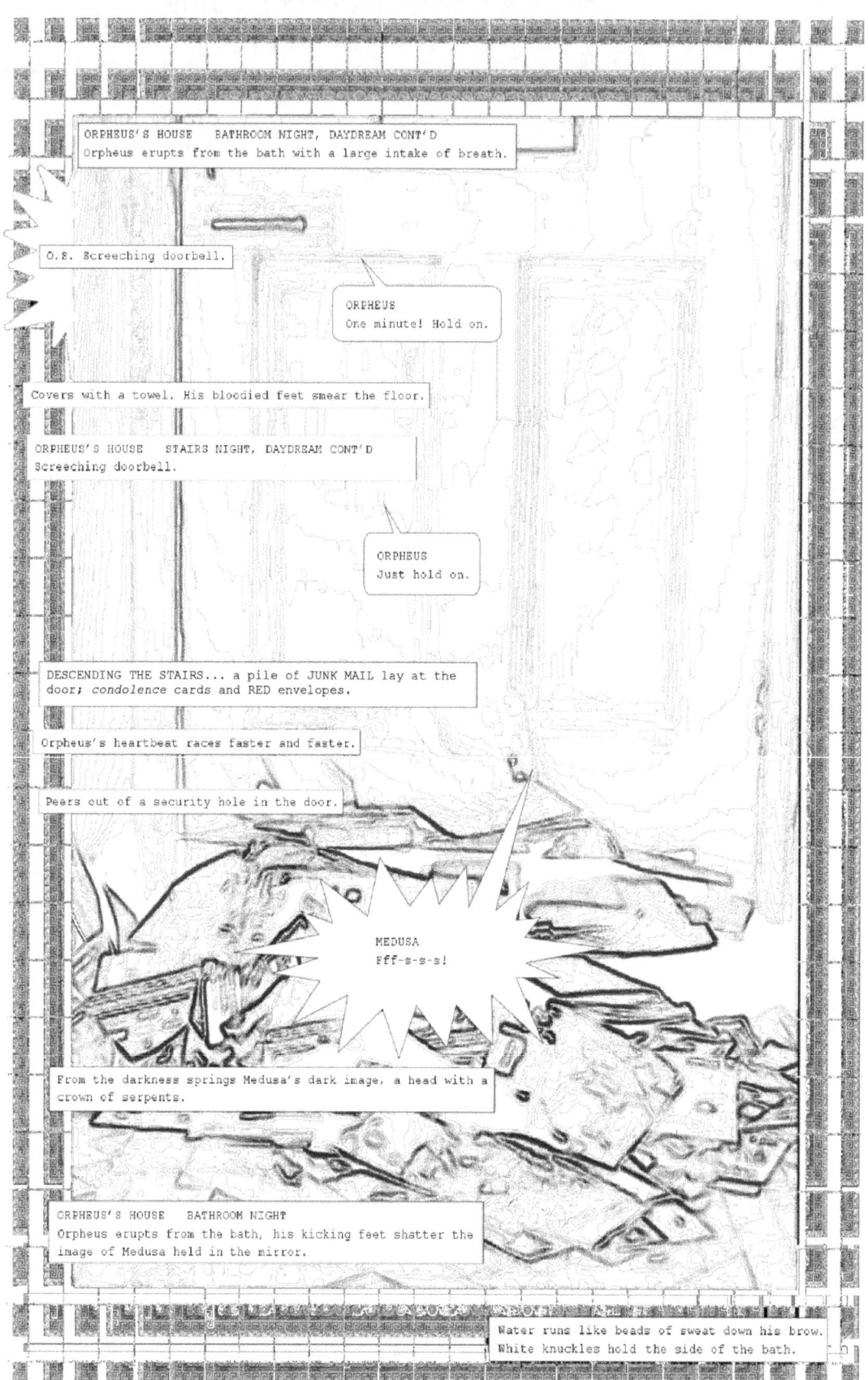

ORPHEUS'S HOUSE   BATHROOM NIGHT, DAYDREAM CONT'D
Orpheus erupts from the bath with a large intake of breath.

O.S. Screeching doorbell.

ORPHEUS
One minute! Hold on.

Covers with a towel. His bloodied feet smear the floor.

ORPHEUS'S HOUSE   STAIRS NIGHT, DAYDREAM CONT'D
Screeching doorbell.

ORPHEUS
Just hold on.

DESCENDING THE STAIRS... a pile of JUNK MAIL lay at the
door; *condolence* cards and RED envelopes.

Orpheus's heartbeat races faster and faster.

Peers out of a security hole in the door.

MEDUSA
Fff-s-s-s!

From the darkness springs Medusa's dark image, a head with a
crown of serpents.

ORPHEUS'S HOUSE   BATHROOM NIGHT
Orpheus erupts from the bath, his kicking feet shatter the
image of Medusa held in the mirror.

Water runs like beads of sweat down his brow.
White knuckles hold the side of the bath.

INT. ORPHEUS'S HOUSE   BATHROOM   NIGHT, DAYDREAM CONT'D

Orpheus erupts from the bath with a large intake of breath.

O.S. Screeching doorbell.

> ORPHEUS
> One minute! Hold on.

Covers with a towel. His bloodied feet smear the floor.

INT. ORPHEUS'S HOUSE   STAIRS   NIGHT, DAYDREAM CONT'D

Screeching doorbell.

> ORPHEUS
> Just hold on.

DESCENDING THE STAIRS... a pile of JUNK MAIL lay at the
door; *condolence* cards and RED envelopes.

Orpheus's heartbeat races faster and faster.

Peers out of a security hole in the door.

From the darkness springs Medusa's dark image, a head with a
crown of serpents.

> MEDUSA
> Fff-s-s-s!

INT. ORPHEUS'S HOUSE   BATHROOM   NIGHT

Orpheus erupts from the bath, his kicking feet shatter the
image of Medusa held in the mirror.

Water runs like beads of sweat down his brow.

White knuckles hold the side of the bath.

1930's... FLASHBACK: TO A PREVIOUS INCARNATION.

ARCHAEOLOGICAL DIG
Orpheus crouches beside dusty skeletal remains and pieces
together jigsaw-like skull parts.
Jason taps a pencil upon a notepad.

ORPHEUS
Slanting brow. Eye sockets crushed.
Upper arm. Possible rock fall?
RECORD and PRESERVE for TRANSPORT.
Unlike any finds I've seen before.

JASON
Got it.

ORPHEUS
This aint no cave Neanderthal.

A buried object catches the light. Swaying —— he catches
the flicker again and spots Hermes's charm in the dirt.
Moving dirt reveals a Greek helmet, and beneath a colorful
flower mosaic.

Lifts helmet.
A STONE head falls from inside and shatters.

ORPHEUS
This aint no excavation, it's a
murder scene.

A gust of wind raises the hairs on their arms.

JUNGLE   CAMP
SOUNDS of EXOTIC CREATURES.
Orpheus squints at a sharp ray of light poking through the
tree canopy and pulls down the brim of his cap. Dew and
sweat run down his brow. Unkempt hair hangs down either side
of his newly acquired moustache and beard.

Looking around he peers at his strange surroundings.

BACK TO PRESENT DAY

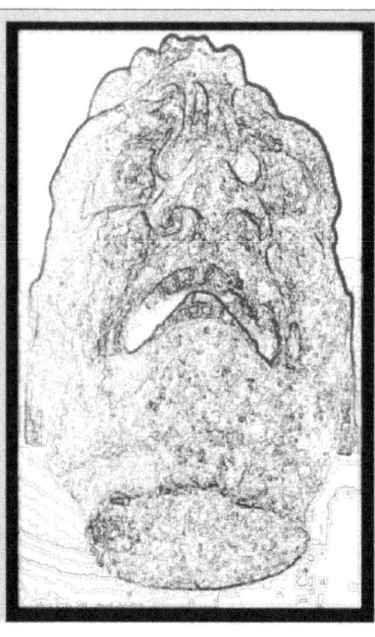

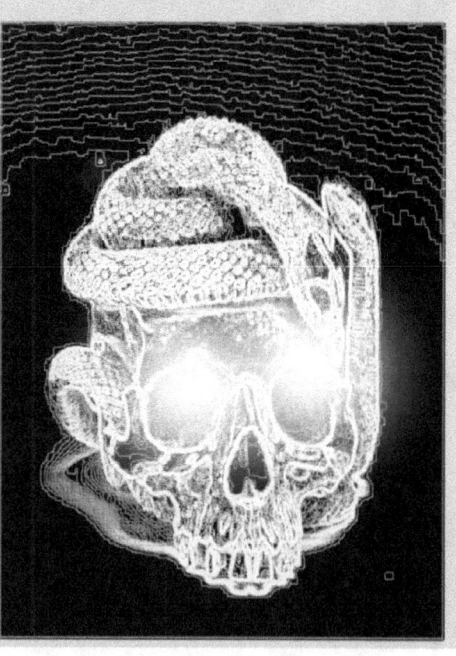

INT. ARCHAEOLOGICAL DIG   DAY, 1930'S

FLASHBACK: TO A PREVIOUS INCARNATION.

Orpheus crouches beside dusty skeletal remains and pieces together jigsaw-like skull parts. Jason taps a pencil upon a notepad.

> ORPHEUS
> Slanting brow. Eye sockets crushed.
> Upper arm. Possible rock fall?
> *RECORD and PRESERVE for TRANSPORT.*
> Unlike any finds I've seen before.

> JASON
> Got it.

> ORPHEUS
> This aint no cave Neanderthal.

A buried object catches the light. Swaying ———— he catches the flicker again and spots Hermes's charm in the dirt.

Moving dirt reveals a Greek helmet, and beneath a colorful flower mosaic.

Lifts helmet.

A STONE head falls from inside and shatters.

> ORPHEUS
> This aint no excavation, it's a
> murder scene.

A gust of wind raises the hairs on their arms.

BACK TO PRESENT DAY

EXT. JUNGLE   CAMP   DAY

SOUNDS of EXOTIC CREATURES.

Orpheus squints at a sharp ray of light poking through the tree canopy and pulls down the brim of his cap. Dew and sweat run down his brow. Unkempt hair hangs down either side of his newly acquired moustache and beard.

Looking around he peers at his strange surroundings.

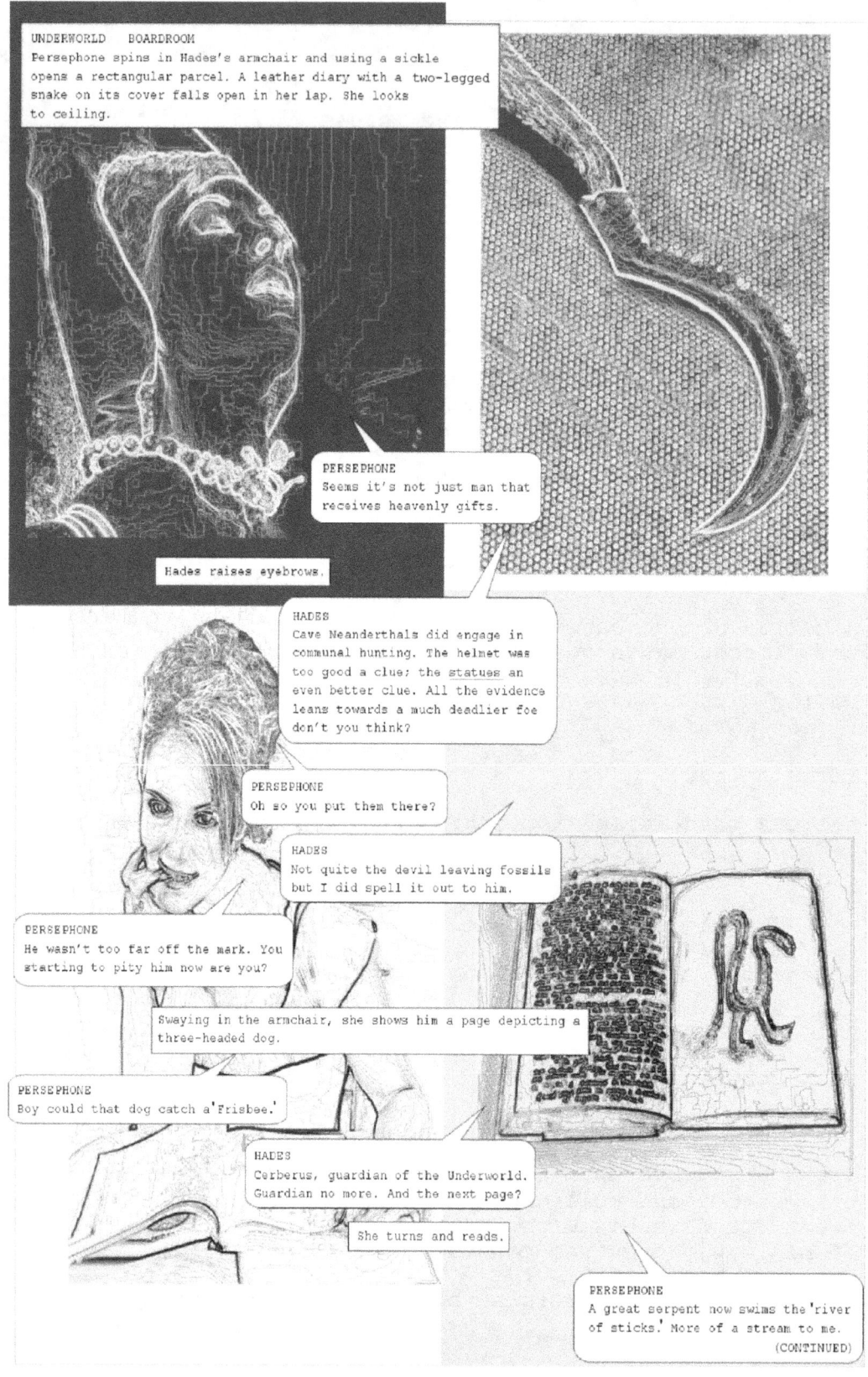

UNDERWORLD   BOARDROOM
Persephone spins in Hades's armchair and using a sickle
opens a rectangular parcel. A leather diary with a two-legged
snake on its cover falls open in her lap. She looks
to ceiling.

PERSEPHONE
Seems it's not just man that
receives heavenly gifts.

Hades raises eyebrows.

HADES
Cave Neanderthals did engage in
communal hunting. The helmet was
too good a clue; the statues an
even better clue. All the evidence
leans towards a much deadlier foe
don't you think?

PERSEPHONE
Oh so you put them there?

HADES
Not quite the devil leaving fossils
but I did spell it out to him.

PERSEPHONE
He wasn't too far off the mark. You
starting to pity him now are you?

Swaying in the armchair, she shows him a page depicting a
three-headed dog.

PERSEPHONE
Boy could that dog catch a 'Frisbee.'

HADES
Cerberus, guardian of the Underworld.
Guardian no more. And the next page?

She turns and reads.

PERSEPHONE
A great serpent now swims the 'river
of sticks.' More of a stream to me.
                              (CONTINUED)

INT. UNDERWORLD   BOARDROOM   DAY

Persephone spins in Hades's armchair and using a sickle opens a rectangular parcel. A leather diary with a two-legged snake on its cover falls open in her lap. She looks to ceiling.

> PERSEPHONE
> Seems it's not just <u>man</u> that receives heavenly gifts.

Hades raises eyebrows.

> HADES
> Cave Neanderthals did engage in communal hunting. The helmet was too good a clue; the <u>statues</u> an even better clue. All the evidence leans towards a much deadlier foe don't you think?

> PERSEPHONE
> Oh so you put them there?

> HADES
> Not quite the devil leaving fossils but I did spell it out to him.

> PERSEPHONE
> He wasn't too far off the mark. You starting to pity him now are you?

Swaying in the armchair, she shows him a page depicting a three-headed dog.

> PERSEPHONE
> Boy could that dog catch a 'Frisbee.'

> HADES
> Cerberus, guardian of the Underworld. Guardian no more. And the next page?

She turns and reads.

> PERSEPHONE
> A great serpent now swims the 'river of sticks.' More of a stream to me.

(CONTINUED)

CONTINUED:
A torn page stub in the spine reveals a missing page.

Flicks through remaining blank pages.

She leaps up and slaps the journal into his chest.

PERSEPHONE
So what's next? You are going to
help him aren't you?

HADES
It's a journey he must make. Not
everyone's fate is set in stone.

Persephone lowers her gaze and bites her lip in thought.

ELSEWHERE...

JUNGLE
Marty, Jason, and Lynx break through thick undergrowth.
Birds chirp and take flight. Night closes in.

A BAT flaps through the trees.

Marty's tranquilizer gun fires into the canopy and makes a
Kung-Fu chop motion with his hand.

Rapid high pitched clicks from Bat.

MARTY
That'll make his eyes water.

Lynx blasts into the trees, the Bat thuds at his feet, and
he dances.

LYNX
You either got it or you aint.

MARTY
You buffoon. I needed that intact.

Lynx makes a fist, and Marty winces.
(CONTINUED)

CONTINUED:

A torn page stub in the spine reveals a missing page.

Flicks through remaining blank pages.

She leaps up and slaps the journal into his chest.

>   PERSEPHONE
>   So what's next? You <u>are</u> going to
>   help him aren't you?

>   HADES
>   It's a journey he must make. Not
>   everyone's fate is set in stone.

Persephone lowers her gaze and bites her lip in thought.

ELSEWHERE...

EXT. JUNGLE   NIGHT

Marty, Jason, and Lynx break through thick undergrowth.
Birds chirp and take flight. Night closes in.

A BAT flaps through the trees.

Marty's tranquilizer gun fires into the canopy and makes a
Kung-Fu chop motion with his hand.

Rapid high pitched clicks from Bat.

>   MARTY
>   That'll make his eyes water.

Lynx blasts into the trees, the Bat thuds at his feet, and
he dances.

>   LYNX
>   You either got it or you aint.

>   MARTY
>   You buffoon. I needed that intact.

Lynx makes a fist, and Marty winces.

>   (CONTINUED)

You and your pansy darts.

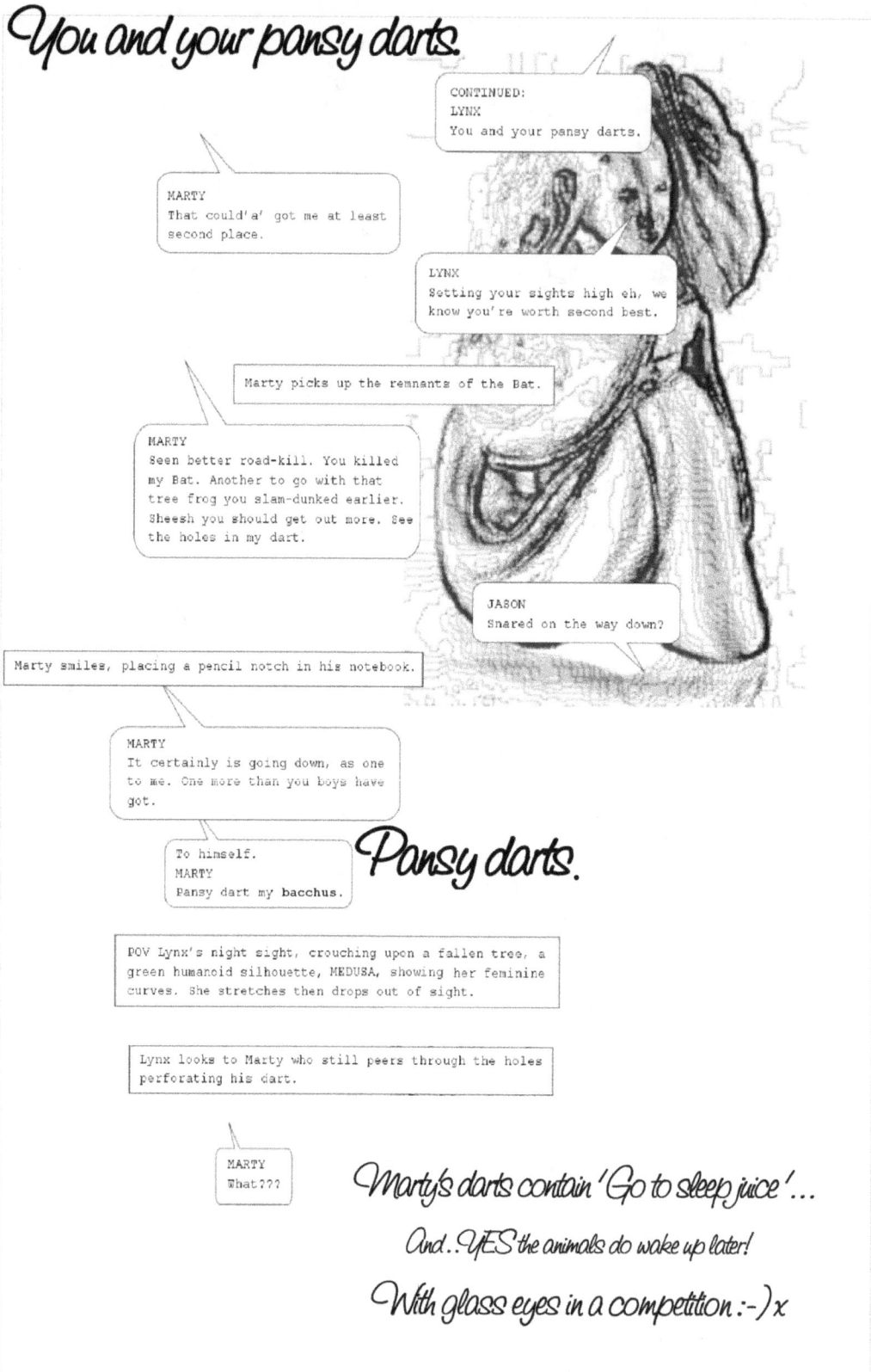

CONTINUED:
LYNX
You and your pansy darts.

MARTY
That could'a' got me at least
second place.

LYNX
Setting your sights high eh, we
know you're worth second best.

Marty picks up the remnants of the Bat.

MARTY
Seen better road-kill. You killed
my Bat. Another to go with that
tree frog you slam-dunked earlier.
Sheesh you should get out more. See
the holes in my dart.

JASON
Snared on the way down?

Marty smiles, placing a pencil notch in his notebook.

MARTY
It certainly is going down, as one
to me. One more than you boys have
got.

To himself.
MARTY
Pansy dart my **bacchus**.

Pansy darts.

POV Lynx's night sight, crouching upon a fallen tree, a
green humanoid silhouette, MEDUSA, showing her feminine
curves. She stretches then drops out of sight.

Lynx looks to Marty who still peers through the holes
perforating his dart.

MARTY
What???

Marty's darts contain 'Go to sleep juice'…

And..YES the animals do wake up later!

With glass eyes in a competition :-)x

CONTINUED:

> LYNX
> You and your pansy darts.

> MARTY
> That could'a' got me at least
> second place.

> LYNX
> Setting your sights high eh, we
> know you're worth second best.

Marty picks up the remnants of the Bat.

> MARTY
> Seen better road-kill. You killed
> my Bat. Another to go with that
> tree frog you slam-dunked earlier.
> Sheesh you should get out more. See
> the holes in my dart.

> JASON
> Snared on the way down?

Marty smiles, placing a pencil notch in his notebook.

> MARTY
> It certainly is going down, as <u>one</u>
> to me. One more than you boys have
> got.

To himself.

> MARTY
> Pansy dart my **bacchus**.

POV Lynx's night sight, crouching upon a fallen tree, a
green humanoid silhouette, MEDUSA, showing her feminine
curves. She stretches then drops out of sight.

Lynx looks to Marty who still peers through the holes
perforating his dart.

> MARTY
> What???

OLYMPUS
Hermes sits like 'The Thinker', Aphrodite tends her nails.

Messenger boy. That is what they call you isn't it?

HERMES
Is it really the power over man that separates us from one another?

APHRODITE
You give them gifts but they hold you in no higher esteem than say, a messenger boy? That is what they call you isn't it? Why do you even appease them?

HERMES
There are more than portfolios of power on the line here. I care. It's not about who's the biggest loser.

It's not about who's the biggest loser.

APHRODITE
Really? You think you can win a battle against this god?

Motes of blue light enter the statue of Orpheus that rests on the game board.

You think you can win a battle against this god?

HERMES
Orpheus is a great storyteller; he tells emotional stories of "The Heroic Age" when Argonauts fought their greatest battle at Troy.

APHRODITE
I have learnt my lesson. Don't get too attached Hermes. This time they're all going down and you're going down with them.

HERMES
They must succeed.

APHRODITE
You planning on helping them?

You planning on helping them?

She licks-lips and twiddles a snake-headed hair pin.

ORPHEUS
Argonaut

HERMES
Messenger of the Gods

EURYDICE

Fate dictates she will be lost forever...
...until now

INT. OLYMPUS   DAY

Hermes sits like 'The Thinker', Aphrodite tends her nails.

                    HERMES
          Is it really the power over man
          that separates us from one another?

                    APHRODITE
          You give them gifts but they hold
          you in no higher esteem than say, a
          messenger boy? That is what they
          call you isn't it? Why do you even
          appease them?

                    HERMES
          There are more than portfolios of
          power on the line here. I care.
          It's not about who's the biggest
          loser.

                    APHRODITE
          Really? You think *you* can win a
          battle against *this* god?

Motes of blue light enter the statue of Orpheus that rests
on the game board.

                    HERMES
          Orpheus is a great storyteller; he
          tells emotional stories of "The
          Heroic Age" when Argonauts fought
          their greatest battle at Troy.

                    APHRODITE
          I have learnt my lesson. Don't get
          too attached Hermes. This time
          they're all going down and you're
          going down with them.

                    HERMES
          They must succeed.

                    APHRODITE
          You planning on helping them?

She licks-lips and twiddles a snake-headed hair pin.

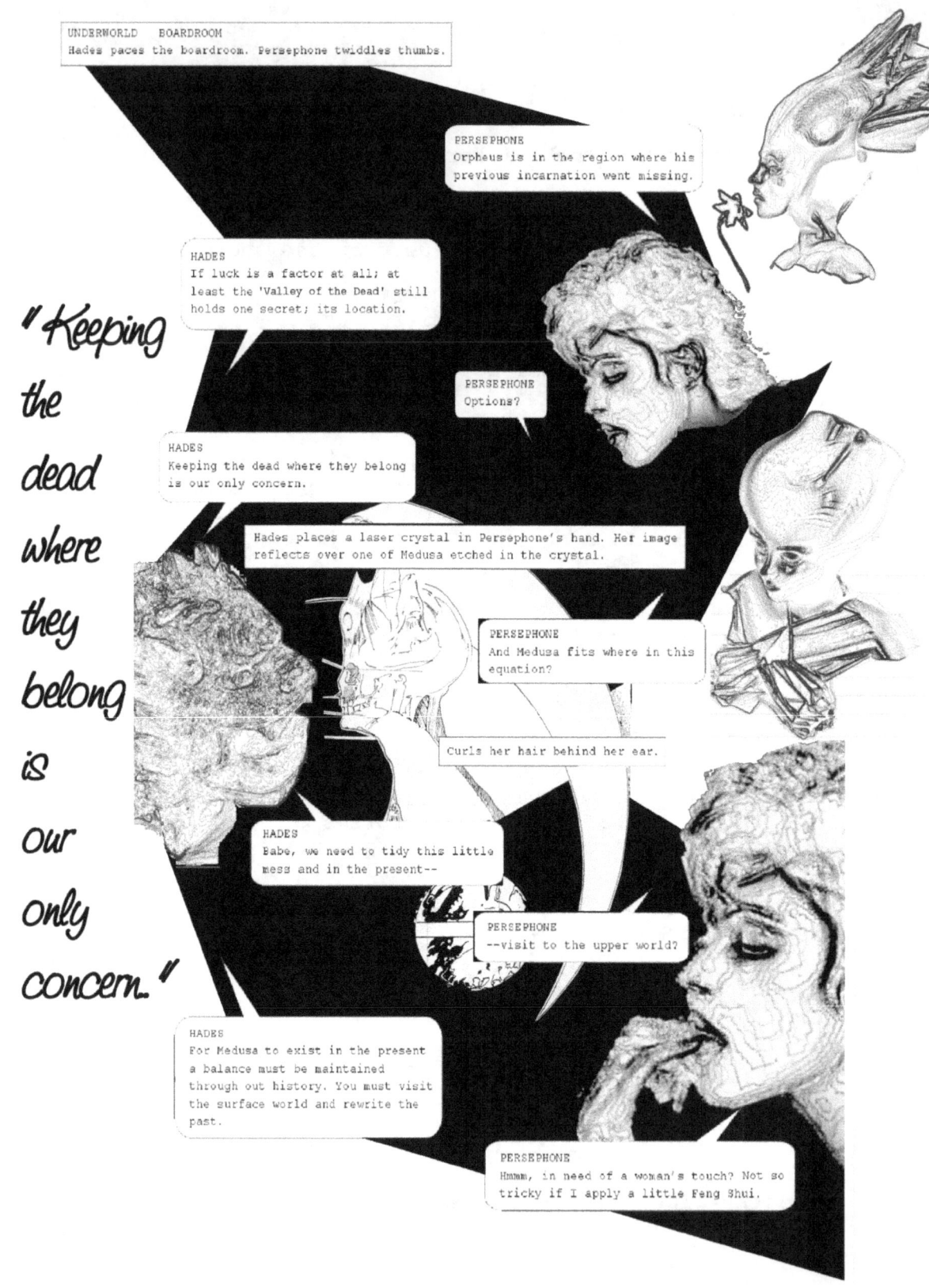

UNDERWORLD   BOARDROOM
Hades paces the boardroom. Persephone twiddles thumbs.

PERSEPHONE
Orpheus is in the region where his
previous incarnation went missing.

HADES
If luck is a factor at all; at
least the 'Valley of the Dead' still
holds one secret; its location.

PERSEPHONE
Options?

HADES
Keeping the dead where they belong
is our only concern.

Hades places a laser crystal in Persephone's hand. Her image
reflects over one of Medusa etched in the crystal.

PERSEPHONE
And Medusa fits where in this
equation?

Curls her hair behind her ear.

HADES
Babe, we need to tidy this little
mess and in the present--

PERSEPHONE
--visit to the upper world?

HADES
For Medusa to exist in the present
a balance must be maintained
through out history. You must visit
the surface world and rewrite the
past.

PERSEPHONE
Hmmm, in need of a woman's touch? Not so
tricky if I apply a little Feng Shui.

"Keeping
the
dead
where
they
belong
is
our
only
concern."

INT. UNDERWORLD   BOARDROOM   DAY

Hades paces the boardroom. Persephone twiddles thumbs.

                    PERSEPHONE
          Orpheus is in the region where his
          previous incarnation went missing.

                    HADES
          If luck is a factor at all; at
          least the 'Valley of the Dead' still
          holds one secret; its location.

                    PERSEPHONE
          Options?

                    HADES
          Keeping the dead where they belong
          is our only concern.

Hades places a laser crystal in Persephone's hand. Her image
reflects over one of Medusa etched in the crystal.

                    PERSEPHONE
          And Medusa fits where in this
          equation?

Curls her hair behind her ear.

                    HADES
          Babe, we need to tidy this little
          mess and in the present--

                    PERSEPHONE
          --visit to the upper world?

                    HADES
          For Medusa to exist in the present
          a balance must be maintained
          through out history. You must visit
          the surface world and rewrite the
          past.

                    PERSEPHONE
          Hmmm, in need of a woman's touch? Not so
          tricky if I apply a little Feng Shui.

200 B.C.
China

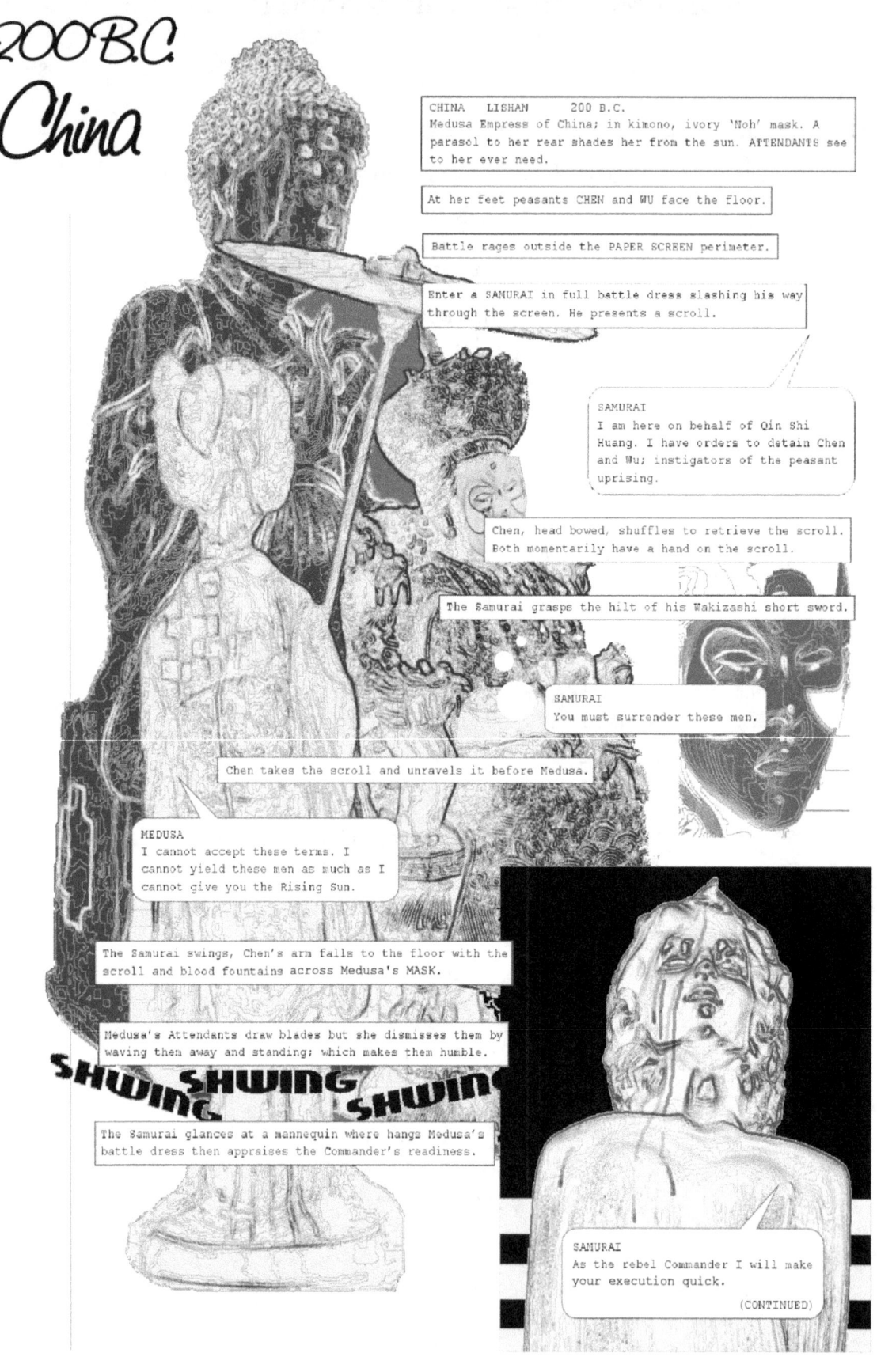

CHINA   LISHAN   200 B.C.
Medusa Empress of China; in kimono, ivory 'Noh' mask. A
parasol to her rear shades her from the sun. ATTENDANTS see
to her ever need.

At her feet peasants CHEN and WU face the floor.

Battle rages outside the PAPER SCREEN perimeter.

Enter a SAMURAI in full battle dress slashing his way
through the screen. He presents a scroll.

SAMURAI
I am here on behalf of Qin Shi
Huang. I have orders to detain Chen
and Wu; instigators of the peasant
uprising.

Chen, head bowed, shuffles to retrieve the scroll.
Both momentarily have a hand on the scroll.

The Samurai grasps the hilt of his Wakizashi short sword.

SAMURAI
You must surrender these men.

Chen takes the scroll and unravels it before Medusa.

MEDUSA
I cannot accept these terms. I
cannot yield these men as much as I
cannot give you the Rising Sun.

The Samurai swings, Chen's arm falls to the floor with the
scroll and blood fountains across Medusa's MASK.

Medusa's Attendants draw blades but she dismisses them by
waving them away and standing; which makes them humble.

SHWING SHWING SHWING SHWING

The Samurai glances at a mannequin where hangs Medusa's
battle dress then appraises the Commander's readiness.

SAMURAI
As the rebel Commander I will make
your execution quick.

(CONTINUED)

EXT. CHINA   LISHAN   DAY, 200 B.C.

Medusa *Empress of China*; in kimono, ivory 'Noh' mask. A
parasol to her rear shades her from the sun. ATTENDANTS see
to her ever need.

At her feet peasants CHEN and WU face the floor.

Battle rages outside the PAPER SCREEN perimeter.

Enter a SAMURAI in full battle dress slashing his way
through the screen. He presents a scroll.

                    SAMURAI
          I am here on behalf of Qin Shi
          Huang. I have orders to detain Chen
          and Wu; instigators of the peasant
          uprising.

Chen, head bowed, shuffles to retrieve the scroll.

Both momentarily have a hand on the scroll.

The Samurai grasps the hilt of his Wakizashi short sword.

                    SAMURAI
          You must surrender these men.

Chen takes the scroll and unravels it before Medusa.

                    MEDUSA
          I cannot accept these terms. I
          cannot yield these men as much as I
          cannot give you the Rising Sun.

The Samurai swings, Chen's arm falls to the floor with the
scroll and blood fountains across Medusa's MASK.

Medusa's Attendants draw blades but she dismisses them by
waving them away and standing; which makes them humble.

The Samurai glances at a mannequin where hangs Medusa's
battle dress then appraises the Commander's readiness.

                    SAMURAI
          As the rebel Commander I will make
          your execution quick.

                                        (CONTINUED)

CONTINUED:
The Samurai blade hovers under Medusa's chin, then cuts
through the arm of her kimono to reveal dragon scales.

SAMURAI
What deception is this?

Samurai looks to the cowering Attendants.

SAMURAI
More cheap trickery.

MEDUSA
If you have any honor, you will
face me.

The Samurai's laughs.

Medusa lifts her mask.

The laughing Samurai solidifies into stone.

CHINA   LISHAN MOUNTAINS
Soldiers camp at the foot .

Medusa climbs the opposing crest and looks down upon the
7,000 strong army made up of soldiers, archers and chariots.

Her snakes rise.
The setting sun picturesquely frames Medusa's silhouette.
The army suffers STONE METAMORPHOSIS on a grand scale.

CONTINUED:

The Samurai blade hovers under Medusa's chin, then cuts
through the arm of her kimono to reveal dragon scales.

> SAMURAI
> What deception is this?

Samurai looks to the cowering Attendants.

> SAMURAI
> More cheap trickery.

> MEDUSA
> If you have any honor, you will
> face me.

The Samurai's laughs.

Medusa lifts her mask.

The laughing Samurai solidifies into stone.

EXT. CHINA   LISHAN MOUNTAINS   NIGHT

Soldiers camp at the foot.

Medusa climbs the opposing crest and looks down upon the
7,000 strong army made up of soldiers, archers and chariots.

Her snakes rise.

The setting sun picturesquely frames Medusa's silhouette.

The army suffers STONE METAMORPHOSIS on a grand scale.

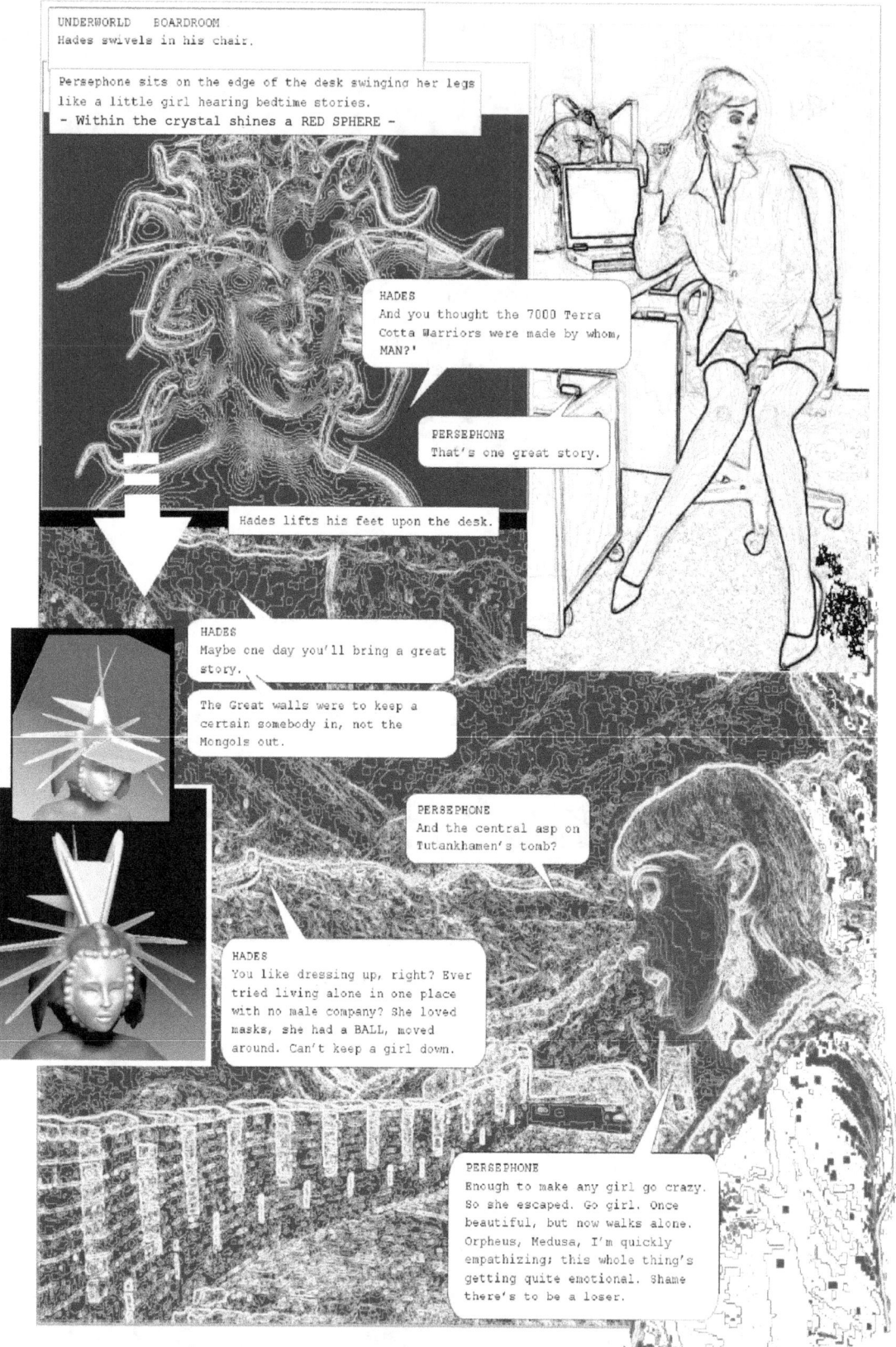

UNDERWORLD   BOARDROOM
Hades swivels in his chair.

Persephone sits on the edge of the desk swinging her legs
like a little girl hearing bedtime stories.
- Within the crystal shines a RED SPHERE -

HADES
And you thought the 7000 Terra
Cotta Warriors were made by whom,
MAN?'

PERSEPHONE
That's one great story.

Hades lifts his feet upon the desk.

HADES
Maybe one day you'll bring a great
story.

The Great walls were to keep a
certain somebody in, not the
Mongols out.

PERSEPHONE
And the central asp on
Tutankhamen's tomb?

HADES
You like dressing up, right? Ever
tried living alone in one place
with no male company? She loved
masks, she had a BALL, moved
around. Can't keep a girl down.

PERSEPHONE
Enough to make any girl go crazy.
So she escaped. Go girl. Once
beautiful, but now walks alone.
Orpheus, Medusa, I'm quickly
empathizing; this whole thing's
getting quite emotional. Shame
there's to be a loser.

INT. UNDERWORLD   BOARDROOM   DAY

Hades swivels in his chair.

Persephone sits on the edge of the desk swinging her legs like a little girl hearing bedtime stories. Within the crystal shines a RED SPHERE.

> HADES
> And you thought the 7000 Terra Cotta Warriors were made by whom, MAN?'

> PERSEPHONE
> That's one great story.

Hades lifts his feet upon the desk.

> HADES
> Maybe one day *you'll* bring a great story.
>> (beat)
> The Great walls were to keep a certain somebody in, not the Mongols out.

> PERSEPHONE
> And the central asp on Tutankhamen's tomb?

> HADES
> You like dressing up, right? Ever tried living alone in one place with no male company? She loved masks, she had a BALL, moved around. Can't keep a girl down.

> PERSEPHONE
> Enough to make any girl go crazy. So she escaped. Go girl. Once beautiful, but now walks alone. Orpheus, Medusa, I'm quickly empathizing; this whole thing's getting quite emotional. Shame there's to be a loser.

JUNGLE   CAMP
Enter Marty at the tree line a twig snaps underfoot causing
a little red laser dot to dance upon his chest.

Orpheus wound like a spring with an itchy trigger-finger.

MARTY
Wo-o-oh it's me, easy tiger.

ORPHEUS
Sorry Hansel, I'm all out of
trailing sweets.

MARTY
A note-it on the fridge saying you
are off in search of "Acherusia
Valley of the Dead" is pushing the
boat out just a bit. And leave a
better trail next time 'cause
you're not the easiest guy to find.

Marty looks around.

MARTY
Just where on Earth are we? What
are you hunting? Have you seen the
huge paw prints around here, loads
of the mothers. A taxidermy project
too far; we're the ones more likely
to be stuffed around here.

Twig snaps.

JUNGLE   CAMP   PERIMETER DAY
Medusa watches from the tree-line, she wears a girlishly
pretty mask and a bronze studded cat suit. She listens in
the direction of Orpheus and Marty.

Watching the watcher is Jason and Lynx who close in to her
vantage point; behind a tree.
(CONTINUED)

EXT. JUNGLE   CAMP   DAY

Enter Marty at the tree line a twig snaps underfoot causing
a little red laser dot to dance upon his chest.

Orpheus wound like a spring with an itchy trigger-finger.

> MARTY
> Wo-o-oh it's me, easy tiger.

> ORPHEUS
> Sorry Hansel, I'm all out of
> trailing sweets.

> MARTY
> A note-it on the fridge saying you
> are off in search of "Acherusia
> Valley of the Dead" is pushing the
> boat out just a bit. And leave a
> better trail next time 'cause
> you're not the easiest guy to find.

Marty looks around.

> MARTY
> Just where on Earth are we? What
> are you hunting? Have you seen the
> huge paw prints around here, loads
> of the mothers. A taxidermy project
> too far; we're the ones more likely
> to be stuffed around here.

Twig snaps.

EXT. JUNGLE   CAMP   PERIMETER   DAY

Medusa watches from the tree-line, she wears a girlishly
pretty mask and a bronze studded cat suit. She listens in
the direction of Orpheus and Marty.

Watching the watcher is Jason and Lynx who close in to her
vantage point; behind a tree.

(CONTINUED)

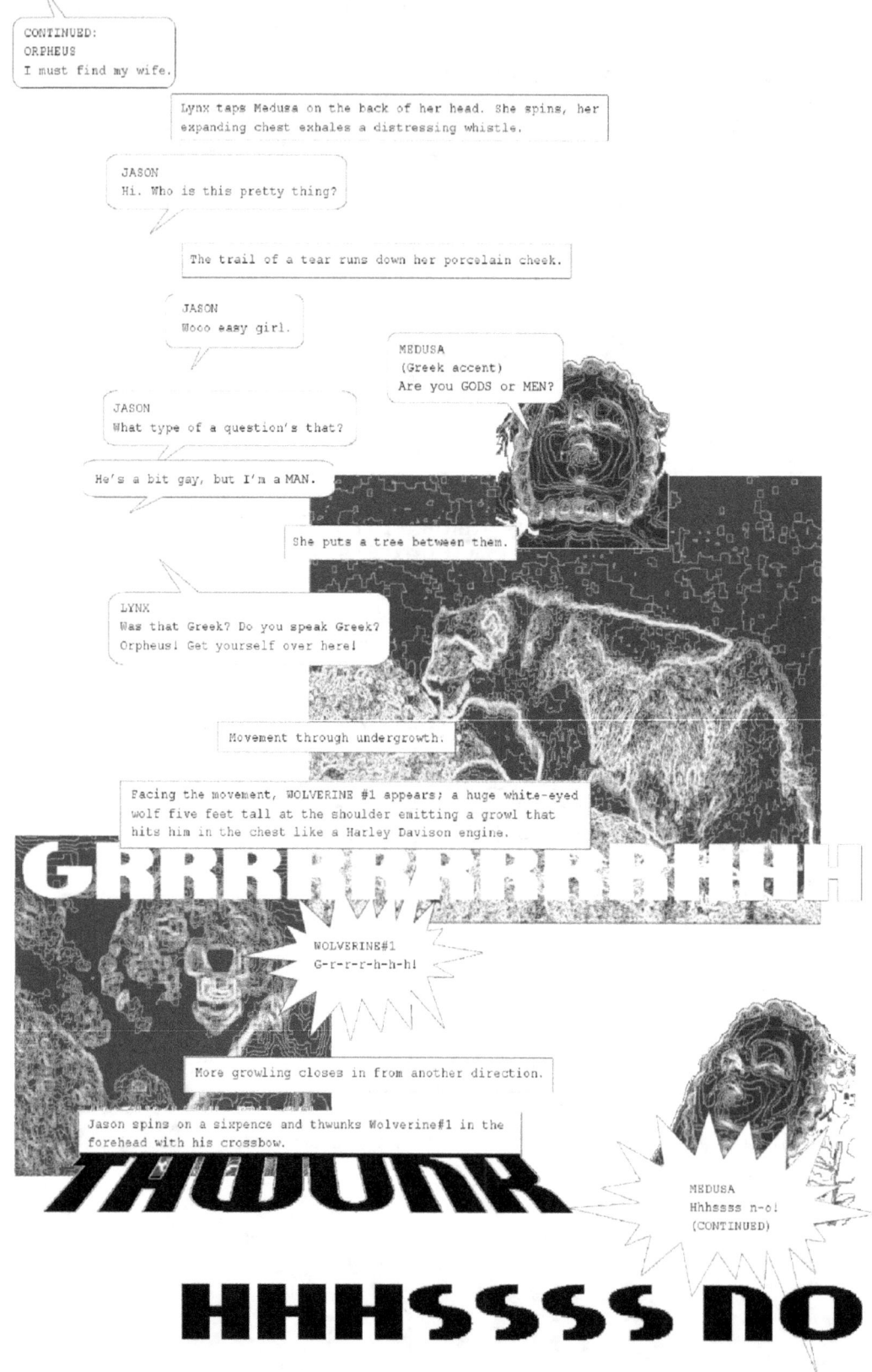

CONTINUED:
ORPHEUS
I must find my wife.

Lynx taps Medusa on the back of her head. She spins, her
expanding chest exhales a distressing whistle.

JASON
Hi. Who is this pretty thing?

The trail of a tear runs down her porcelain cheek.

JASON
Wooo easy girl.

MEDUSA
(Greek accent)
Are you GODS or MEN?

JASON
What type of a question's that?

He's a bit gay, but I'm a MAN.

She puts a tree between them.

LYNX
Was that Greek? Do you speak Greek?
Orpheus! Get yourself over here!

Movement through undergrowth.

Facing the movement, WOLVERINE #1 appears; a huge white-eyed
wolf five feet tall at the shoulder emitting a growl that
hits him in the chest like a Harley Davison engine.

GRRRRAWRRRBHHH

WOLVERINE#1
G-r-r-r-h-h-h!

More growling closes in from another direction.

Jason spins on a sixpence and thwunks Wolverine#1 in the
forehead with his crossbow.

THWUNK

MEDUSA
Hhhssss n-o!
(CONTINUED)

HHHSSSS NO

CONTINUED:

>   ORPHEUS
>   I must find my wife.

Lynx taps Medusa on the back of her head. She spins, her
expanding chest exhales a distressing whistle.

>   JASON
>   Hi. Who is this pretty thing?

The trail of a tear runs down her porcelain cheek.

>   JASON
>   Wooo easy girl.

>   MEDUSA
>   (Greek accent)
>   Are you GODS or MEN?

>   JASON
>   What type of a question's that?
>   He's a bit gay, but I'm a MAN.

She puts a tree between them.

>   LYNX
>   Was that Greek? Do you speak Greek?
>   Orpheus! Get yourself over here!

Movement through undergrowth.

Facing the movement, WOLVERINE #1 appears; a huge white-eyed
wolf five feet tall at the shoulder emitting a growl that
hits him in the chest like a Harley Davison engine.

>   WOLVERINE#1
>   G-r-r-r-h-h-h!

More growling closes in from another direction.

Jason spins on a sixpence and thwunks Wolverine#1 in the
forehead with his crossbow.

>   MEDUSA
>   Hhhssss n-o!

>   (CONTINUED)

CONTINUED:
Lynx fires a FLARE in the direction of Marty hurdling
through the undergrowth.

MARTY
It's me! It's only me!

Orpheus with dagger hurdles in behind. WOLVERINE #2 pursues.

Orpheus turns and the creature body-checks him, sandwiching
him against a tree.

Long pause.
The creature's head flops to one side, falling dead to the
floor. Orpheus's dagger sticks out of its throat.
Orpheus shwings it free.

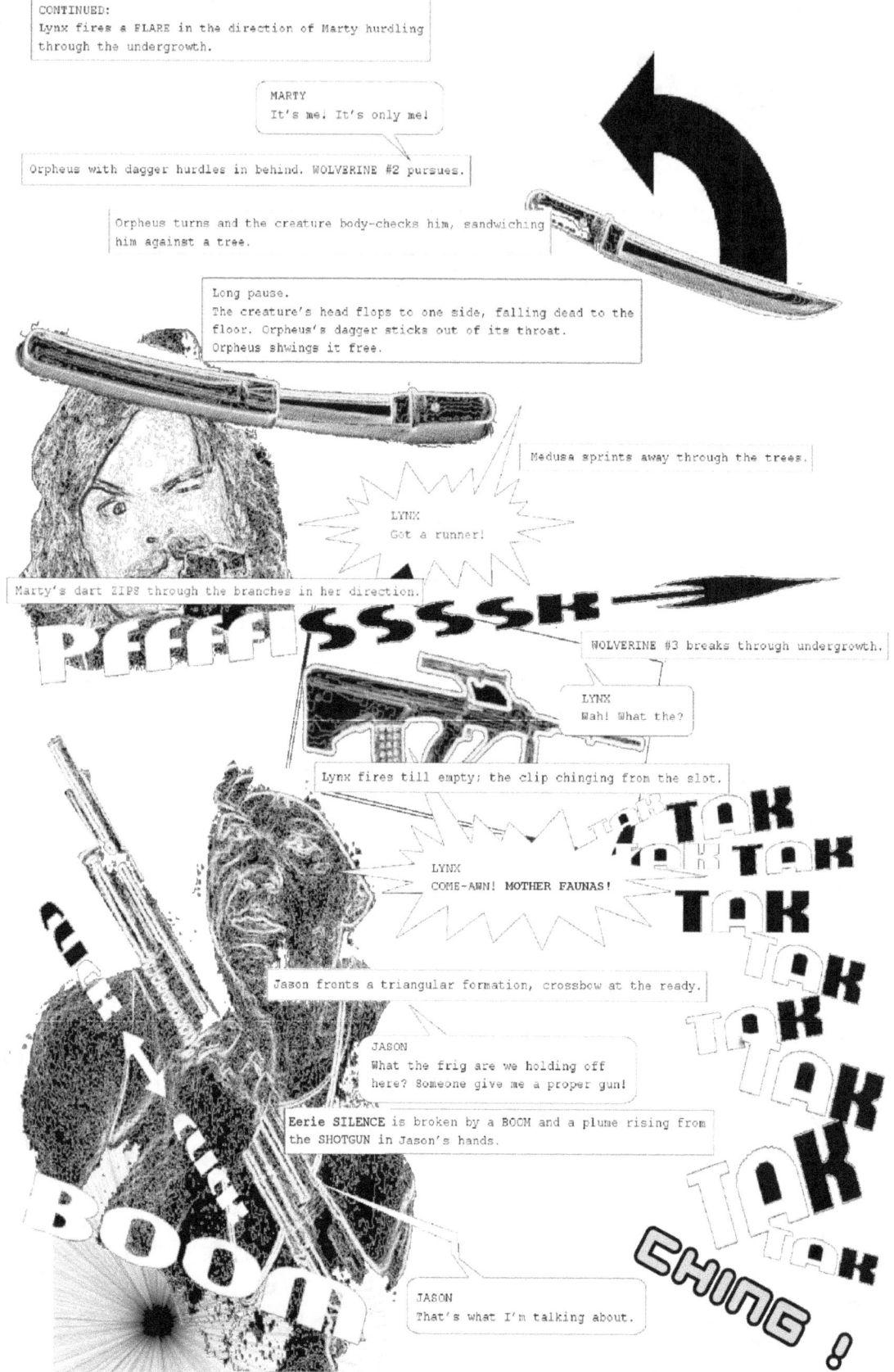

Medusa sprints away through the trees.

LYNX
Got a runner!

Marty's dart ZIPS through the branches in her direction.

RFFFISSSSH

WOLVERINE #3 breaks through undergrowth.

LYNX
Wah! What the?

Lynx fires till empty; the clip chinging from the slot.

TAK TAK TAK
TAK
TAK
TAK
TAK
CHING !

LYNX
COME-AWN! MOTHER FAUNAS!

Jason fronts a triangular formation, crossbow at the ready.

JASON
What the frig are we holding off
here? Someone give me a proper gun!

Eerie SILENCE is broken by a BOOM and a plume rising from
the SHOTGUN in Jason's hands.

BOOM

JASON
That's what I'm talking about.

CONTINUED:

Lynx fires a FLARE in the direction of Marty hurdling through the undergrowth.

                    MARTY
          It's me! It's only me!

Orpheus with dagger hurdles in behind. WOLVERINE #2 pursues.

Orpheus turns and the creature body-checks him, sandwiching him against a tree.

Long pause.

The creature's head flops to one side, falling dead to the floor. Orpheus's dagger sticks out of its throat.

Orpheus shwings it free.

Medusa sprints away through the trees.

                    LYNX
          Got a runner!

Marty's dart ZIPS through the branches in her direction.

WOLVERINE #3 breaks through undergrowth.

                    LYNX
          Wah! What the?

Lynx fires till empty; the clip chinging from the slot.

                    LYNX
          COME-AWN! MOTHER FAUNAS!

Jason fronts a triangular formation, crossbow at the ready.

                    JASON
          What the frig are we holding off
          here? Someone give me a proper gun!

Eerie SILENCE is broken by a BOOM and a plume rising from the SHOTGUN in Jason's hands.

                    JASON
          That's what I'm talking about.

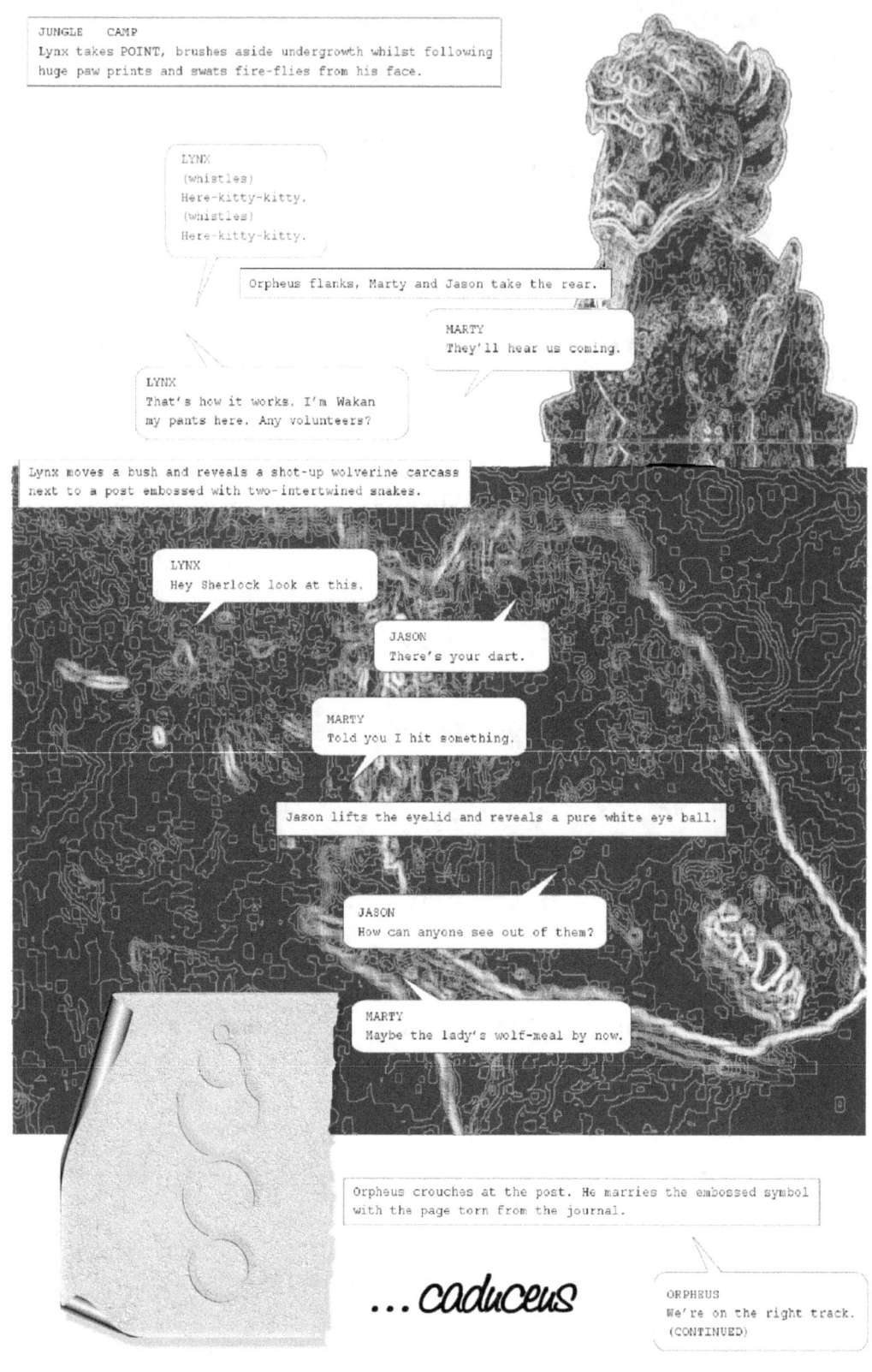

JUNGLE   CAMP
Lynx takes POINT, brushes aside undergrowth whilst following
huge paw prints and swats fire-flies from his face.

LYNX
 (whistles)
 Here-kitty-kitty.
 (whistles)
 Here-kitty-kitty.

Orpheus flanks, Marty and Jason take the rear.

MARTY
 They'll hear us coming.

LYNX
 That's how it works. I'm Wakan
 my pants here. Any volunteers?

Lynx moves a bush and reveals a shot-up wolverine carcass
next to a post embossed with two-intertwined snakes.

LYNX
 Hey Sherlock look at this.

JASON
 There's your dart.

MARTY
 Told you I hit something.

Jason lifts the eyelid and reveals a pure white eye ball.

JASON
 How can anyone see out of them?

MARTY
 Maybe the lady's wolf-meal by now.

Orpheus crouches at the post. He marries the embossed symbol
with the page torn from the journal.

... *caduceus*

ORPHEUS
 We're on the right track.
 (CONTINUED)

EXT. JUNGLE   CAMP   NIGHT

Lynx takes POINT, brushes aside undergrowth whilst following huge paw prints and swats fire-flies from his face.

> LYNX
> (whistles)
> Here-kitty-kitty.
> (whistles)
> Here-kitty-kitty.

Orpheus flanks, Marty and Jason take the rear.

> MARTY
> They'll hear us coming.

> LYNX
> That's how it works. I'm Wakan
> my pants here. Any volunteers?

Lynx moves a bush and reveals a shot-up wolverine carcass next to a post embossed with two- intertwined snakes.

> LYNX
> Hey Sherlock look at this.

> JASON
> There's your dart.

> MARTY
> Told you I hit something.

Jason lifts the eyelid and reveals a pure white eye ball.

> JASON
> How can anyone see out of them?

> MARTY
> Maybe the lady's wolf-meal by now.

Orpheus crouches at the post. He marries the embossed symbol with the page torn from the journal.

> ORPHEUS
> We're on the right track.

(CONTINUED)

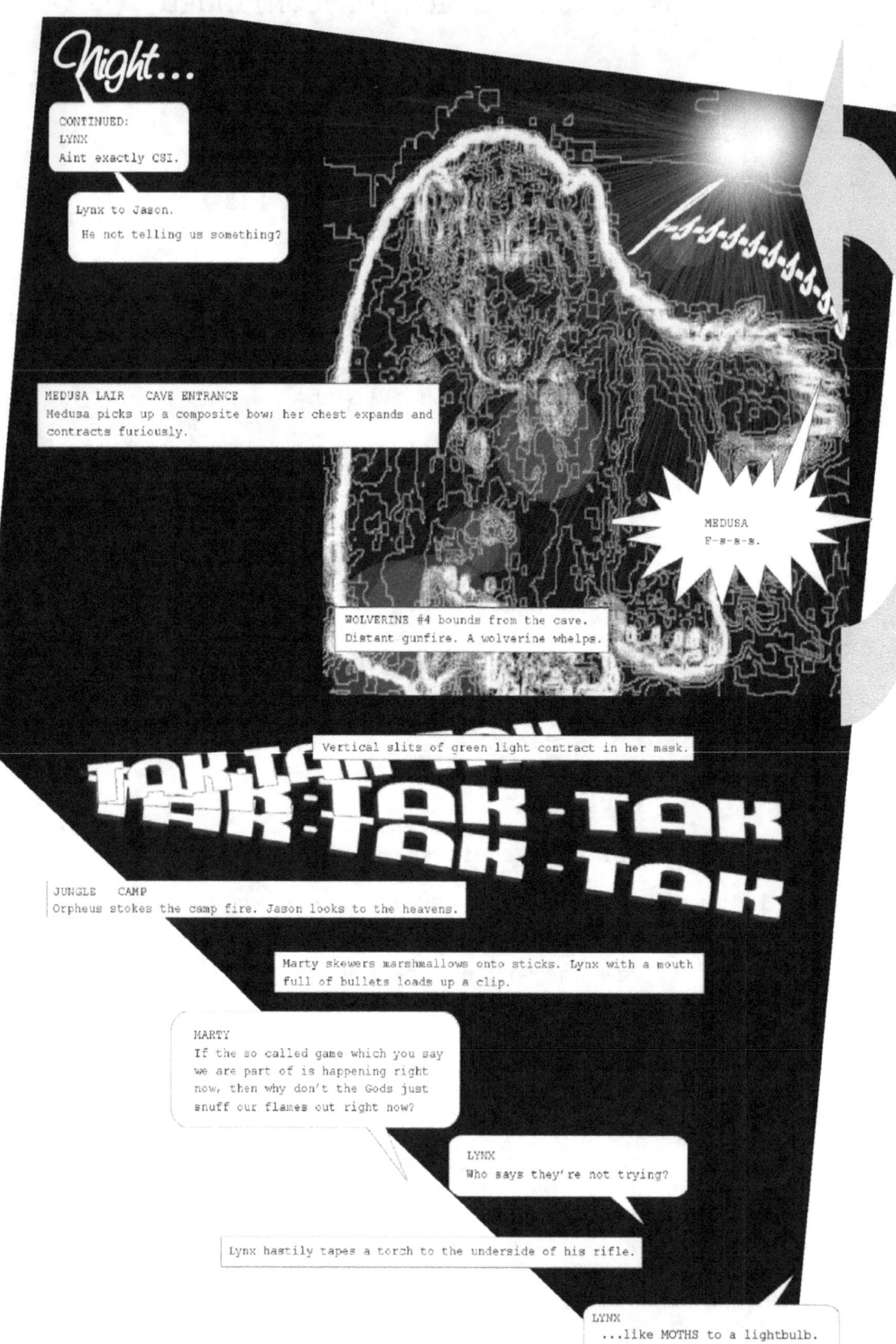

Night...

CONTINUED:
LYNX
Aint exactly CSI.

Lynx to Jason.
He not telling us something?

MEDUSA LAIR CAVE ENTRANCE
Medusa picks up a composite bow; her chest expands and
contracts furiously.

f-s-s-s-s-s-s-s-s

MEDUSA
F-s-s-s.

WOLVERINE #4 bounds from the cave.
Distant gunfire. A wolverine whelps.

Vertical slits of green light contract in her mask.

TAK-TAK-TAK-TAK
TAK-TAK-TAK

JUNGLE CAMP
Orpheus stokes the camp fire. Jason looks to the heavens.

Marty skewers marshmallows onto sticks. Lynx with a mouth
full of bullets loads up a clip.

MARTY
If the so called game which you say
we are part of is happening right
now, then why don't the Gods just
snuff our flames out right now?

LYNX
Who says they're not trying?

Lynx hastily tapes a torch to the underside of his rifle.

LYNX
...like MOTHS to a lightbulb.
(CONTINUED)

CONTINUED:

> LYNX
> Aint exactly CSI.

Lynx to Jason.

> LYNX
> He not telling us something?

INT. MEDUSA LAIR - CAVE ENTRANCE   NIGHT

Medusa picks up a composite bow; her chest expands and
contracts furiously.

> MEDUSA
> F-s-s-s.

WOLVERINE #4 bounds from the cave.

Distant gunfire. A wolverine whelps.

Vertical slits of green light contract in her mask.

EXT. JUNGLE   CAMP   NIGHT

Orpheus stokes the camp fire. Jason looks to the heavens.
Marty skewers marshmallows onto sticks. Lynx with a mouth
full of bullets loads up a clip.

> MARTY
> If the so called game which you say
> we are part of is happening right
> now, then why don't the Gods just
> snuff our flames out right now?

> LYNX
> Who says they're not trying?

Lynx hastily tapes a torch to the underside of his rifle.

> LYNX
> ...like MOTHS to a lightbulb.

(CONTINUED)

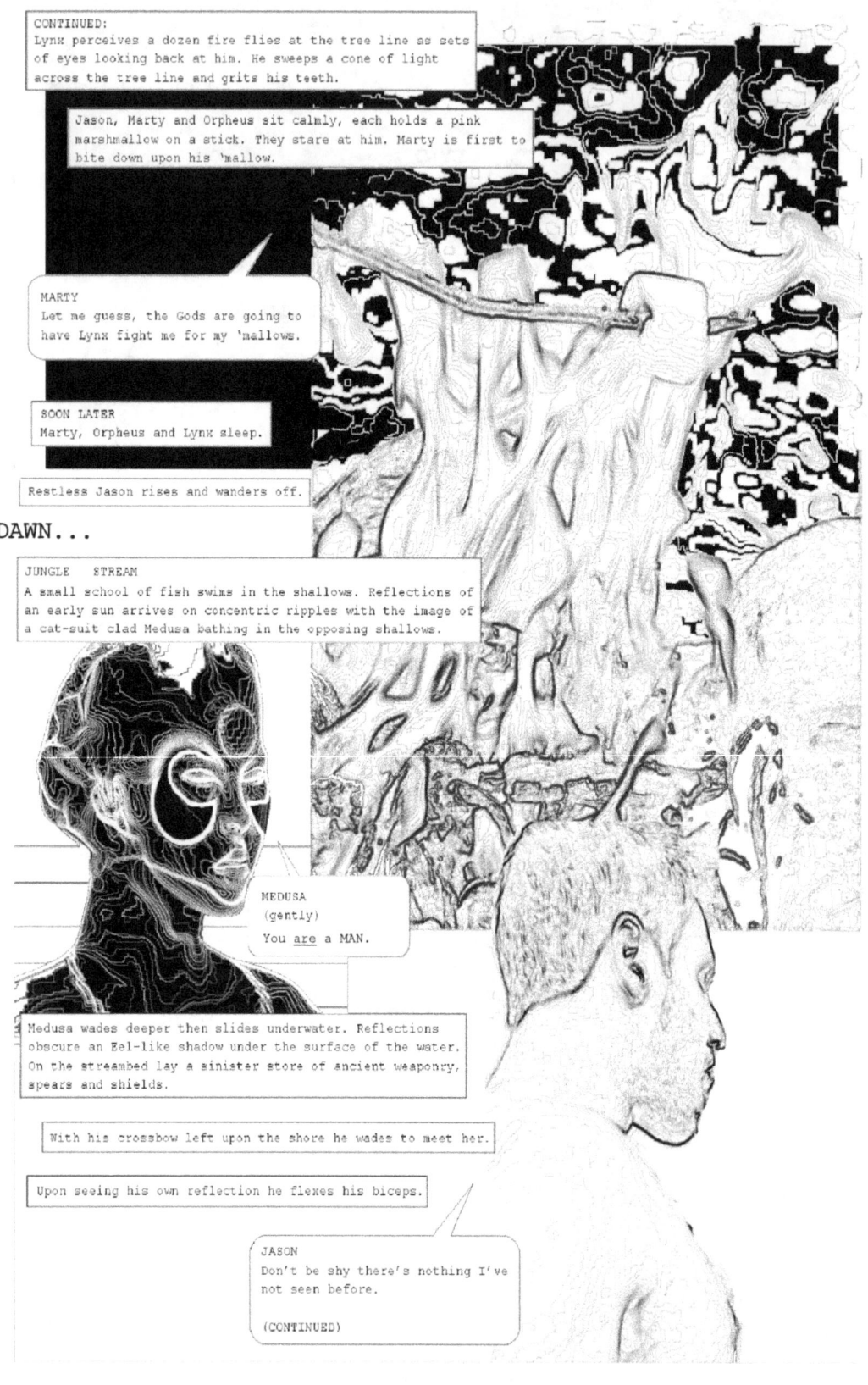

CONTINUED:
Lynx perceives a dozen fire flies at the tree line as sets
of eyes looking back at him. He sweeps a cone of light
across the tree line and grits his teeth.

Jason, Marty and Orpheus sit calmly, each holds a pink
marshmallow on a stick. They stare at him. Marty is first to
bite down upon his 'mallow.

MARTY
Let me guess, the Gods are going to
have Lynx fight me for my 'mallows.

SOON LATER
Marty, Orpheus and Lynx sleep.

Restless Jason rises and wanders off.

DAWN...

JUNGLE   STREAM
A small school of fish swims in the shallows. Reflections of
an early sun arrives on concentric ripples with the image of
a cat-suit clad Medusa bathing in the opposing shallows.

MEDUSA
(gently)
You are a MAN.

Medusa wades deeper then slides underwater. Reflections
obscure an Eel-like shadow under the surface of the water.
On the streambed lay a sinister store of ancient weaponry,
spears and shields.

With his crossbow left upon the shore he wades to meet her.

Upon seeing his own reflection he flexes his biceps.

JASON
Don't be shy there's nothing I've
not seen before.

(CONTINUED)

CONTINUED:

Lynx perceives a dozen fire flies at the tree line as sets of eyes looking back at him. He sweeps a cone of light across the tree line and grits his teeth.

Jason, Marty and Orpheus sit calmly, each holds a pink marshmallow on a stick. They stare at him. Marty is first to bite down upon his 'mallow.

> MARTY
> Let me guess, the Gods are going to have Lynx fight me for my 'mallows.

SOON LATER

Marty, Orpheus and Lynx sleep.

Restless Jason rises and wanders off.

EXT. JUNGLE   STREAM   DAY

A small school of fish swims in the shallows. Reflections of an early sun arrives on concentric ripples with the image of a cat-suit clad Medusa bathing in the opposing shallows.

> MEDUSA
> (gently)
> You <u>are</u> a MAN.

Medusa wades deeper then slides underwater. Reflections obscure an Eel-like shadow under the surface of the water.

On the streambed lay a sinister store of ancient weaponry, spears and shields.

With his crossbow left upon the shore he wades to meet her.

Upon seeing his own reflection he flexes his biceps.

> JASON
> Don't be shy there's nothing I've not seen before.

(CONTINUED)

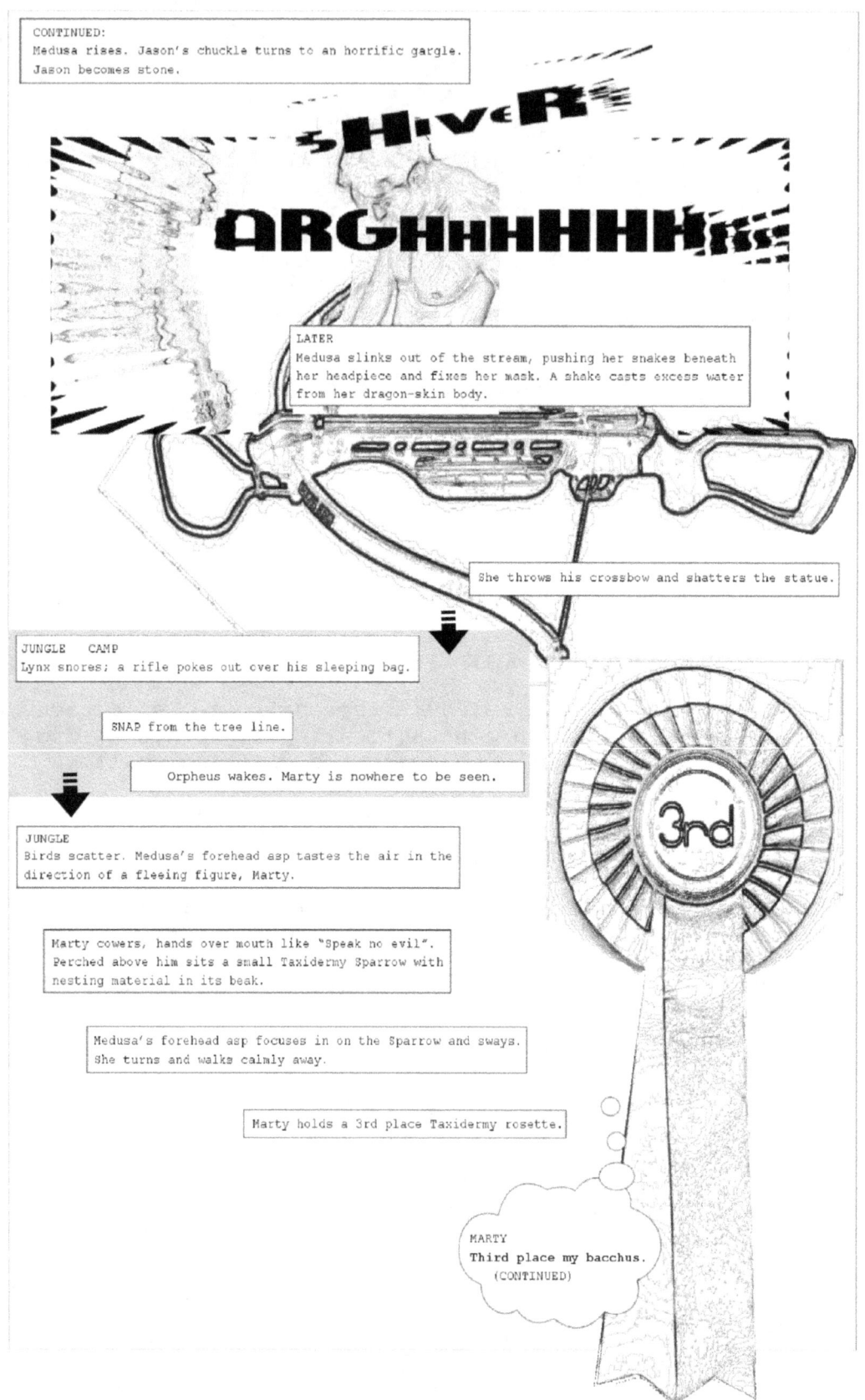

CONTINUED:
Medusa rises. Jason's chuckle turns to an horrific gargle.
Jason becomes stone.

sHiveR

ARGHhHHHHHH

LATER
Medusa slinks out of the stream, pushing her snakes beneath
her headpiece and fixes her mask. A shake casts excess water
from her dragon-skin body.

She throws his crossbow and shatters the statue.

JUNGLE   CAMP
Lynx snores; a rifle pokes out over his sleeping bag.

SNAP from the tree line.

Orpheus wakes. Marty is nowhere to be seen.

JUNGLE
Birds scatter. Medusa's forehead asp tastes the air in the
direction of a fleeing figure, Marty.

Marty cowers, hands over mouth like "Speak no evil".
Perched above him sits a small Taxidermy Sparrow with
nesting material in its beak.

Medusa's forehead asp focuses in on the Sparrow and sways.
She turns and walks calmly away.

Marty holds a 3rd place Taxidermy rosette.

MARTY
Third place my bacchus.
(CONTINUED)

CONTINUED:

Medusa rises. Jason's chuckle turns to an horrific gargle.

Jason becomes stone.

LATER

Medusa slinks out of the stream and pushes her snakes beneath her headpiece; a single shake casts excess water from her dragon-skin body.

She throws his crossbow and shatters the statue.

EXT. JUNGLE   CAMP   NIGHT

Lynx snores; a rifle pokes out over his sleeping bag.

SNAP from the tree line.

Orpheus wakes. Marty is nowhere to be seen.

EXT. JUNGLE   DAY

Birds scatter. Medusa's forehead asp tastes the air in the direction of a fleeing figure, Marty.

Marty cowers, hands over mouth like "Speak no evil".

Perched above him sits a small Taxidermy Sparrow with nesting material in its beak.

Medusa's forehead asp focuses in on the Sparrow and sways.

She turns and walks calmly away.

Marty holds a 3rd place Taxidermy rosette.

> MARTY
> Third-place my **bacchus**.

(CONTINUED)

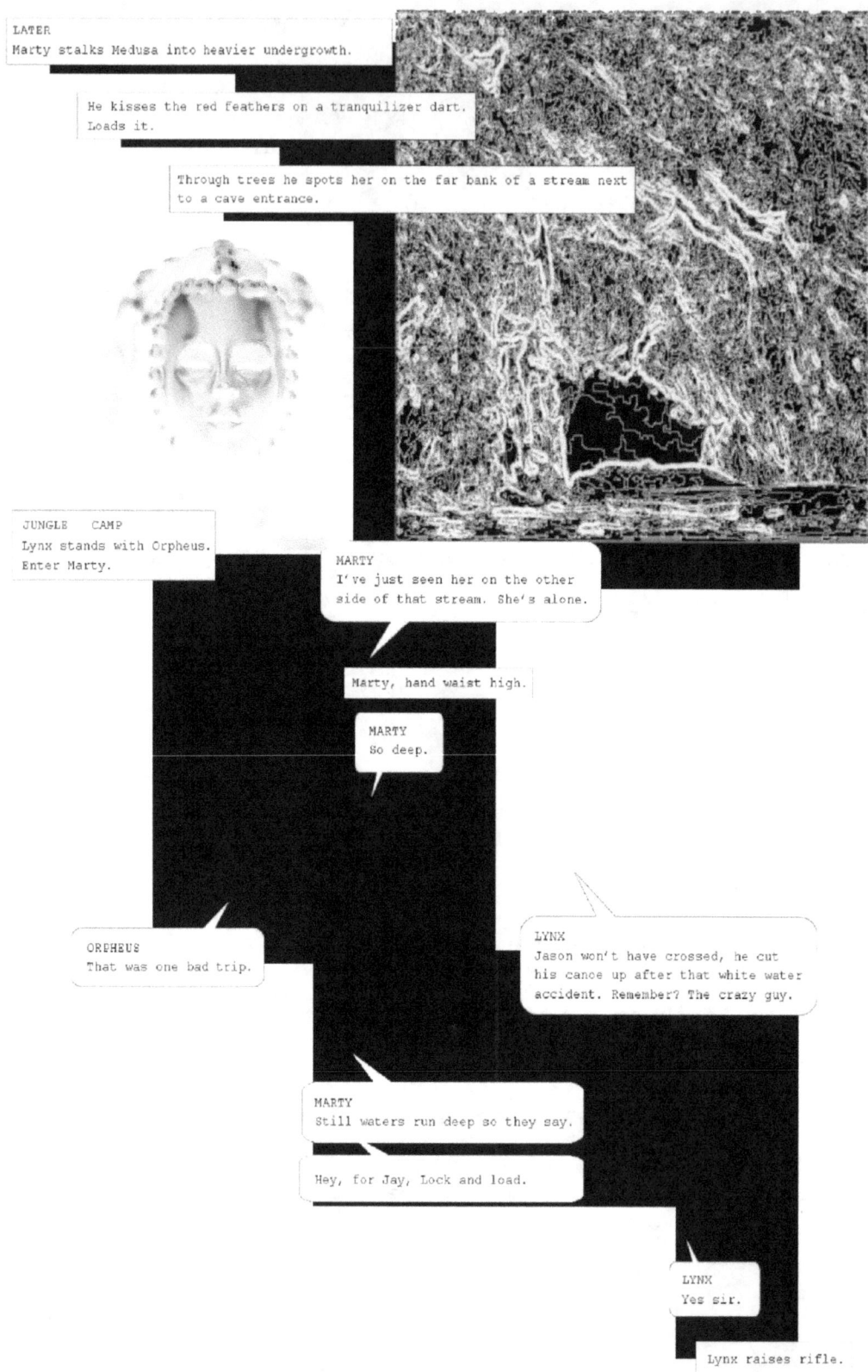

LATER
Marty stalks Medusa into heavier undergrowth.

He kisses the red feathers on a tranquilizer dart.
Loads it.

Through trees he spots her on the far bank of a stream next
to a cave entrance.

JUNGLE   CAMP
Lynx stands with Orpheus.
Enter Marty.

MARTY
I've just seen her on the other
side of that stream. She's alone.

Marty, hand waist high.

MARTY
So deep.

ORPHEUS
That was one bad trip.

LYNX
Jason won't have crossed, he cut
his canoe up after that white water
accident. Remember? The crazy guy.

MARTY
Still waters run deep so they say.

Hey, for Jay, Lock and load.

LYNX
Yes sir.

Lynx raises rifle.

CONTINUED:

LATER

Marty stalks Medusa into heavier undergrowth.

He kisses the red feathers on a tranquilizer dart.

Loads it.

Through trees he spots her on the far bank of a stream next to a cave entrance.

EXT. JUNGLE   CAMP   DAY

Lynx stands with Orpheus.

Enter Marty.

> MARTY
> I've just seen her on the other
> side of that stream. She's alone.

Marty, hand waist high.

> MARTY
> So deep.

> LYNX
> Jason won't have crossed, he cut
> his canoe up after that white water
> accident. Remember? The crazy guy.

> ORPHEUS
> That was one bad trip.

> MARTY
> Still waters run deep so they say.
> (beat)
> Hey, for Jay, Lock and load.

> LYNX
> Yes sir.

Lynx raises rifle.

JUNGLE   STREAM
Using cover Orpheus and Marty look across the stream. Lynx
at the waters edge spots a footprint in the streambed and
kisses his lucky man-symbol.

LYNX
She entered here and exited there.

Lynx wades in; his feet stir a mound of silt and he sinks.

LYNX
You CAN all swim right?

MEDUSA LAIR   CAVE ENTRANCE
Orpheus and Marty wait. Lynx inserts an ear-piece.

LYNX
Jay! Jason?

Rising growl from WOLVERINE #5 in cave.

Lynx checks his rifle clip. Presses play delivering an uptempo
music track that almost drowns out the growling.

The eyes of WOLVERINE #5 appear in the darkness.

He sings along to the tune, giving facial attitude.

LYNX
Come on you big mother.

WOLVERINE #6 appears.

Steady burst...
Increasing to full-auto...
A large shadow falling over him makes him wince.

EXT. JUNGLE   STREAM   DAY

Using cover Orpheus and Marty look across the stream. Lynx
at the waters edge spots a footprint in the streambed and
kisses his lucky man-symbol.

                    LYNX
          She entered here and exited there.

Lynx wades in; his feet stir a mound of silt and he sinks.

                    LYNX
          You <u>CAN</u> all swim right?

EXT. MEDUSA LAIR   CAVE ENTRANCE   DAY

Orpheus and Marty wait. Lynx inserts an ear-piece.

                    LYNX
          Jay! Jason?

Rising growl from WOLVERINE #5 in cave.

Lynx checks his rifle clip. Presses play delivering an uptempo music track that almost drowns out the growling.

The eyes of WOLVERINE #5 appear in the darkness.

He sings along to the tune, giving facial attitude.

                    LYNX
          Come on you big mother.

WOLVERINE #6 appears.

Steady burst...

Increasing to full-auto...

A large shadow falling over him makes him wince.

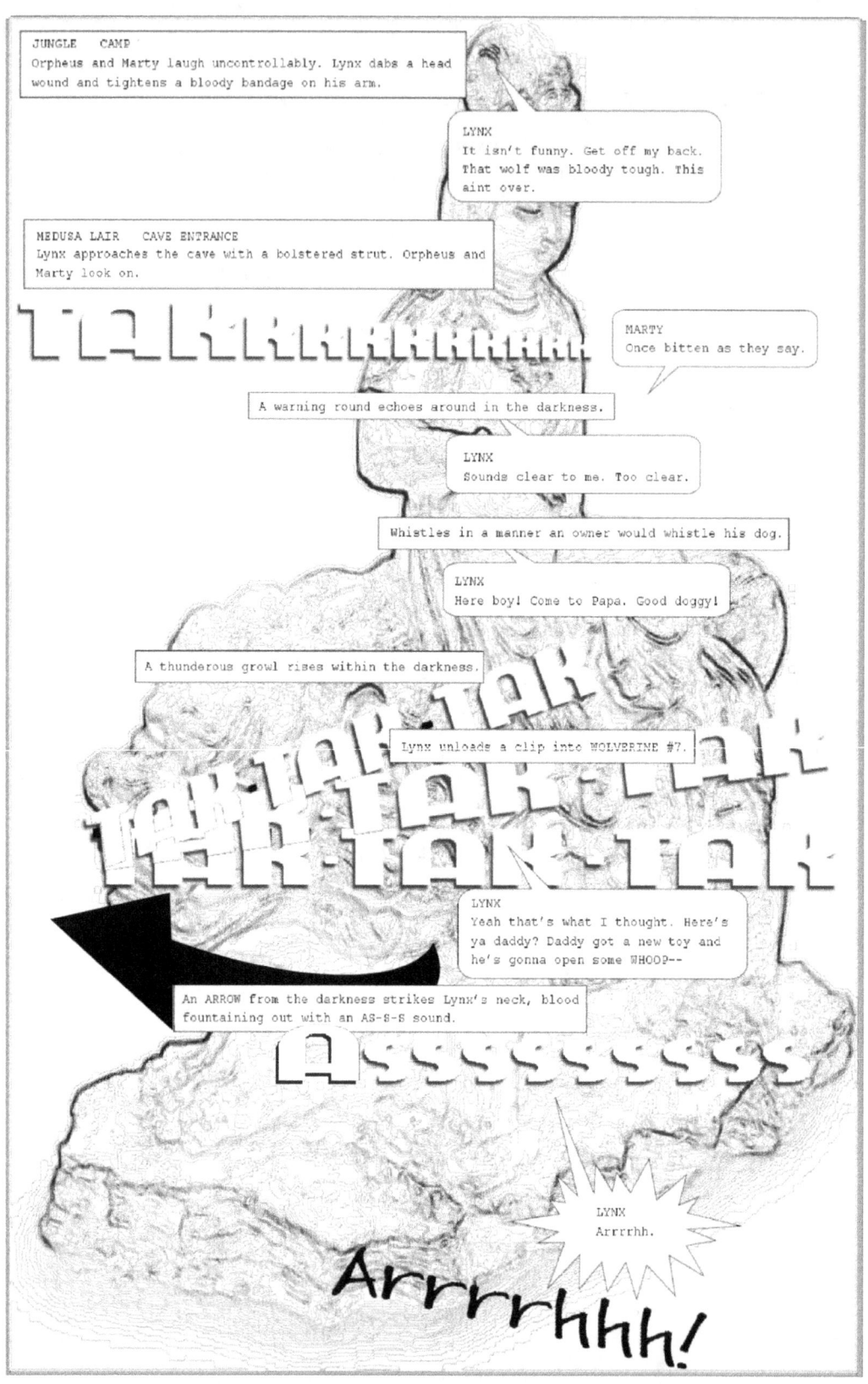

JUNGLE   CAMP
Orpheus and Marty laugh uncontrollably. Lynx dabs a head
wound and tightens a bloody bandage on his arm.

LYNX
It isn't funny. Get off my back.
That wolf was bloody tough. This
aint over.

MEDUSA LAIR   CAVE ENTRANCE
Lynx approaches the cave with a bolstered strut. Orpheus and
Marty look on.

MARTY
Once bitten as they say.

A warning round echoes around in the darkness.

LYNX
Sounds clear to me. Too clear.

Whistles in a manner an owner would whistle his dog.

LYNX
Here boy! Come to Papa. Good doggy!

A thunderous growl rises within the darkness.

Lynx unloads a clip into WOLVERINE #7.

LYNX
Yeah that's what I thought. Here's
ya daddy? Daddy got a new toy and
he's gonna open some WHOOP--

An ARROW from the darkness strikes Lynx's neck, blood
fountaining out with an AS-S-S sound.

LYNX
Arrrrhh.

EXT. JUNGLE   CAMP   NIGHT

Orpheus and Marty laugh uncontrollably. Lynx dabs a head
wound and tightens a bloody bandage on his arm.

> LYNX
> It isn't funny. Get off my back.
> That wolf was bloody tough. This
> aint over.

EXT. MEDUSA LAIR   CAVE ENTRANCE   DAY

Lynx approaches the cave with a bolstered strut. Orpheus and
Marty look on.

> MARTY
> Once bitten as they say.

A warning round echoes around in the darkness.

> LYNX
> Sounds clear to me. Too clear.

Whistles in a manner an owner would whistle his dog.

> LYNX
> Here boy! Come to Papa. Good doggy!

A thunderous growl rises within the darkness.

Lynx unloads a clip into WOLVERINE #7.

> LYNX
> Yeah that's what I thought. Here's
> ya daddy? Daddy got a new toy and
> he's gonna open some WHOOP--

An ARROW from the darkness strikes Lynx's neck, blood
fountaining out with an AS-S-S sound.

> LYNX
> Arrrrhh.

Stumbling, hand bracing his neck, blood pumps through his
fingers. He drags his rifle by the barrel.

(CONTINUED)

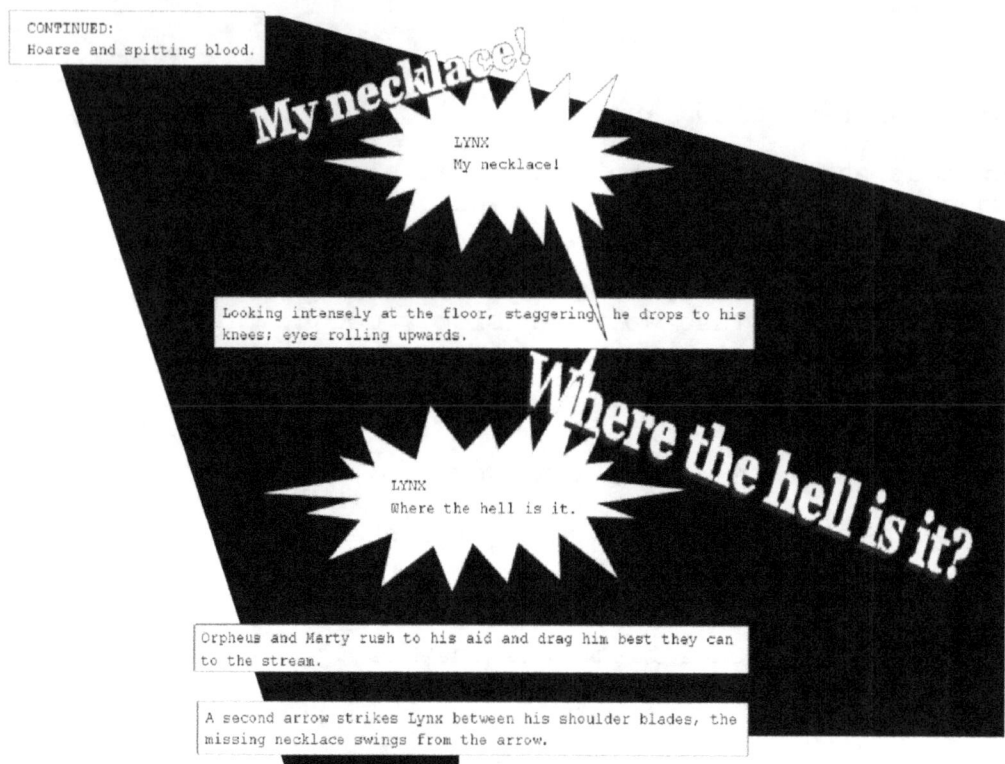

CONTINUED:
Hoarse and spitting blood.

My necklace!

LYNX
My necklace!

Looking intensely at the floor, staggering, he drops to his
knees; eyes rolling upwards.

Where the hell is it?

LYNX
Where the hell is it.

Orpheus and Marty rush to his aid and drag him best they can
to the stream.

A second arrow strikes Lynx between his shoulder blades, the
missing necklace swings from the arrow.

JUNGLE   STREAM
Marty SPLASHES through the stream like an hysteric
child. Orpheus pursues.

IN THE RELATIVE SAFETY OF CAMP...

JUNGLE   CAMP
Orpheus watches a tearful Marty gather his belongings.

MARTY
I must be insane. This whole thing;
insane. We came looking for you
Orpheus. We found you! Now let's get
the hell out of here!

I MUST BE INSANE.

THIS WHOLE THING; INSANE.

WE CAME LOOKING FOR YOU ORPHEUS.

WE FOUND YOU! NOW LET'S GET

THE HELL OUTTA HERE!

Marty pulls on the caduceus around Orpheus's neck.

MARTY
I sure hope to GOD...that piece of
WICCAN doesn't get us all killed.
I'm turning back.

(CONTINUED)

CONTINUED:

Hoarse and spitting blood.

> LYNX
> My necklace!

Looking intensely at the floor, staggering, he drops to his knees; eyes rolling upwards.

> LYNX
> Where the hell is it.

Orpheus and Marty rush to his aid and drag him best they can to the stream.

A second arrow strikes Lynx between his shoulder blades, the missing necklace swings from the arrow.

EXT. JUNGLE   STREAM   DAY

Marty SPLASHES through the stream like an hysteric child. Orpheus pursues.

IN THE RELATIVE SAFETY OF CAMP...

EXT. JUNGLE   CAMP   DAY

Orpheus watches a tearful Marty gather his belongings.

> MARTY
> I must be insane. This whole thing;
> insane. We came looking for you
> Orpheus. We found you! Now let's get
> the hell out of here!

Marty pulls on the caduceus around Orpheus's neck.

> MARTY
> I sure hope to GOD...that piece of
> WICCAN doesn't get us all killed.
> I'm turning back.

                                        (CONTINUED)

CONTINUED:
ORPHEUS
You can't turn back.

MARTY
Wrong! You're turning back, and I'm
gonna follow you. So let's get the
hell outta here, alive!

Marty throws his tranquilizer gun at Orpheus and takes-off
briskly towards the edge of camp.

MARTY
Game over.

A tranquilizer dart thwacks Marty in the thigh.

MARTY
Argh? What the ...?

Looking down a dart protrudes from his thigh.

MARTY
I'm feelin' kinda wooz--

Marty falls like a log.

JUNGLE   CAMP
Orpheus secures Marty within his own sleeping bag.
Lifting his eyelid, a PENLIGHT makes his pupils shrink.
Left to sleep, his rifle ribbon flutters from a breeze.

Tranquilizer...

ORPHEUS
If nowhere was a place, we're
getting there real quick.

Come on Orpheus keep your head.

CONTINUED:

>   ORPHEUS
>   You can't turn back.

>   MARTY
>   Wrong! You're turning back, and I'm
>   gonna follow you. So let's get the
>   hell outta here, alive!

Marty throws his tranquilizer gun at Orpheus and takes-off
briskly towards the edge of camp.

>   MARTY
>   Game over.

A tranquilizer dart thwacks Marty in the thigh.

>   MARTY
>   Argh? What the @#!

Looking down a dart protrudes from his thigh.

>   MARTY
>   I'm feelin' kinda **woozy**.

Marty falls like a log.

EXT. JUNGLE   CAMP   NIGHT

Orpheus secures Marty within his own sleeping bag.
Lifting his eyelid, a PENLIGHT makes his pupils shrink.
Left to sleep, his rifle ribbon flutters from a breeze.

>   ORPHEUS
>   If nowhere was a place, we're
>   getting there real quick.
>   (beat)
>   Come on Orpheus keep your head.

DAWN...

JUNGLE   CAMP
Tweeting birds.

Arrrrhhh! I've lost my arms!

Orpheus jerks awake to the sound of Marty hyperventilating.

MARTY
Wah-h-h my arms. I've lost my arms.

Orpheus slaps Marty's cheek. Marty lay bound in rope

MARTY
(whispers)
Somethin' there in the trees
took my ribbon.

Both look to the trees.

He unties Marty.

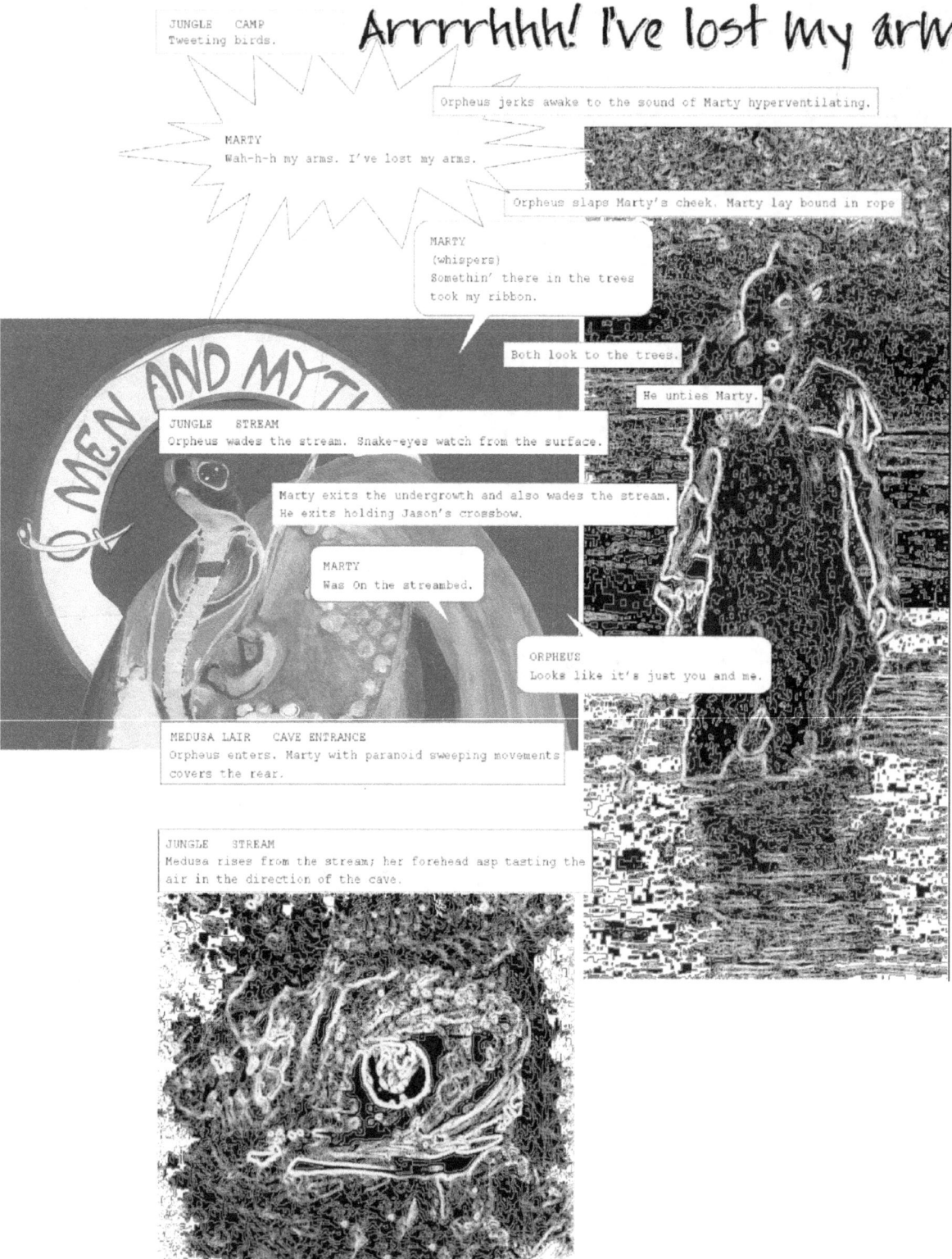

JUNGLE   STREAM
Orpheus wades the stream. Snake-eyes watch from the surface.

Marty exits the undergrowth and also wades the stream.
He exits holding Jason's crossbow.

MARTY
Was On the streambed.

ORPHEUS
Looks like it's just you and me.

MEDUSA LAIR   CAVE ENTRANCE
Orpheus enters. Marty with paranoid sweeping movements
covers the rear.

JUNGLE   STREAM
Medusa rises from the stream; her forehead asp tasting the
air in the direction of the cave.

EXT. JUNGLE   CAMP   DAY

Tweeting birds.

Orpheus jerks awake to the sound of Marty hyperventilating.

>   MARTY
>   Wah-h-h my arms. I've lost my arms.

Orpheus slaps Marty's cheek. Marty lay bound in rope

>   MARTY
>   (whispers)
>   Somethin' there in the trees
>   took my ribbon.

Both look to the trees.

He unties Marty.

EXT. JUNGLE   STREAM   DAY

Orpheus wades the stream. Snake-eyes watch from the surface.

Marty exits the undergrowth and also wades the stream.

He exits holding Jason's crossbow.

>   MARTY
>   Was On the streambed.

>   ORPHEUS
>   Looks like it's just you and me.

INT. MEDUSA LAIR   CAVE ENTRANCE   DAY

Orpheus enters. Marty with paranoid sweeping movements
covers the rear.

EXT. JUNGLE   STREAM   DAY

Medusa rises from the stream; her forehead asp tasting the
air in the direction of the cave.

"CAN CANEM"

MEDUSA LAIR   CAVE ENTRANCE
Orpheus on POINT ; Marty follows. Earthen floor underfoot
abruptly becomes a mosaic of the words "Can Canem".

ORPHEUS
Beware of the dog!

Beware of the dog.

MARTY
You sure?

You sure?

ORPHEUS
Trust me, that's what it says.

Trust me, that's what it says.

... The rising sun.

MEDUSA LAIR   INNER SANCTUM
A large tapestry hangs at the entrance. Various statues
exist frozen in horrific poses.

Orpheus kicks a pile of miscellaneous dusty weapons.

On his knees he blows away dust from a mosaic to reveal the
petals of a flower emulating the sun's rays.

ORPHEUS
The rising sun.

INT. MEDUSA LAIR   CAVE ENTRANCE   DAY

Orpheus on POINT; Marty follows. Earthen floor underfoot
abruptly becomes a mosaic of the words "Can Canem".

                    ORPHEUS
          Beware of the dog!

                    MARTY
          You sure?

                    ORPHEUS
          Trust me, that's what it says.

INT. MEDUSA LAIR   INNER SANCTUM   DAY

A large tapestry hangs at the entrance. Various statues
exist frozen in horrific poses.

Orpheus kicks a pile of miscellaneous dusty weapons.

On his knees he blows away dust from a mosaic to reveal the
petals of a flower emulating the sun's rays.

                    ORPHEUS
          The rising sun.

BEFORE THE CURSE...
Ancient Greece...

MEDUSA'S HOME, ANCIENT GREECE
Medusa, pretty, stands on a sunflower mosaic. Around her arm
she strokes a pet snake. A LOOKING GLASS held by a statue of
Aphrodite angles the suns rays from the above skylight to
her bare feet.

MEDUSA
The sun rising in the distant east,
some say its morning rays are
gentler; more beautiful. Could
there be such beauty?

OLYMPUS
Aphrodite curtsies to Zeus.

A swift wind announces the arrival of Hermes who then
presents a pretty clay figurine of a Greek lady with snake
upon her arm to Aphrodite.

HERMES
(sarcastically)
Thank you Hermes.

APHRODITE
How dare a mortal proclaim the Sun's
rays more beautiful than I?
(venomously)
Lord I ask permission to forbid the
Sun's rays from ever bathing upon
her oh so beautiful face.

Aphrodite caresses the snake on the figurine.

ZEUS
Vanity is not one of your comely
traits. And how do you wish to
carry out such a sentence?

Aphrodite removes an asp-shaped-hairpin from her hair and
drives it into the idol's head causing the face to chip
away.

Zeus looks away in disgust.

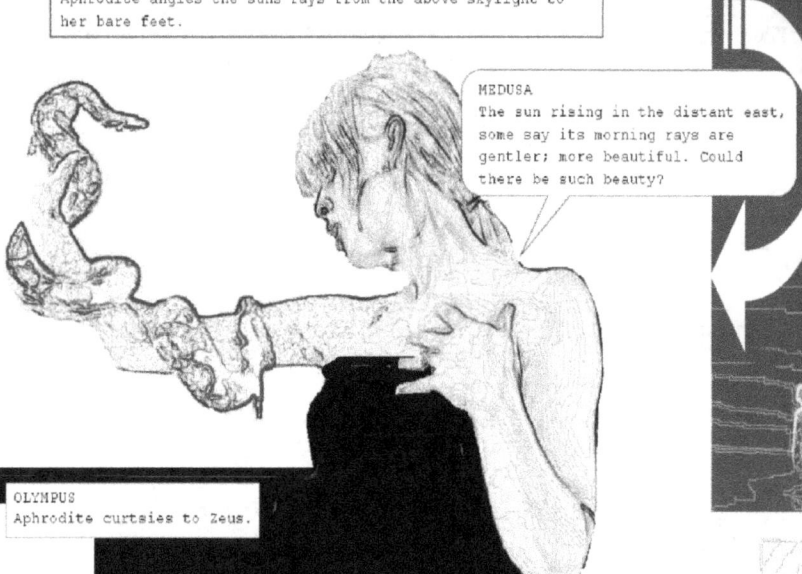
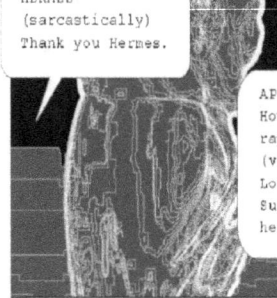

BEFORE THE CURSE...

INT. MEDUSA LAIR   INNER SANCTUM   DAY, ANCIENT GREECE

Medusa, pretty, stands on a sunflower mosaic. Around her arm
she strokes a pet snake. A 'LOOKING GLASS' held by a statue of
Aphrodite angles the suns rays from the above skylight to
her bare feet.

                         MEDUSA
               The sun rising in the distant east,
               some say its morning rays are
               gentler; more beautiful. Could
               there be such beauty?

INT. OLYMPUS   DAY

Aphrodite curtsies to Zeus.

A swift wind announces the arrival of Hermes who presents a
pretty clay figurine of a Greek lady with snake upon her arm
to Aphrodite.

                         HERMES
                    (sarcastically)
               Thank you Hermes.

                         APHRODITE
               How dare a mortal proclaim the suns
               rays more beautiful than I?
                    (venomously)
               Lord I ask permission to forbid the
               Sun's rays from ever bathing upon
               her oh so beautiful face.

Aphrodite caresses the snake on the figurine.

                         ZEUS
               Vanity is not one of your comely
               traits. And how do you wish to
               carry out such a sentence?

Aphrodite removes an asp-shaped-hairpin from her hair and
drives it into the idol's head causing the face to chip
away.

Zeus looks away in disgust.

THE BIRTH OF THE MEDUSA...

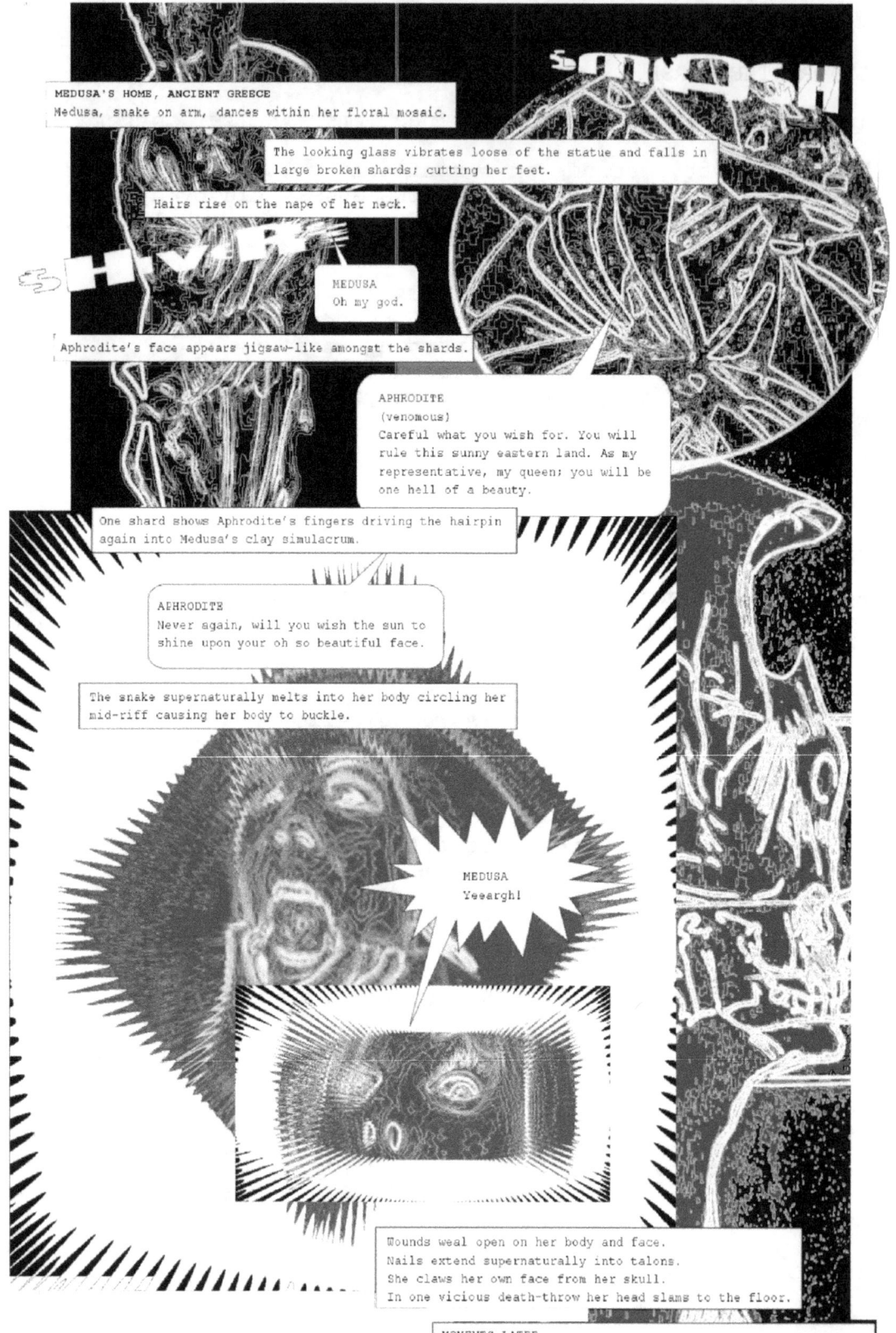

MEDUSA'S HOME, ANCIENT GREECE
Medusa, snake on arm, dances within her floral mosaic.

The looking glass vibrates loose of the statue and falls in large broken shards; cutting her feet.

Hairs rise on the nape of her neck.

MEDUSA
Oh my god.

Aphrodite's face appears jigsaw-like amongst the shards.

APHRODITE
(venomous)
Careful what you wish for. You will rule this sunny eastern land. As my representative, my queen; you will be one hell of a beauty.

One shard shows Aphrodite's fingers driving the hairpin again into Medusa's clay simulacrum.

APHRODITE
Never again, will you wish the sun to shine upon your oh so beautiful face.

The snake supernaturally melts into her body circling her mid-riff causing her body to buckle.

MEDUSA
Yeeargh!

Wounds weal open on her body and face.
Nails extend supernaturally into talons.
She claws her own face from her skull.
In one vicious death-throw her head slams to the floor.

MOMENTS LATER
A snake explodes from Medusa's forehead; one gasp from the asp causes her torso to expand into life.

(CONTINUED)

THE BIRTH OF THE MEDUSA...   136.

INT. MEDUSA LAIR   INNER SANCTUM   DAY, ANCIENT GREECE

Medusa, snake on arm, dances within her floral mosaic.

The looking glass vibrates loose of the statue and falls in
large broken shards; cutting her feet.

Hairs rise on the nape of her neck.

                    MEDUSA
          Oh my god.

Aphrodite's face appears jigsaw-like amongst the shards.

                    APHRODITE
               (venomous)
          Careful what you wish for. You will
          rule this sunny eastern land. As my
          representative, my queen; you will be
          one hell of a beauty.

One shard shows Aphrodite's fingers driving the hairpin
again into Medusa's clay simulacrum.

                    APHRODITE
          Never again, will you wish the sun to
          shine upon your oh so beautiful face.

The snake supernaturally melts into her body circling her
mid-riff causing her body to buckle.

                    MEDUSA
          Yeeargh!

Wounds weal open on her body and face.

Nails extend supernaturally into talons.

She claws her own face from her skull.

In one vicious death-throw her head slams to the floor.

MOMENTS LATER

A snake explodes from Medusa's forehead; one gasp from the
asp causes her torso to expand into life.

                                        (CONTINUED)

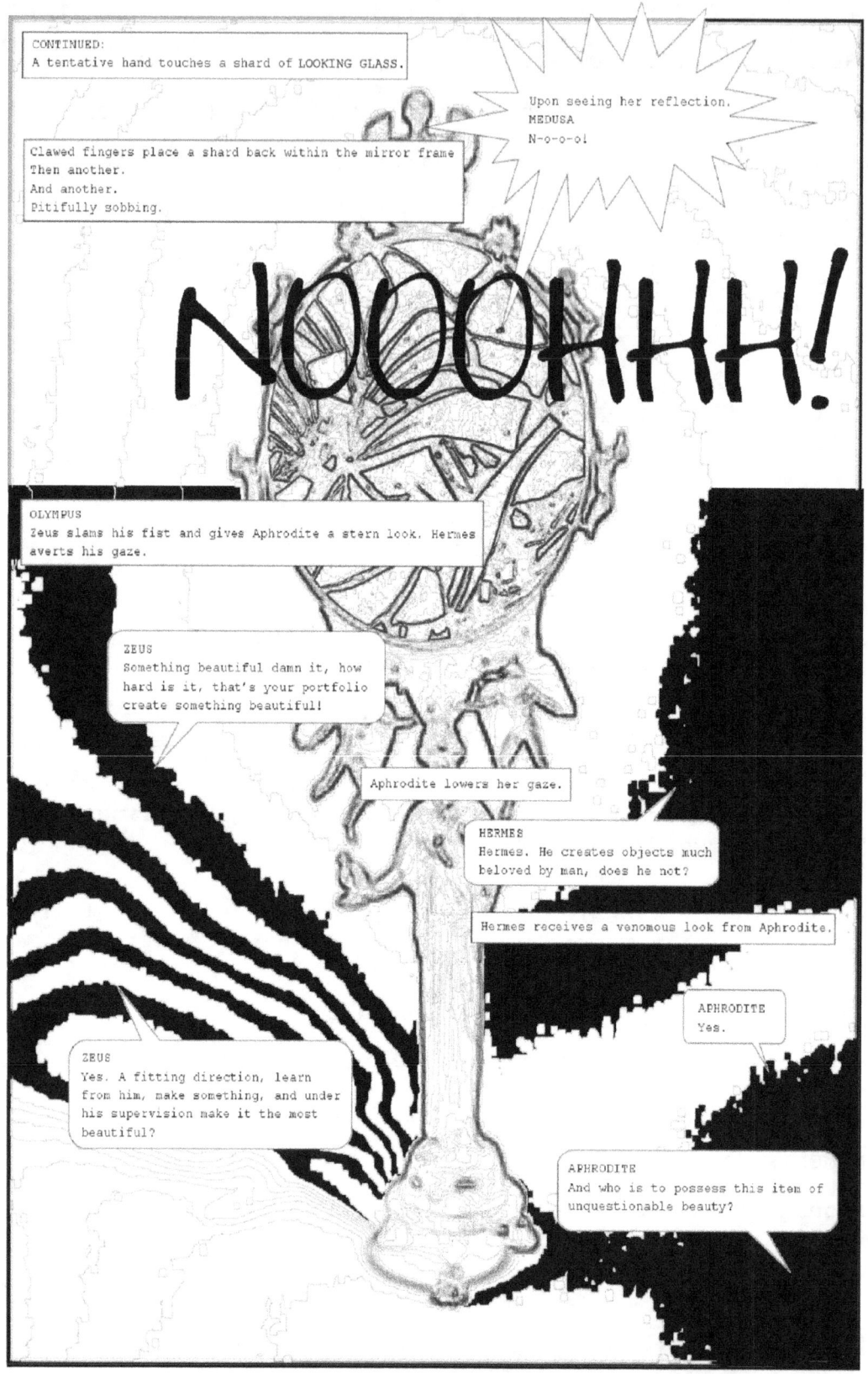

CONTINUED:

A tentative hand touches a shard of LOOKING GLASS.

Upon seeing her reflection.

>   MEDUSA
>   N-o-o-o!

Clawed fingers place a shard back within the mirror frame

Then another.

And another.

Pitifully sobbing.

INT. OLYMPUS   DAY

Zeus slams his fist and gives Aphrodite a stern look. Hermes
averts his gaze.

>   ZEUS
>   Something beautiful damn it, how
>   hard is it, that's your portfolio
>   create something beautiful!

Aphrodite lowers her gaze.

>   HERMES
>   Hermes. He creates objects much
>   beloved by man, does he not?

Hermes receives a venomous look from Aphrodite.

>   APHRODITE
>   Yes.

>   ZEUS
>   Yes. A fitting direction, learn
>   from him, make something, and under
>   his supervision make it the most
>   beautiful?

>   APHRODITE
>   And who is to possess this item of
>   unquestionable beauty?

PRESENT DAY...

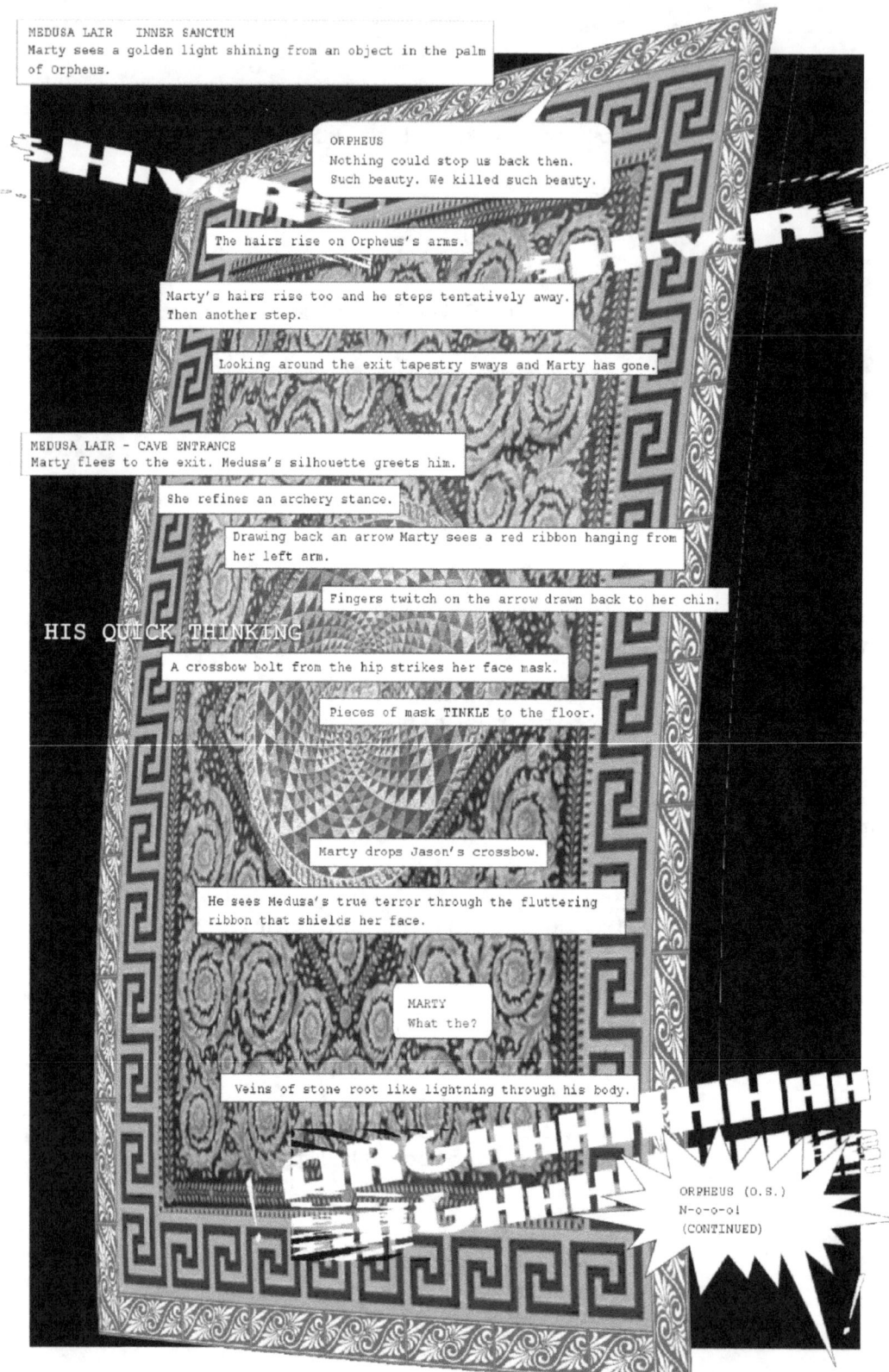

MEDUSA LAIR   INNER SANCTUM
Marty sees a golden light shining from an object in the palm
of Orpheus.

ORPHEUS
Nothing could stop us back then.
Such beauty. We killed such beauty.

The hairs rise on Orpheus's arms.

Marty's hairs rise too and he steps tentatively away.
Then another step.

Looking around the exit tapestry sways and Marty has gone.

MEDUSA LAIR - CAVE ENTRANCE
Marty flees to the exit. Medusa's silhouette greets him.

She refines an archery stance.

Drawing back an arrow Marty sees a red ribbon hanging from
her left arm.

Fingers twitch on the arrow drawn back to her chin.

HIS QUICK THINKING

A crossbow bolt from the hip strikes her face mask.

Pieces of mask TINKLE to the floor.

Marty drops Jason's crossbow.

He sees Medusa's true terror through the fluttering
ribbon that shields her face.

MARTY
What the?

Veins of stone root like lightning through his body.

ORPHEUS (O.S.)
N-o-o-o!
(CONTINUED)

INT. MEDUSA LAIR   INNER SANCTUM   DAY, PRESENT

Marty sees a golden light shining from an object in the palm of Orpheus.

> ORPHEUS
> Nothing could stop us back then.
> Such beauty. We killed such beauty.

The hairs rise on Orpheus's arms.

Marty's hairs rise too and he steps tentatively away.

Then another step.

Looking around the exit tapestry sways and Marty has gone.

INT. MEDUSA LAIR   CAVE ENTRANCE   DAY

Marty flees to the exit. Medusa's silhouette greets him.

She refines an archery stance.

Drawing back an arrow Marty sees a red ribbon hanging from her left arm.

Fingers twitch on the arrow drawn back to her chin.

QUICK THINKING...

A crossbow bolt from the hip strikes her face mask.

Pieces of mask TINKLE to the floor.

Marty drops Jason's crossbow.

He sees Medusa's true terror through the fluttering ribbon that shields her face.

> MARTY
> What the?

Veins of stone root like lightning through his body.

> ORPHEUS (O.S.)
> N-o-o-o!

(CONTINUED)

CONTINUED:
Sound of footsteps running away.

Medusa tears the ribbon from her wrist and discards it to
the floor.

MEDUSA
You pussy-cat, meow.

MEDUSA LAIR   INNER SANCTUM
Orpheus changes directions to the sound of scuffing feet.

A mosaic depicts a man holding aloft a snake-infested head.

MEDUSA
Coming ready or not.

MEDUSA LAIR   CAVE ENTRANCE
A new mask depicting a venomous expression slides over
Medusa's face.

Her forehead asp licks the air towards the INNER SANCTUM.

MEDUSA LAIR   INNER SANCTUM
Medusa's forehead-asp licks the air in the direction of a
pile of shields. She pulls one away.

Reveal a cowering Orpheus with hands over his eyes.

MEDUSA
Peek-a-boo.

Medusa peels back a finger to reveal a blindfold.
(CONTINUED)

CONTINUED:

Sound of footsteps running away.

Medusa tears the ribbon from her wrist and discards it to
the floor.

                    MEDUSA
          You pussy-cat, meow.

INT. MEDUSA LAIR   INNER SANCTUM   DAY

Orpheus changes directions to the sound of scuffing feet.

A mosaic depicts a man holding aloft a snake-infested head.

                    MEDUSA
          Coming ready or not.

INT. MEDUSA LAIR   CAVE ENTRANCE   DAY

A new mask depicting a venomous expression slides over
Medusa's face.

Her forehead asp licks the air towards the INNER SANCTUM.

INT. MEDUSA LAIR   INNER SANCTUM   DAY

Medusa's forehead-asp licks the air in the direction of a
pile of shields. She pulls one away.

Reveal a cowering Orpheus with hands over his eyes.

                    MEDUSA
          Peek-a-boo.

Medusa peels back a finger to reveal a blindfold.

(CONTINUED)

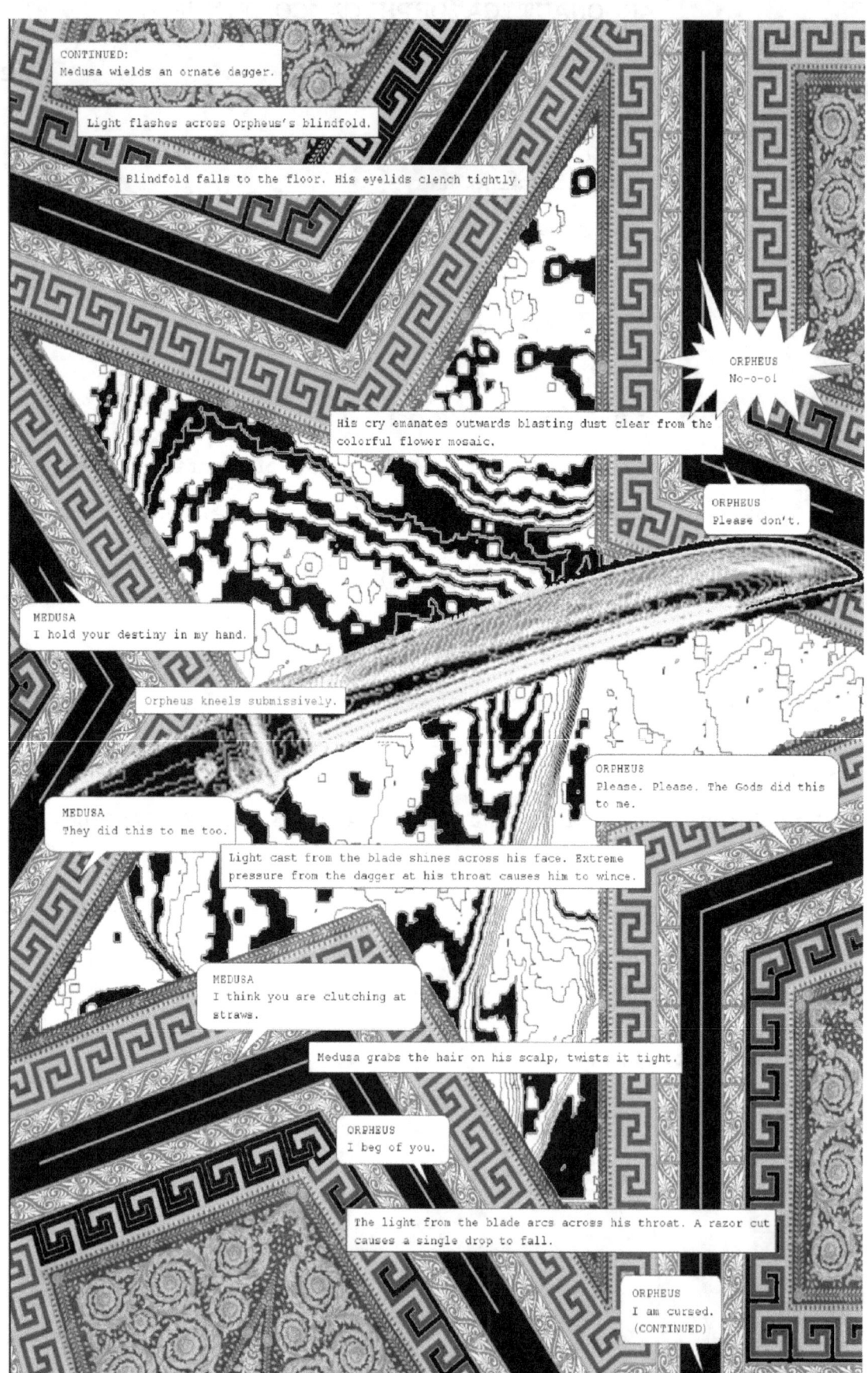

CONTINUED:

Medusa wields an ornate dagger.

Light flashes across Orpheus's blindfold.

Blindfold falls to the floor. His eyelids clench tightly.

> ORPHEUS
> NO-O-O!

His cry emanates outwards blasting dust clear from the colorful flower mosaic.

> ORPHEUS
> Please don't.

> MEDUSA
> I hold your destiny in my hand.

Orpheus kneels submissively.

> ORPHEUS
> Please. Please. The Gods did this
> to me.

> MEDUSA
> They did this to me too.

Light cast from the blade shines across his face. Extreme pressure from the dagger at his throat causes him to wince.

> MEDUSA
> I think you are clutching at
> straws.

Medusa grabs the hair on his scalp, twists it tight.

> ORPHEUS
> I beg of you.

The light from the blade arcs across his throat. A razor cut causes a single drop to fall.

> ORPHEUS
> I am cursed.

(CONTINUED)

THE AWAKENING OF THE GOLDEN FLEECE...

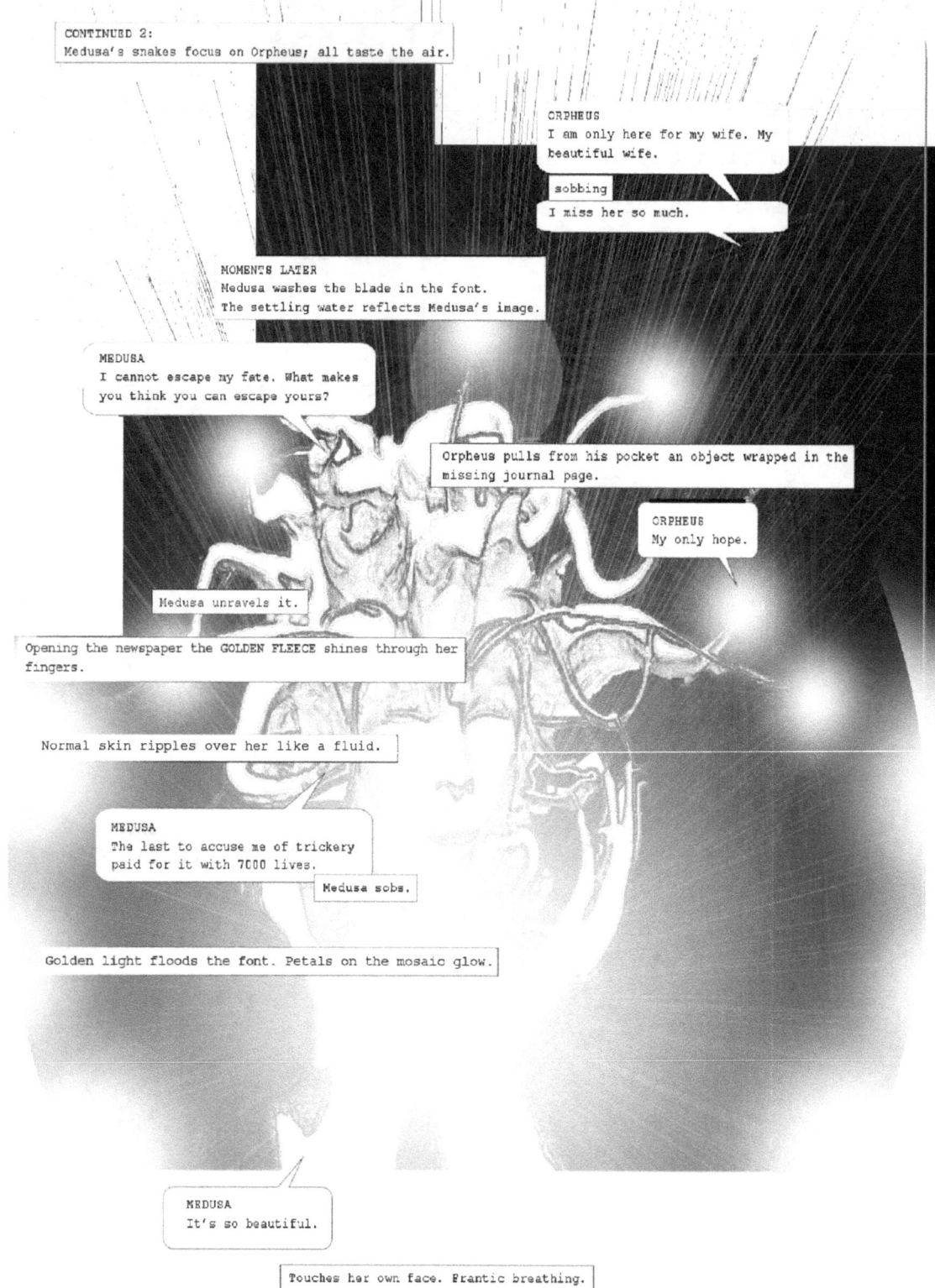

CONTINUED 2:
Medusa's snakes focus on Orpheus; all taste the air.

ORPHEUS
I am only here for my wife. My
beautiful wife.

sobbing
I miss her so much.

MOMENTS LATER
Medusa washes the blade in the font.
The settling water reflects Medusa's image.

MEDUSA
I cannot escape my fate. What makes
you think you can escape yours?

Orpheus pulls from his pocket an object wrapped in the
missing journal page.

ORPHEUS
My only hope.

Medusa unravels it.

Opening the newspaper the GOLDEN FLEECE shines through her
fingers.

Normal skin ripples over her like a fluid.

MEDUSA
The last to accuse me of trickery
paid for it with 7000 lives.

Medusa sobs.

Golden light floods the font. Petals on the mosaic glow.

MEDUSA
It's so beautiful.

Touches her own face. Frantic breathing.

The cut on Orpheus's throat heals; hairs on his arms lower
(CONTINUED)

CONTINUED 2:   146.

THE AWAKENING OF THE GOLDEN FLEECE...

Medusa's snakes focus on Orpheus; all taste the air.

> ORPHEUS
> I am only here for my wife. My
> beautiful wife.
> (sobbing)
> I miss her so much.

MOMENTS LATER

Medusa washes the blade in the font.

The settling water reflects Medusa's image.

> MEDUSA
> I cannot escape my fate. What makes
> you think you can escape yours?

Orpheus pulls from his pocket an object wrapped in the
missing journal page.

> ORPHEUS
> My only hope.

Medusa unravels it.

Opening the newspaper the GOLDEN FLEECE shines through her
fingers.

Normal skin ripples over her like a fluid.

> MEDUSA
> The last to accuse me of trickery
> paid for it with 7000 lives.

Medusa sobs.

Golden light floods the font. Petals on the sun mosaic glow.

> MEDUSA
> It's so beautiful.

Touches her own face. Frantic breathing.

The cut on Orpheus's throat heals; hairs on his arms lower

                                              (CONTINUED)

CONTINUED 3:

> MEDUSA
> (whisper)
> Do not open your eyes.

Medusa takes him by the hand.

She leads him into darkness.

Distant droning from underworld guardians.

> MEDUSA
> Whatever your heart feels,
> you must not open your eyes!

Loud droning from underworld guardians.

Echoing screams of tortured souls.

> SOUL OF LYNX
> Orpheus you abandoned us.

> SOUL OF MARTY
> Left us to die.

> SOUL OF JASON
> Murderer!

> MEDUSA
> (distant echo)
> Whatever your heart feels,
> you must not open your eyes!

DISTANT ENCHANTING MUSIC...

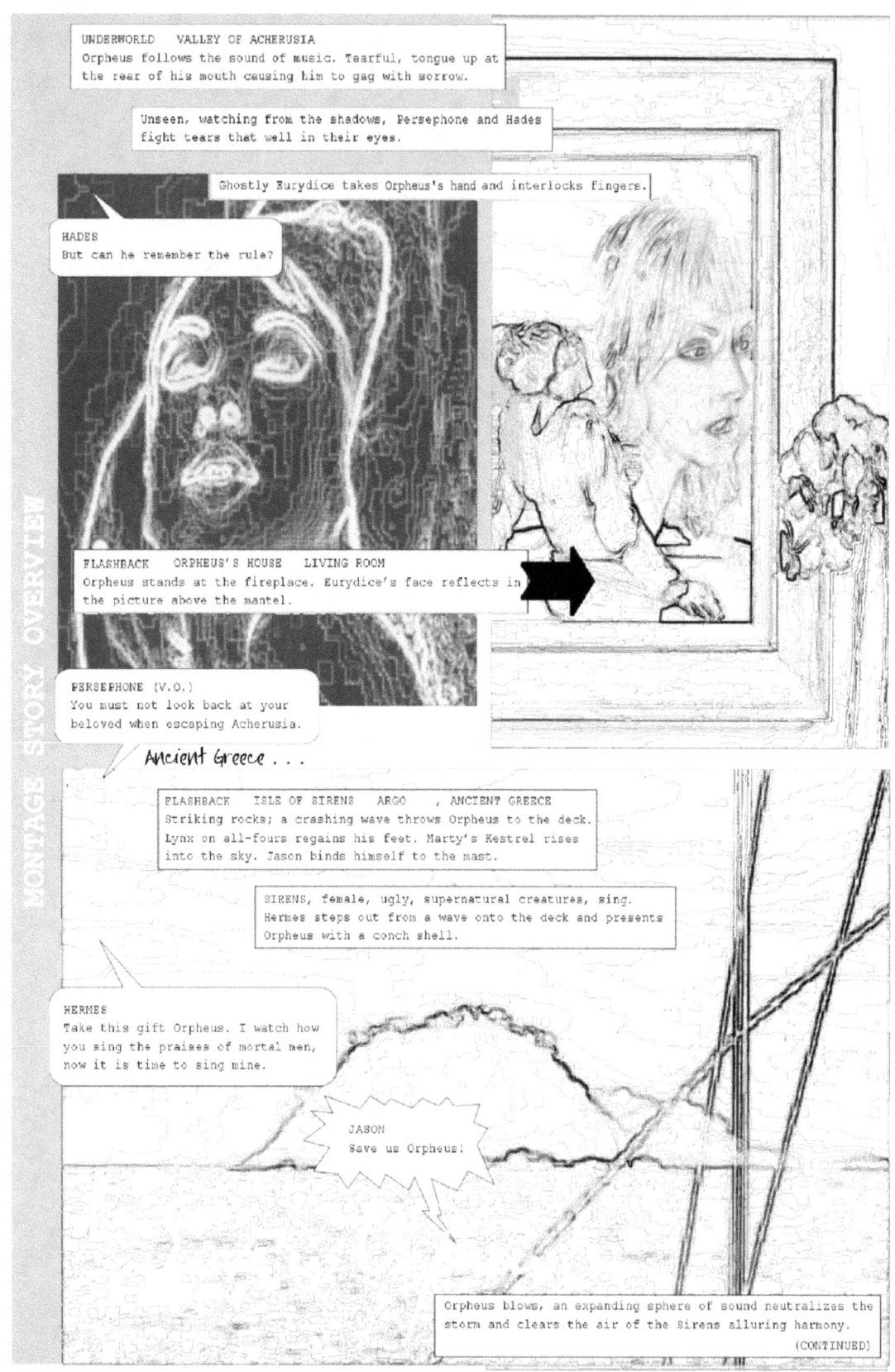

MONTAGE STORY OVERVIEW

UNDERWORLD   VALLEY OF ACHERUSIA
Orpheus follows the sound of music. Tearful, tongue up at
the rear of his mouth causing him to gag with sorrow.

Unseen, watching from the shadows, Persephone and Hades
fight tears that well in their eyes.

Ghostly Eurydice takes Orpheus's hand and interlocks fingers.

HADES
But can he remember the rule?

FLASHBACK   ORPHEUS'S HOUSE   LIVING ROOM
Orpheus stands at the fireplace. Eurydice's face reflects in
the picture above the mantel.

PERSEPHONE (V.O.)
You must not look back at your
beloved when escaping Acherusia.

Ancient Greece . . .

FLASHBACK   ISLE OF SIRENS   ARGO   , ANCIENT GREECE
Striking rocks; a crashing wave throws Orpheus to the deck.
Lynx on all-fours regains his feet. Marty's Kestrel rises
into the sky. Jason binds himself to the mast.

SIRENS, female, ugly, supernatural creatures, sing.
Hermes steps out from a wave onto the deck and presents
Orpheus with a conch shell.

HERMES
Take this gift Orpheus. I watch how
you sing the praises of mortal men,
now it is time to sing mine.

JASON
Save us Orpheus!

Orpheus blows, an expanding sphere of sound neutralizes the
storm and clears the air of the Sirens alluring harmony.
(CONTINUED)

BEGIN MONTAGE STORY OVERVIEW...

INT. UNDERWORLD   VALLEY OF ACHERUSIA   DAY

Orpheus follows the sound of music. Tearful, tongue up at
the rear of his mouth causing him to gag with sorrow.

Unseen, watching from the shadows, Persephone and Hades
fight tears that well in their eyes.

Ghostly Eurydice takes Orpheus's hand and interlocks fingers.

> HADES
> But can he remember the rule?

FLASHBACK   INT. ORPHEUS'S HOUSE   LIVING ROOM   DAY

Orpheus stands at the fireplace. Eurydice's face reflects in
the picture above the mantel.

> PERSEPHONE (V.O.)
> You must not look back at your
> beloved when escaping Acherusia.

FLASHBACK   EXT. ISLE OF SIRENS   ARGO   DAY, ANCIENT GREECE

Striking rocks; a crashing wave throws Orpheus to the deck.
Lynx on all-fours regains his feet. Marty's Kestrel rises
into the sky. Jason binds himself to the mast.

SIRENS, female, ugly, supernatural creatures, sing.

Hermes steps out from a wave onto the deck and presents
Orpheus with a conch shell.

> HERMES
> Take this gift Orpheus. I watch how
> you sing the praises of mortal men,
> now it is time to sing mine.

> JASON
> Save us Orpheus!

Orpheus blows, an expanding sphere of sound neutralizes the
storm and clears the air of the Sirens alluring harmony.

(CONTINUED)

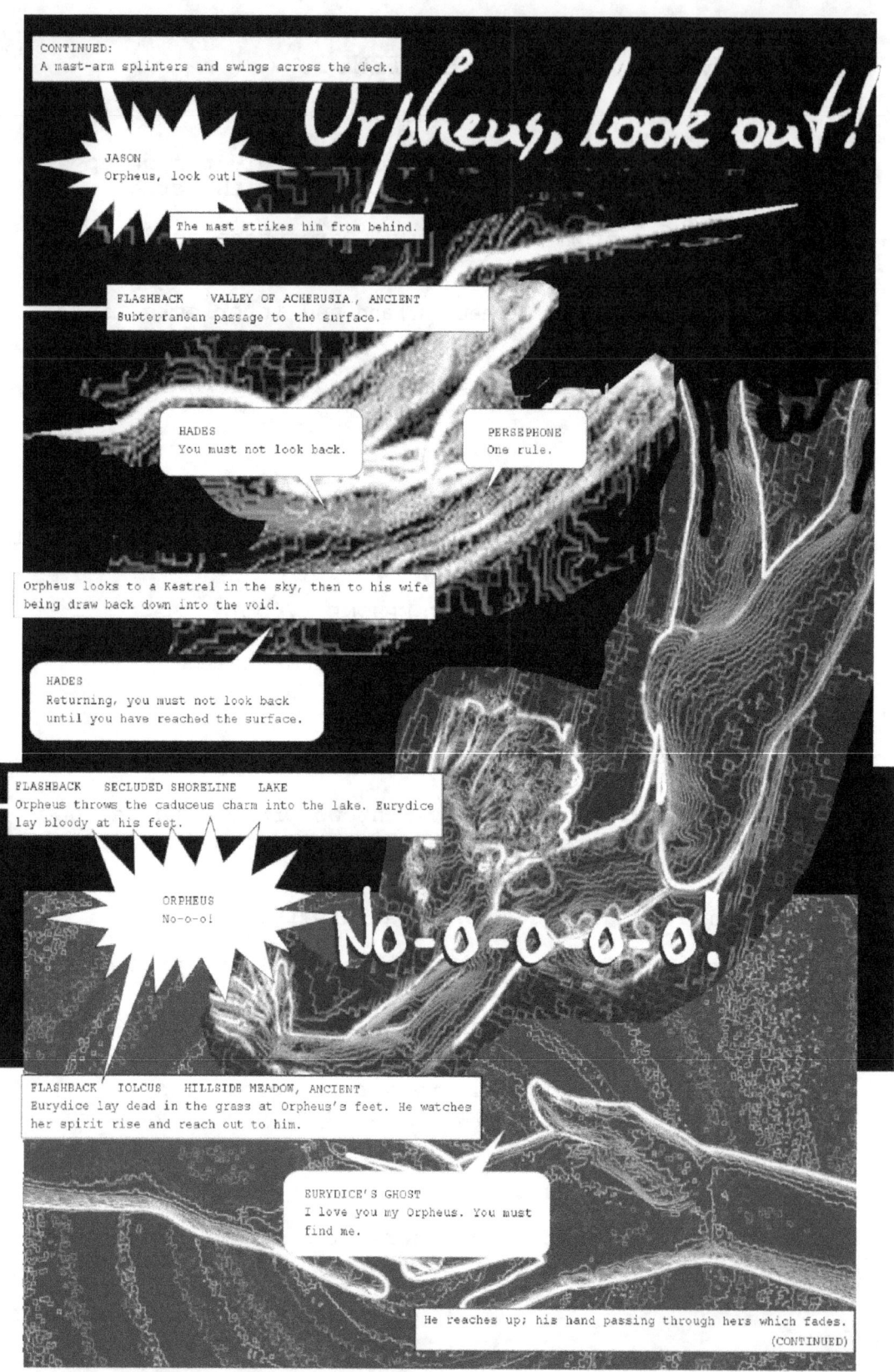

CONTINUED:
A mast-arm splinters and swings across the deck.

JASON
Orpheus, look out!

The mast strikes him from behind.

FLASHBACK   VALLEY OF ACHERUSIA , ANCIENT
Subterranean passage to the surface.

HADES
You must not look back.

PERSEPHONE
One rule.

Orpheus looks to a Kestrel in the sky, then to his wife
being draw back down into the void.

HADES
Returning, you must not look back
until you have reached the surface.

FLASHBACK   SECLUDED SHORELINE   LAKE
Orpheus throws the caduceus charm into the lake. Eurydice
lay bloody at his feet.

ORPHEUS
No-o-o!

FLASHBACK   IOLCUS   HILLSIDE MEADOW, ANCIENT
Eurydice lay dead in the grass at Orpheus's feet. He watches
her spirit rise and reach out to him.

EURYDICE'S GHOST
I love you my Orpheus. You must
find me.

He reaches up; his hand passing through hers which fades.
                                        (CONTINUED)

CONTINUED:

A mast-arm splinters and swings across the deck.

                    JASON
              Orpheus, look out!

The mast strikes him from behind.

FLASHBACK   INT. VALLEY OF ACHERUSIA   DAY, ANCIENT

Subterranean passage to the surface.

          HADES (V.O.)   PERSEPHONE (V.O.)
     You must not look back.   One rule.

Orpheus looks to a Kestrel in the sky, then to his wife
being draw back down into the void.

                    HADES (V.O.)
              Returning, you must not look back
              until you have reached the surface.

FLASHBACK   EXT. SECLUDED SHORELINE   LAKE   DAY

Orpheus throws the caduceus charm into the lake. Eurydice
lay bloody at his feet.

                    ORPHEUS
              NO-O-O!

FLASHBACK   EXT. IOLCUS   HILLSIDE MEADOW   DAY, ANCIENT

Eurydice lay dead in the grass at Orpheus's feet. He watches
her spirit rise and reach out to him.

                    EURYDICE'S GHOST
              I love you my Orpheus. You must
              find me.

He reaches up; his hand passing through hers which fades.

                                        (CONTINUED)

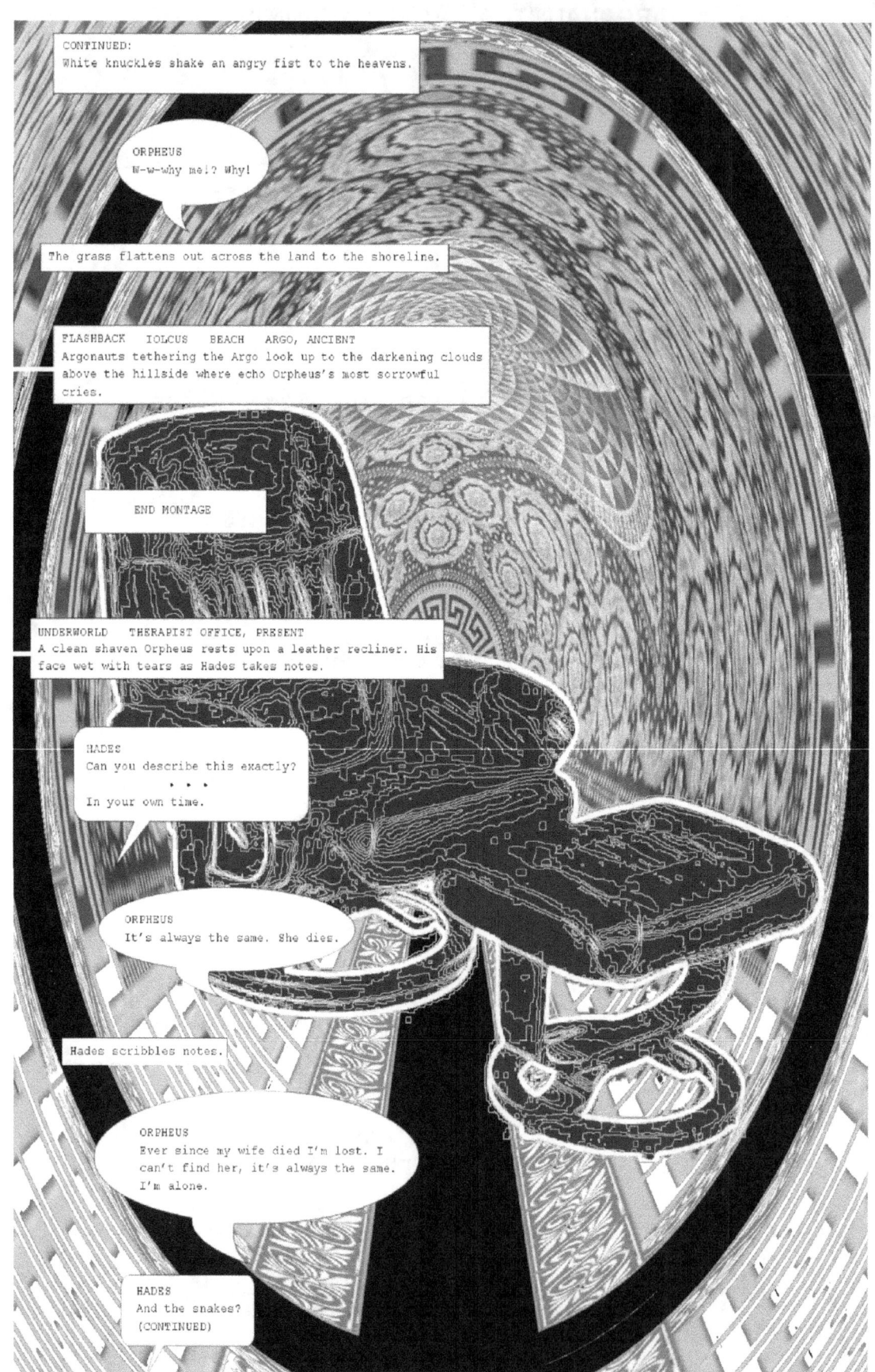

CONTINUED:

White knuckles shake an angry fist to the heavens.

                    ORPHEUS
              W-w-why me!? Why!

The grass flattens out across the land to the shoreline.

FLASHBACK   EXT. IOLCUS   BEACH   ARGO   DAY, ANCIENT

Argonauts tethering the Argo look up to the darkening clouds
above the hillside where echo Orpheus's most sorrowful
cries.

END MONTAGE

INT. UNDERWORLD   THERAPIST OFFICE   DAY, PRESENT

A clean shaven Orpheus rests upon a leather recliner. His
face wet with tears as Hades takes notes.

                    HADES
              Can you describe this exactly?
                    (beat)
              In your own time.

                    ORPHEUS
              It's always the same. She dies.

Hades scribbles notes.

                    ORPHEUS
              Ever since my wife died I'm lost. I
              can't find her, it's always the same.
              I'm alone.

                    HADES
              And the snakes?

                                        (CONTINUED)

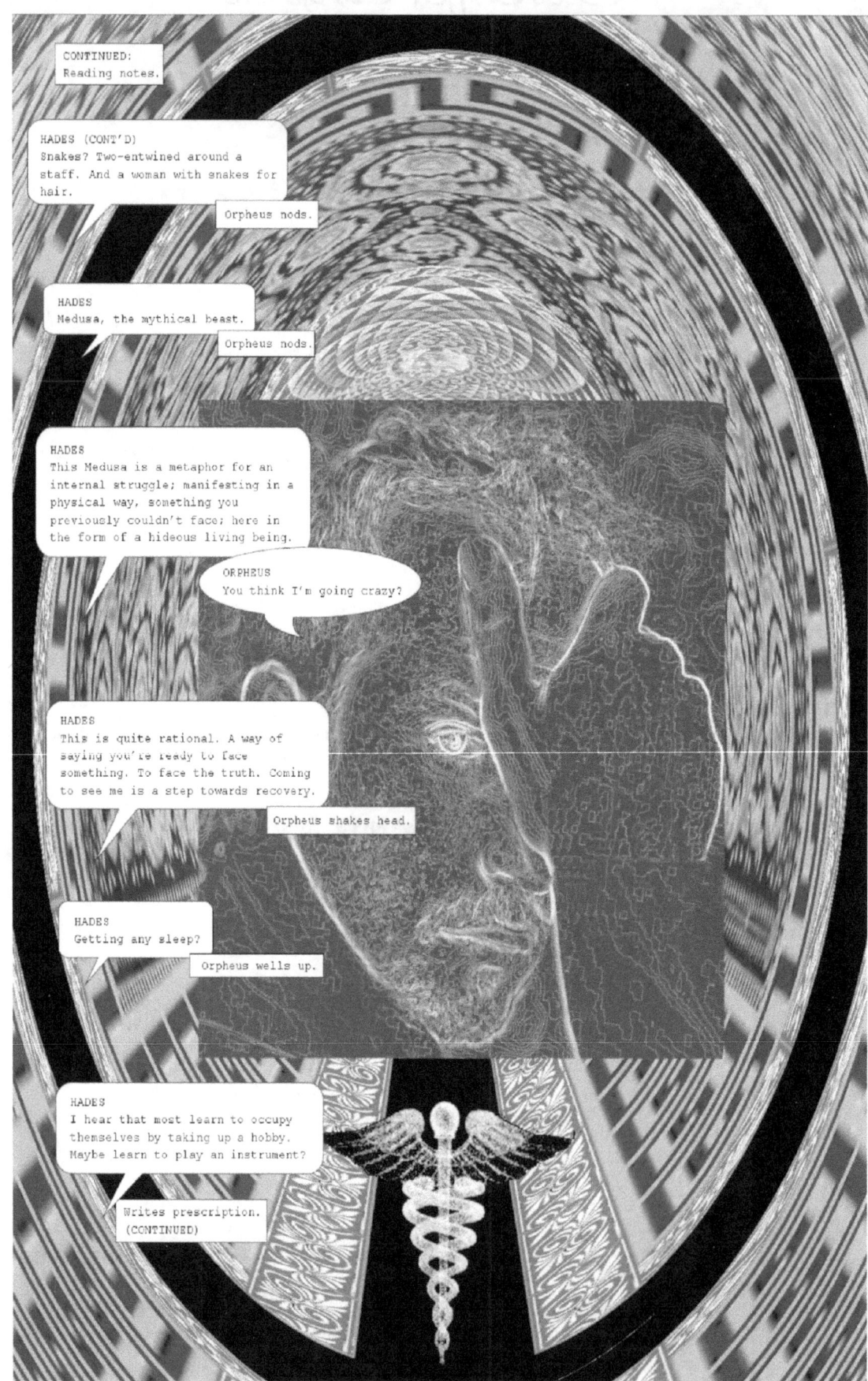

CONTINUED:

Reading notes.

> HADES (CONT'D)
> Snakes? Two-entwined around a
> staff. And a woman with snakes for
> hair.

Orpheus nods.

> HADES
> Medusa, the mythical beast.

Orpheus nods.

> HADES
> This Medusa is a metaphor for an
> internal struggle; manifesting in a
> physical way, something you
> previously couldn't face; here in
> the form of a hideous living being.

> ORPHEUS
> You think I'm going crazy?

> HADES
> This is quite rational. A way of
> saying you're ready to face
> something. To face the truth. Coming
> to see me is a step towards recovery.

Orpheus shakes head.

> HADES
> Getting any sleep?

Orpheus wells up.

> HADES
> I hear that most learn to occupy
> themselves by taking up a hobby.
> Maybe learn to play an instrument?

Writes prescription.

(CONTINUED)

CONTINUED 2:

                        HADES
              Only one rule.

Orpheus looks at him more seriously.

                        HADES
              Take one before sleeping. Don't
              lift anything heavy or plan
              anything adventurous.

Hades hands over a CD with a tight sympathetic smile.

                        HADES
              You may find comfort in music.

BACK IN RECEPTION...

INT. UNDERWORLD   RECEPTION   DAY

Orpheus looks at Persephone who returns a sympathetic smile.

Electronic buzzer unlocks door.

                        PERSEPHONE
              Don't look back.

Orpheus pauses without turning.

                        ORPHEUS
              Say something?

                        PERSEPHONE
              Excuse me???

Orpheus breathes deep.

Fashion Show … music pipes-up …

Orpheus sits in the crowd. Relaxing, smiling.
Lights dim.

His face reflects in the hard CD case.

The lights dim further causing him to abandon his reading.

An emerging SUPERMODEL bathes in a heavenly light.
She moves like his wife, the wind machine catches her dress.
He hones in on her seductive smile.

Orpheus's face transforms from merry to haunted. Tears roll
down his cheeks.

People around clap and cheer as other MODELS join her on the
catwalk.

The Supermodel walks slowly towards him,
Seconds expand.
Slow tears.
Music.

in his mind …

… Eurydice

INT. FASHION SHOW   DAY

Music.

Orpheus sits in the crowd. Relaxing, smiling.

Lights dim.

His face reflects in the hard CD case.

The lights dim further causing him to abandon his reading.

An emerging SUPERMODEL bathes in a heavenly light.

She moves like his wife, the wind machine catches her dress.

He hones in on her seductive smile.

Orpheus's face transforms from merry to haunted. Tears roll down his cheeks.

People around clap and cheer.

More MODELS join her on the catwalk.

The Supermodel walks slowly towards him...

Seconds expand.

Slow tears.

Music.

PRESENT

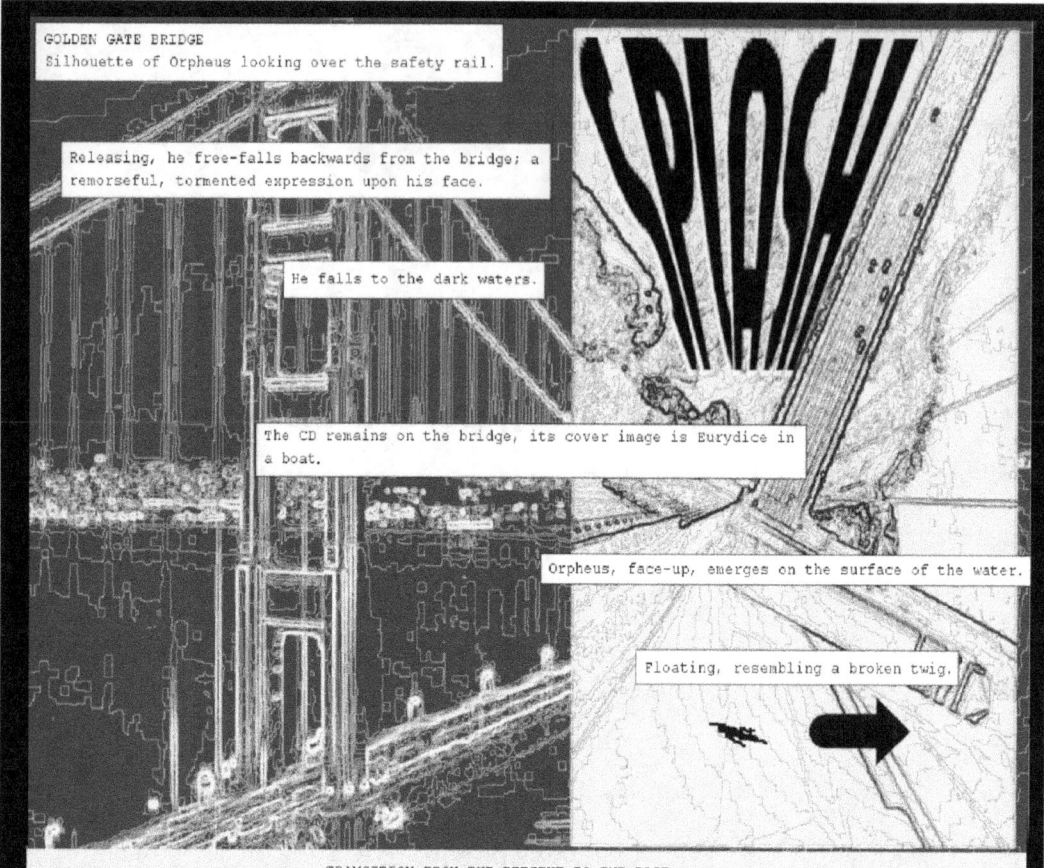

GOLDEN GATE BRIDGE
Silhouette of Orpheus looking over the safety rail.

Releasing, he free-falls backwards from the bridge; a remorseful, tormented expression upon his face.

He falls to the dark waters.

The CD remains on the bridge, its cover image is Eurydice in a boat.

Orpheus, face-up, emerges on the surface of the water.

Floating, resembling a broken twig.

. . . TRANSITION FROM THE PRESENT TO THE PAST . . .

IOLCUS BRIDGE, ANCIENT GREECE
Eurydice looks down to a twig emerging on the water.

Orpheus's hand touches her back.
She spins.

EURYDICE
My love.

They embrace.

EURYDICE
I thought you were off to rescue
Helen of Troy?

ORPHEUS
There is no better beauty I seek
than the one I hold in my arms.

Embracing, a sandal slips off Eurydice's foot.

ORPHEUS
I would move heaven and hell to
find you.

PAST

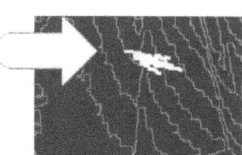

PRESENT...

EXT. GOLDEN GATE BRIDGE   NIGHT

Silhouette of Orpheus looking over the safety rail.

Releasing, he free-falls backwards from the bridge; a
remorseful, tormented expression upon his face.

He falls to the dark waters.

The CD remains on the bridge, its cover image is Eurydice in
a boat; beside which lay a pill bottle with its pill intact.

Orpheus, face-up, emerges on the surface of the water.

Floating, resembling a broken twig.

PAST...

INT. IOLCUS   BRIDGE   DAY, ANCIENT GREECE

Eurydice looks down to a twig emerging on the water.

Orpheus's hand touches her back.

She spins.

              EURYDICE
    My love.

They embrace.

              EURYDICE
    I thought you were off to rescue
    Helen of Troy?

              ORPHEUS
    There is no better beauty I seek
    than the one I hold in my arms.

Embracing, a sandal slips off Eurydice's foot.

              ORPHEUS
    I would move heaven and hell to
    find you.

OBSERVING FROM MOUNT OLYMPUS...

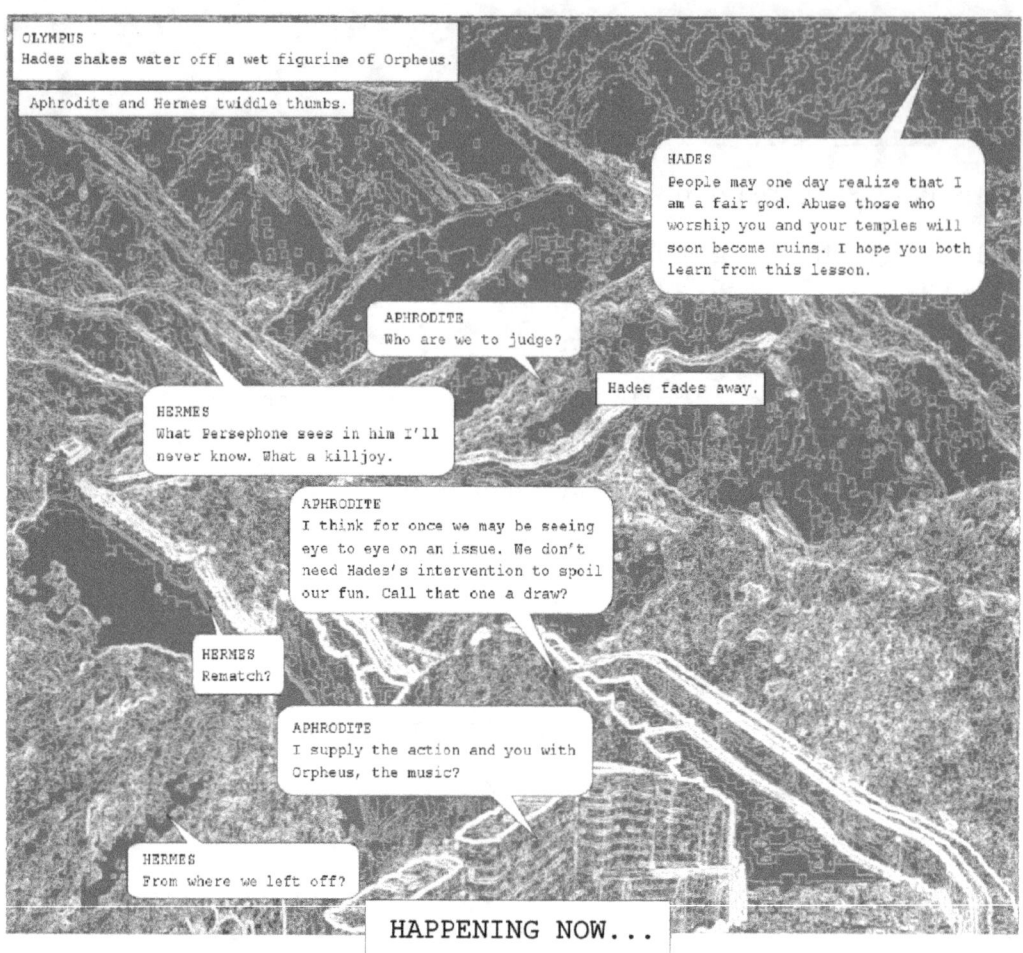

OLYMPUS
Hades shakes water off a wet figurine of Orpheus.

Aphrodite and Hermes twiddle thumbs.

HADES
People may one day realize that I am a fair god. Abuse those who worship you and your temples will soon become ruins. I hope you both learn from this lesson.

APHRODITE
Who are we to judge?

Hades fades away.

HERMES
What Persephone sees in him I'll never know. What a killjoy.

APHRODITE
I think for once we may be seeing eye to eye on an issue. We don't need Hades's intervention to spoil our fun. Call that one a draw?

HERMES
Rematch?

APHRODITE
I supply the action and you with Orpheus, the music?

HERMES
From where we left off?

HAPPENING NOW...

METROPOLITAN MUSEUM GALLERY#2 "THE SILK ROAD"
The Museum's double doors bursts inwards from a gail.

Beneath the poster of the 'Great Wall of China' stands Medusa all in black with a veil obscuring her face.

Medusa

SHIVER

The hairs rise on the Students' arms.
(CONTINUED)

OBSERVING FROM MOUNT OLYMPUS...

INT. OLYMPUS   DAY

Hades shakes water off a wet figurine of Orpheus.

Aphrodite and Hermes twiddle thumbs.

> HADES
> People may one day realize that I
> am a fair god. Abuse those who
> worship you and your temples will
> soon become ruins. I hope you both
> learn from this lesson.

> APHRODITE
> Who are we to judge?

Hades fades away.

> HERMES
> What Persephone sees in him I'll
> never know. What a killjoy.

> APHRODITE
> I think for once we may be seeing
> eye to eye on an issue. We don't
> need Hades's intervention to spoil
> our fun. Call that one a draw?

> HERMES
> Rematch?

> APHRODITE
> I supply the action and you with
> Orpheus, the music?

> HERMES
> From where we left off?

HAPPENING NOW...

INT. METROPOLITAN MUSEUM   GALLERY#2 "THE SILK ROAD"   DAY

The Museum's double doors bursts inwards from a gale.

Beneath the poster of the 'Great Wall of China' stands
Medusa all in black with a veil obscuring her face.

The hairs rise on the Students' arms.

(CONTINUED)

CONTINUED:
Screams from Students.

A hand on Young Eurydice's shoulder causes her to jump.

METROPOLITAN MUSEUM   STEPS
Heavy rain.
The Teacher counts the Students onboard a waiting bus.

MEDUSA
This is for you young Eurydice.

Eurydice, last to descend.

Medusa hands her a parcel.

Medusa atop the steps shelters beneath a wide brimmed hat.

TEACHER
(to Young Eurydice)
Hurry up please.

(to DRIVER)
That's everyone. Good to go. The
heavens are opening.

Onboard, children's names grow
in the condensation upon the windows.

Young Eurydice wipes condensation off the rear window and
peers through a pillbox slot to Medusa ...
　　　　　　　　　...then opens the parcel tentatively.

A golden light illuminates her face. The glow tickles her
fingertips. Miraculously the port-wine birthmark vanishes.

Young Eurydice writes in the condensation.

THANK YOU

CONTINUED:

Screams from Students.

A hand on Young Eurydice's shoulder causes her to jump.

                    MEDUSA
        This is for you young Eurydice.

Medusa hands her a parcel.

EXT. METROPOLITAN MUSEUM   STEPS   DAY

Heavy rain.

The Teacher counts the Students onboard a waiting bus.

Eurydice, last to descend.

Medusa atop the steps shelters beneath a wide brimmed hat.

Onboard, children's names grow in the condensation upon the
windows.

                    TEACHER
               (to Young Eurydice)
        Hurry up please.
               (to DRIVER)
        That's everyone. Good to go. The
        heavens are opening.

INT. METROPOLITAN MUSEUM   STEPS   BUS   DAY

Young Eurydice wipes condensation off the rear window and
peers through a pillbox slot to Medusa; then opens the
parcel tentatively.

A golden light illuminates her face. The glow tickles her
fingertips. Miraculously the port-wine birthmark vanishes.

Young Eurydice writes in the condensation.

EXT. METROPOLITAN MUSEUM   STEPS   DAY

Medusa sees the words 'Thank you' upon the bus window.
Young Eurydice looks through the lettering.

> MEDUSA
> You're very welcome. And tomorrow
> the sun <u>will</u> shine on your oh so
> beautiful face.

Bus departs.

Medusa raises her arms to the heavens, spins and dances
happily. Arms open, embracing the rain like it were the most
beautiful experience on Earth.

EXT. SUBURBS   DAY

The SCHOOL BUS stops on the corner.

Young Eurydice steps off and rushes through the rain to
greet her mother at the front door.

> YOUNG EURYDICE
> Mum!

Mother gasps.

Young Eurydice draws attention to her cheek.

Mother cups her face.

CAR PULLS UP ACROSS THE ROAD, bumper sticker reads 'ARGO
music festival.'

Young Orpheus steps out dragging a guitar case.

> HERMES
> Chin-up Orpheus! You're young; you
> can't be expected to remember all
> the words all of the time. Don't
> worry, the competition runs next
> year. Chin up; you have your whole
> life ahead of you.

(CONTINUED)

CONTINUED:

HERMES (CONT'D)
You practice now! There's always
another day.

YOUNG ORPHEUS
I will sir. Thank you for the ride.

The car pulls away.

Young Orpheus drags his guitar through the rain.

YOUNG ORPHEUS'S HOUSE   LIVING ROOM
Young Orpheus doesn't bother to hang his coat correctly; the
wet coat slips off the hook to the floor.

MOTHER
How'd it go honey?

Sucked!

YOUNG ORPHEUS
Sucked! I'm a loser.

Young Orpheus in front of TV, back to his mother.
She picks up his coat.

MOTHER
Don't worry son. Sometimes when you
win you don't have half as much
fun. At least everyone knows who
you are now.

BRRRRRRR

What, a loser?

YOUNG ORPHEUS
What, a loser?

MOTHER
A great musician. Son, don't put
yourself down.

She kisses the top of his head.
(CONTINUED)

CONTINUED:

> HERMES (CONT'D)
> You <u>practice</u> now! There's always
> another day.

> YOUNG ORPHEUS
> I will sir. Thank you for the ride.

The car pulls away.

Young Orpheus drags his guitar through the rain.

INT. YOUNG ORPHEUS'S HOUSE LIVING ROOM   DAY

Young Orpheus doesn't bother to hang his coat correctly; the
wet coat slips off the hook to the floor.

> MOTHER
> How'd it go honey?

> YOUNG ORPHEUS
> Sucked! I'm a loser.

Young Orpheus in front of TV, back to his mother. She picks
up his coat.

> MOTHER
> Don't worry son. Sometimes when you
> win you don't have half as much
> fun. At least everyone knows who
> you are now.

> YOUNG ORPHEUS
> What, a loser?

> MOTHER
> A great musician. Son, don't put
> yourself down.

She kisses the top of his head.

(CONTINUED)

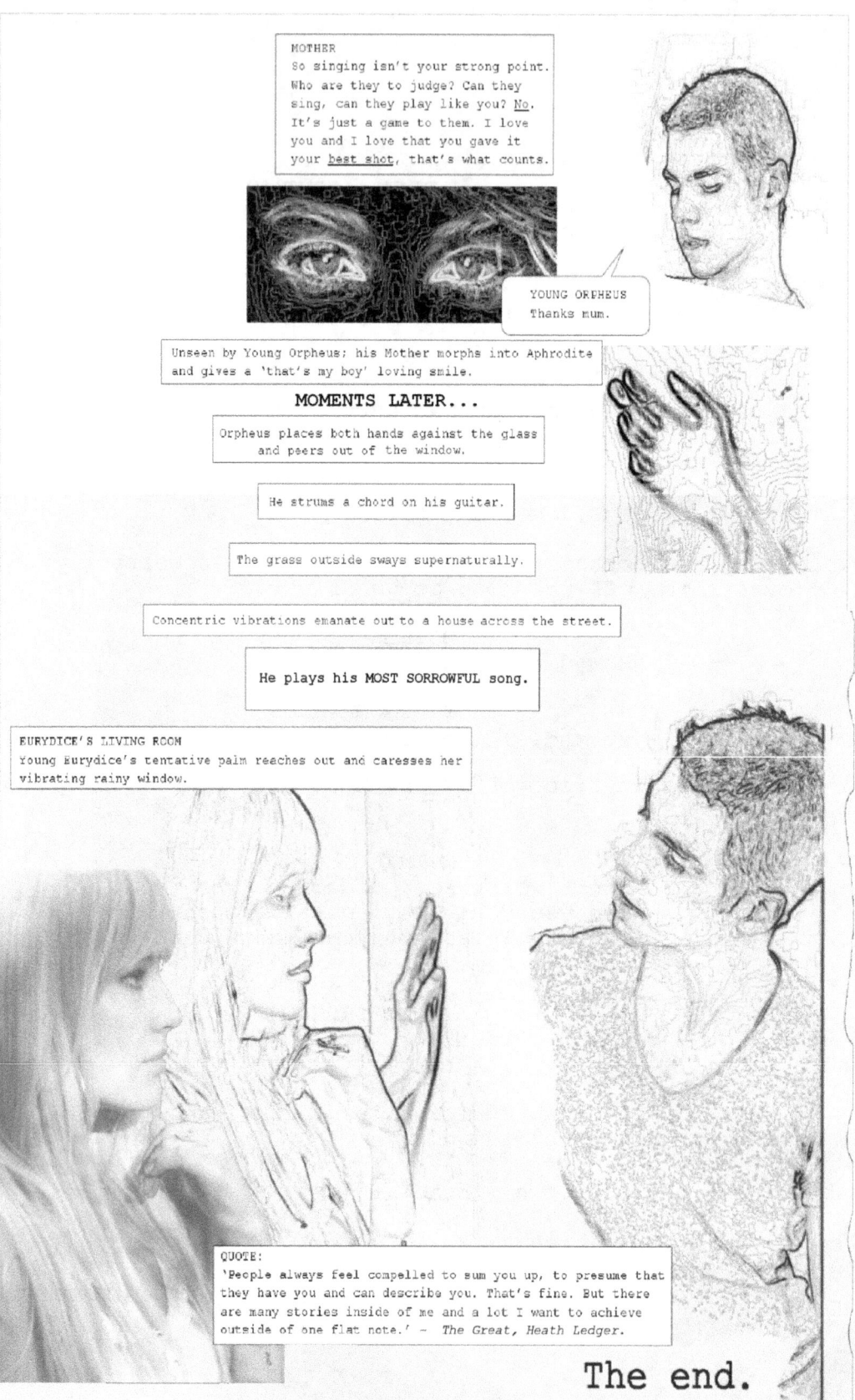

MOTHER
So singing isn't your strong point.
Who are they to judge? Can they
sing, can they play like you? No.
It's just a game to them. I love
you and I love that you gave it
your best shot, that's what counts.

YOUNG ORPHEUS
Thanks mum.

Unseen by Young Orpheus; his Mother morphs into Aphrodite
and gives a 'that's my boy' loving smile.

MOMENTS LATER...

Orpheus places both hands against the glass
and peers out of the window.

He strums a chord on his guitar.

The grass outside sways supernaturally.

Concentric vibrations emanate out to a house across the street.

He plays his MOST SORROWFUL song.

EURYDICE'S LIVING ROOM
Young Eurydice's tentative palm reaches out and caresses her
vibrating rainy window.

QUOTE:
'People always feel compelled to sum you up, to presume that
they have you and can describe you. That's fine. But there
are many stories inside of me and a lot I want to achieve
outside of one flat note.' – *The Great, Heath Ledger.*

The end.

CONTINUED: 172.

> MOTHER
> So singing isn't your strong point.
> Who are they to judge? Can they
> sing, can they play like you? No.
> It's just a game to them. I love
> you and I love that you gave it
> your best shot, that's what counts.

> YOUNG ORPHEUS
> Thanks mum.

Unseen by Young Orpheus; his Mother morphs into Aphrodite
and gives a 'that's my boy' loving smile.

MOMENTS LATER...

Orpheus places both hands against the glass and peers out of
the window.

He strums a chord on his guitar.

The grass outside sways supernaturally.

Concentric vibrations emanate out to a house across the
street.

He plays his most sorrowful song. (*guitar solo)

EXT./INT. STREET/EURYDICE'S LIVING ROOM   DAY

Young Eurydice's tentative palm reaches out and caresses her
vibrating rainy window.

                                                      FADE OUT:

THE END

QUOTE:
'People always feel compelled to sum you up, to presume that
they have you and can describe you. That's fine. But there
are many stories inside of me and a lot I want to achieve
outside of one flat note.'
                              The late/great - Heath Ledger

*guitar solo
Senza Una Donna "Without A Woman" - Zucchero & Paul Young

SERIAL POOL ATTENDANT

Synopsis:
On an L.A. beach Alex (pool attendant) meets her idol, the notorious Shark (real name Henry, a high profile killer on parole). Shark mentors Alex in the art of 'murder' and in 'not getting caught'. Cultural references lead to his catchphrase . . .

"A CLASSIC!"

The big reveal: Shark is not just a serial killer but a puppet taking orders from Victoria (once screenplay tutor to Alex) and mission director of an assassin-like organisation known as the . . .

'SERIAL POOL'

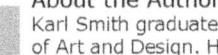

It is not mere chance that brings Alex and Henry together.

Siblings with a flair for death. Shark takes his sister under his wing.

Hitmen liaising as *real CLEANERS.*

"IF YOUR PROBLEM IS TOO BIG TO FILTER . . .YOU CALL THE POOL ATTENDANT"

Concept:
Two loyal Psycho's team up to create the L.A. version of "Miami Vice". Add a sexy mission director... Victoria... a sprinkling of "Mission Impossible" and that's ENTERTAINMENT!

"YOU'LL DIE LAUGHING"
"...lunatic brother-sister psychology at its finest."

About the Author
Karl Smith graduated with a degree in Fine Art from Cleveland College of Art and Design. His fresh fusion of action and emotion when screenwriting is surely to be seen in a cinema near you soon. Bet your mortgage on it!

ASK YOUR LOCAL BOOK STORE TO STOCK OTHER ORPHIC HOUSE TITLES

SERIAL POOL ATTENDANT:
SCREENPLAY & TV SERIES BIBLE

HARDBACK
ISBN 978-0-9566156-7-1

PAPERBACK
ISBN 978-0-9566156-2-6

California, L.A.

Television plays

Hardcover

ORPHIC HOUSE

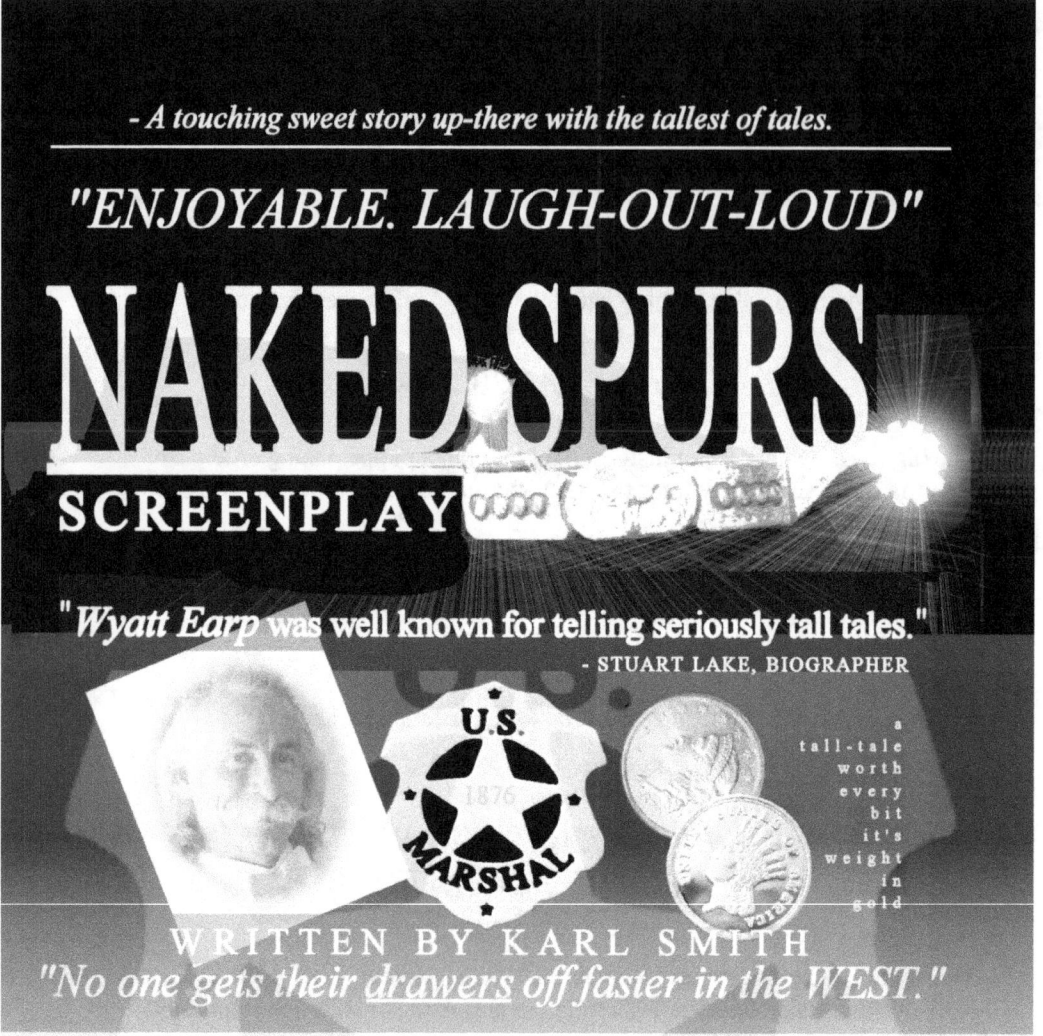

- *A touching sweet story up-there with the tallest of tales.*

"ENJOYABLE. LAUGH-OUT-LOUD"

NAKED SPURS
SCREENPLAY

"Wyatt Earp was well known for telling seriously tall tales."
- STUART LAKE, BIOGRAPHER

U.S. 1876 MARSHAL

a tall-tale worth every bit it's weight in gold

WRITTEN BY KARL SMITH
"No one gets their <u>drawers</u> off faster in the WEST."

"Naked but for a pair of spurs"

"Did one man truely outwit the greatest gunslingers in history?"

"I do sincerely wish it were true."

- California 1876 -

NAKED SPURS

"NO ONE GETS THEIR DRAWERS OFF FASTER IN THE WEST"

CALIFORNIA 1876

A COAST MIWOK WARRIOR
AND THE PRISON THAT WAS TO BE NAMED AFTER HIM

Saint ...  *... Quentin*

A YOUNG ARTIST creates a Wild West diorama and tells the seriously tall tale of NAKED SPURS, his great-great grandfather.

NAKED SPURS is the plausible tale of the BEAT THE BOUNTY competition a contest attracting the fastest guns in the West to the largest manhunt in history.

As the streaking inmate of San Quentin penitentiary NAKED SPURS must run for his life along with other criminals.

This is one story he cannot run away from.

"FROM THE MAN WITH BALLS IS BORN A LEGEND."

Inspiration:

Wyatt Earp told his memoirs to his biographer Stuart Lake.
In one story he was suspected of fixing a prize fight in which he was the judge.
The book was suspected to be entirely fictional.

Concept:

'The Good, the Bad and the Ugly' meets *'My name is Earl'* ... well, Earp actually.

About the Author
Karl Smith graduated with a degree in Fine Art from Cleveland College of Art and Design. His fresh fusion of action and emotion when screenwriting is surely to be seen in a cinema near you soon. Bet your mortgage on it!

Karl Peter Smith

HARDBACK
THE SOUND OF NAKED SPURS:
A SPAGHETTI WESTERN SCREENPLAY
ISBN 978-0-9566156-8-8

PAPERBACK
NAKED SPURS: SCREENPLAY
ISBN 978-0-9566156-2-6

Miwok Indians

California drama

California prison

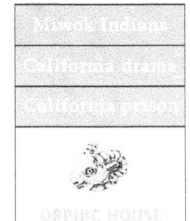

ORPHIC HOUSE

A HISTORY OF FEAR
SCREENPLAY

SCREENPLAY
WRITTEN BY
karl smith

"Will put the frighteners up you."
"A GRIPPING TALE!"

A HISTORY OF FEAR

Synopsis:
A wish melds the soul of a kind-hearted simpleton to a toy BEAR. A secret for three generations, the seven foot GUARDIAN wakes in time of need.

Surviving the sinking of the TITANIC a toy BEAR passes into the hands of the JEWISH COMMUNITY. Aboard the rescue ship CARPATHIA it travels on to the gas chambers of AUSCHWITZ.

The BEAR brings something with it…A HISTORY OF FEAR.

When TRICK OR TREATERS uncover an SS OFFICER in the neighborhood . . .

HALLOWEEN IS ABOUT TO GET A LITTLE HAIRY

Concept:
'Gremlins' meets 'Schindler's List' / 'The Golem of Prague'.

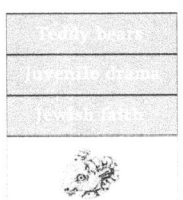

email: orphichouse@yahoo.co.uk   titles available from all good book stores

Teddy bears

Juvenile drama

Jewish faith

ORPHIC HOUSE

A HISTORY OF FEAR:
SCREENPLAY

HARDBACK
ISBN 978-0-9566156-9-5

PAPERBACK
ISBN 978-0-9566156-3-3

KARL SMITH

'Moving words around a page is like painting.'
To learn this process check out... *Print-on-demand Technical Guide: Screenplay Publishing*

Karl Peter Smith

E-PORTFOLIO:
1. Search for Eurydice - Romance with Bite
2. Serial Pool Attendant - Crime
3. Naked Spurs - Western
4. A History of Fear - Horror
5. Purge the Soul – Thriller
6. Memoirs of Dirty Max - Romance
7. Bikini THREE-20 (Thunderbirds) – Sci-Fi
8. Bill and Ted's Idiot's Guide to Screenwriting - Comedy

EDUCATION
UNIVERSITY OF TEESSIDE, Cleveland, England.
Bachelor of Fine Art - Printing, Drawing and Painting.
Specialized in Sculpture

HONOURS
Cleveland College of Art and Design used my sculptures to advertise the college in the UCAS prospectus; a national publication attracting future students to campus.

"I cried whilst writing."
A History Of Fear
"...the blonde ponytail."

Thanks Helen x

Pencil Drawing of Miss. Helen Shepley by K.S. 2006